The Waiting

Carol James

Contact Information: titleadmin@pelicanbookgroup.com

Cover Art by Nicola Martinez

White Rose Publishing, a division of Pelican Ventures, LLC
www.pelicanbookgroup.com PO Box 1738 *Aztec, NM * 87410

White Rose Publishing Circle and Rosebud logo is a trademark of Pelican Ventures, LLC

Publishing History
First White Rose Edition, 2019
Electronic Edition ISBN 978-1-5223-0124-0
Paperback Edition ISBN 978-1-5223-0143-1

Published in the United States of America

Dedication

To Jimmy, my greatest encourager and supporter —
My One.

"When I am forced into God's waiting room to wait for answers to hard questions in silence, He waits with me."
Alice Chapin

1

Katherine Herrington eased her most prized possession—a rainbow stack of spiral notebooks—out of the cardboard moving box and gently placed them on the upper shelf in her old closet. Sandwiched between an outdated combination CD-cassette player and two stacked shoe boxes full of fashion dolls and their twenty-year-old ensembles, those irreplaceable pages contained the last fifteen years of her life.

As the sweet perfume of Mom's star jasmine drifted in through the gauzy sheers billowing across the open bedroom window, the evening breeze carried the memory of the words she'd heard so often. *Katherine, enjoy the moment. Be spontaneous.* Mom had always thought she was inflexible, too rigid, but that wasn't true. She was just a planner. While some people kept journals, she made lists. Looking back at all the check-marked entries and seeing what she had accomplished was satisfying.

Besides, had Mom been more like her and a little less spontaneous, she might still be with them.

After all, having your life in order, wanting to know what to expect, was no crime. Organization was a good thing. In fact, tomorrow she'd go to the store, buy some plastic containers, and whip this closet into shape. She would have done it tonight, except for...The Date.

"Beth?"

Katherine smiled. Cassie was the only one who still called her that.

"Can I come in?" The door cracked open just enough for Katherine to see her sister's blue eyes dancing with excitement.

"Sure, sweetie."

Cassie burst through the door and dove into the middle of the old iron bed with the level of enthusiasm only a thirteen-year-old girl who hadn't yet been on her first date could have. "Aren't you excited?" Sitting cross-legged, she bounced with anticipation.

No. "Cassie, it's just a date. Nothing more." Katherine was long over the tears of frustration she'd shed privately after Dad had told her he and one of the church ladies had set up this date with Crescent Bluff's newest bachelor. Dad was the only person she'd do this for. She was sick of blind dates.

The women at her church in Dallas had meddled in the same way. They meant well but hadn't seemed to understand that, if and when He wanted to, God would bring the man she'd prayed for since middle school into her life. He wouldn't need their help, or anyone else's for that matter. A year ago, she thought He had, but now—maybe not.

Anyway, tonight was the last blind date of her life. "I'm only going because Dad set it up, and I don't want to hurt his feelings. He means well."

"But, Beth. This guy could be The One." Stars filled Cassie's eyes.

Katherine smiled. Who was she to destroy Cassie's fairytale optimism? "You're right. You never know, do you? I imagine he could be." She sat down on the bed and hugged her little sister.

Cassie's head rested on Katherine's shoulder. Her voice was hushed. "I'm glad you lost your job." She bolted up. "I mean, not glad you're not working but glad you could come back home. I miss Mom so much." Her eyes filled with tears.

"I know. Me, too." Katherine eased her sister's head back down onto her shoulder and stroked her flaxen hair. Losing Mom had been heartbreaking, yet Katherine had, at Dad's insistence, returned to Dallas and resumed some semblance of a normal life. But now with no job, she'd had no other choice but to come back home. That is, unless she counted collecting unemployment and living with friends or on the street viable options.

The deep hum of a car engine vibrated the old wood-framed windows. He was here.

Cassie jumped up and peeked between the curtains. "Wow! Awesome car." She turned back and grinned, the tears gone. "Come look."

Katherine moved behind her sister and peered over her shoulder. Some sort of red sports car sat at the top of the circular drive. Impressive to guys maybe, but not to her. Cars were a means of transportation, nothing more. They should be reliable and sensible, not flashy.

As the driver's side door opened, Katherine held her breath. *Here we go.* A man dressed in jeans and a plaid western shirt stepped out. Her heart groaned. Not only was he short, but he was bald. Or maybe his head was shaven, but the only reason a twenty-five or thirty-something-year-old man shaved his head was because he was either bald or balding. Short and hairless were not on "The List." A knot formed in her stomach. Unfortunately, it was too late to conjure up an illness.

"Oh, he's so cute." Cassie placed her fingertips together and clapped them excitedly.

They couldn't be looking at the same man. Katherine blinked slowly and then refocused her eyes. No, nothing had changed.

Cassie jumped up. "I'll go let him in, but you hurry. Hurry." Twirling out of the room, she closed the door.

Katherine kicked off her heels and placed them on the rack in the closet. Then she slipped on a pair of flat sandals. Hopefully the change in shoes would solve the height problem.

As the doorbell rang, Cassie's footsteps echoed down the hall through the closed bedroom door.

After taking one final look in the mirror, Katherine retouched her lip gloss and ran her fingers through her hair. She sat on the edge of the bed, took a deep breath, and counted slowly to ten—and on to twenty. For Dad, she could stand almost anything for a few hours. Plastering a smile on her face, she opened the door and inched down the hall toward the living room. *Let the fun begin.*

Cassie was curled up on one end of the couch with her feet tucked under her, and the back of The Date's bald head arched above the top of the leather recliner. Wonder how Dad would have reacted if he'd come home and seen a stranger trespassing in his chair. Terms like "PK, dribbling, striker" were flying back and forth between the two. Soccer. Maybe The Date had more in common with Cassie than with her. If Cassie were only a little older.

"Oh, hi, Beth." Cassie jumped up. Her grin was almost wider than her face.

The Date stood and turned toward her, a large bundle of pink tulips in his hands. He was actually kind of cute...for a short, bald guy. "Hello, there," he said. "I'm Sam. Sam Tucker." His voice was deep, his accent unusual.

Certainly not Texan, not even southern. Midwestern...Northeastern...She couldn't quite place it. "You look lovely this evening. These are for you." He held out the rosy bouquet, and as he smiled, his eyes sparkled like sunlight on ocean waves.

It was like looking into the Caribbean from the deck of a ship. She fought to keep her balance as the deep aquamarine pools pulled at her like an undertow at South Padre.

He cleared his throat as he pushed the bouquet closer. "Perhaps you'd like to place them in some water?"

"Beth?" Cassie stepped forward and took the flowers from him. "Here, I'll do that for you. Thanks, Sam."

"Greatly appreciate it, Cassie."

"You guys have fun." Waltzing into the kitchen, Cassie left them alone.

"So, Beth, is it?" He held out his hand and smiled again.

Oh, great, she'd made a stellar first impression. As she found her breath, her voice followed. "No. Katherine. Katherine Herrington." She grasped his outstretched hand. "Nice to meet you, Sam." The sightline from her eyes to his was an upward angle. He wasn't short after all. He was definitely taller than she was, just not as tall as Clark. She had changed shoes for no reason.

"Katherine." He cocked his head to the side, raised his eyebrows, and pressed his lips together. "OK. Katherine it is then. Pleased to meet you, as well." He extended his crooked elbow for her to take. "Ready?"

Or not... "Ready." She took his arm, and he led her out the door to his car. The clean scent of his cologne was like a fresh summer breeze.

As he held her door open, he spoke. "So, Cassie tells me you like Tex-Mex."

What else could Cassie possibly have told him in those few seconds they were alone? She shouldn't have stalled and let her sister greet him.

"There's an old restaurant on the highway toward Fort Worth," he continued. "The Cantina. I haven't been there in a while, but they used to have live music and the best fajitas around. Or if you're not in the mood for Mexican, we could do sushi in Dallas."

Sam closed the passenger door and walked around to the driver's side. He must not have put much thought into planning their date if he hadn't even decided on a restaurant. But being given a choice was kind of nice, and while she didn't really have a preference, The Cantina was closer and would most likely mean an earlier night and a shorter date. So, Mexican, it was.

After climbing into the car, he buckled his seatbelt and placed the key in the ignition. He turned to face her. "So, what's your preference, Katherine?"

"How about The Cantina? I haven't been there in quite a while, either."

"All right! Tex-Mex it is." As he pushed the

gearshift forward, he smiled and winked at her. "Spoken by a man in a state of great relief. Not much of a sushi fan, I must say."

She stared out the windshield. He'd set himself up, and she wouldn't pass up the opportunity to take advantage of his admission. "Of course, I've always heard it's a woman's prerogative to change her mind." Glancing left out of the corner of her eye, she continued, "And I do love sushi." As his face reddened, she sighed for effect. "Let me think. You know, on second thought, sushi actually sounds wonderful." The redness now covered his entire head. He was quite cute when he was embarrassed. "Dallas is farther away, but it's early. Maybe I would like sushi, after all."

As they reached the stop sign at the intersection of the highways, he turned toward her, one arm resting on the seat back, the other on the door. "Decision time. Which is it? Left toward Fort Worth or right toward Dallas? You decide."

"Let's see...such a hard choice." As the pick-up behind them honked, she jumped. "Left."

His eyes laughed. "Only if you're sure. I certainly wouldn't want to make you do anything you wouldn't enjoy."

They needed to go. "Yes, I'm sure. Left. Go left."

He made no effort to grasp the steering wheel. "I mean, if you really want sushi, I'd be happy to oblige."

The truck honked again. "Sam! Left, left."

His forehead wrinkled in thought. "Oh, I don't know. Maybe I should give sushi another try. I might learn to like it, you know."

The driver behind them laid on the horn. "Sam, left, please. Left. Now."

A smug look covered his face. "Only because you insist, Katherine. Only because you insist." The car burst out onto the highway.

Sam shifted quickly through the gears until the car flew up the road toward Fort Worth.

Probably trying to impress her. She sank back into the quilted, black leather seat that felt more like a wingback chair in a den than a car seat. OK, she'd humor him. "Nice car."

He smiled. "Thanks. It's my new work car."

Certainly not the typical company car, at least not like any she'd seen before. "So, tell me, what exactly do you do?"

As he shifted one more time, she gripped the arm rest and ignored the inner voice demanding she look at the speedometer.

"Nothing at the moment. I'm on medical leave, and I've come to my aunt's to recuperate for a few months."

"Medical leave?" The lack of hair...oh no, chemo. She'd been so judgmental, so insensitive earlier. But she couldn't possibly have known. Other than the bald head he looked so healthy.

"Yeah, knee surgery. Blew it out playing football."

So, knee surgery wasn't exactly life-threatening, but the ride to the restaurant might be. Her heart raced while fence posts, highway signs, mesquite trees, all whizzed past her window as one continuous green-brown-gray blur. They were going way too fast.

"But to answer your question, I'm currently in PR—Public Relations, that is—for an athletic organization."

"I know what PR means." He must think she'd been living under a rock somewhere. "I have a business degree."

"Me, too. An MBA. That is—"

"I know what that means, too." Even though he tried to cover his mouth, she saw his grin. He was baiting her.

"So, how about you, Katherine? What do you do?"

As she grabbed the console, she finally obeyed the voice of self-preservation. The needle reached to almost one hundred on a dial that ended at two hundred. "Please tell me the numbers on the speedometer are in kilometers."

The revving of the engine eased as he looked down toward the dashboard and downshifted. "Whoops. Sorry. I've only had the car a few days, and I'm still getting used to the feel. Had no idea we were going that fast. Didn't mean to scare you."

She relaxed her grip and took a deep breath. "Oh, no. I wasn't scared. I just don't want you to get a ticket. The highway patrol routinely has a speed trap set a few miles up the road."

The smirk on his face told her he wasn't buying her explanation. "Thanks for your concern." The speedometer now hovered at seventy. "So, what do you do?"

"At the moment, I guess you could say I'm on leave, too. Not medical, though. Economical. About nine months ago, I went to work for an auditing company in Dallas, and when the economy tanked, so did my job. Last to be added, first to be subtracted." That was more than enough information for a first— and only—date.

"Well, that's a good reason to move back home. You plan to look for a job here?"

The sun had slipped behind the horizon setting the

few stray clouds on fire. She couldn't see sunsets like this among the skyscrapers in Dallas. "No. My boss—ex-boss—said he'd call me when things picked back up. Plus, my dad needs my help right now. He has to go overseas for a few weeks, so I'll take care of Cassie. Then we'll see what happens."

The car slowed slightly. "My aunt told me about your mom. I'm terribly sorry."

Despite her will, tears filled her eyes, and she turned to look out the window at some pretend point of interest. "Thank you." She couldn't say any more. She wanted to go home. She wasn't ready to do this, after all. The pain was still too raw to share something so intimate with a stranger. But then again, she couldn't let Dad down.

He had only arranged this date because he loved her, and no matter how uncomfortable the next few hours would be, she would not disappoint him.

2

Sam ate the last bite of fajitas. When she'd been so quiet in her house, he hadn't been sure. But, no—she didn't remember him, and that was definitely a good thing.

Finding Beth...Katherine...had been too easy. She was the real reason he'd come back to Crescent Bluff. Rehab was only an excuse. When he'd casually asked about her last week, Aunt Ginny's eyes had sparkled with understanding. She'd set up the blind date, passed the ball to him, and now it was his job to get it in the goal.

Her hair was shorter, more contemporary, and her eyes an even richer brown. Other than that, she hadn't changed much at all. Except that she was even more beautiful now than she'd been in ninth grade, and she'd been gorgeous then. The beginning of high school...what a weird time of life when most girls had become women and most guys were still boys. She'd always been about a head taller than any of the guys in school, but he'd definitely surpassed her.

He had come back to Crescent Bluff searching. These last few years, the world would say he'd made it. Yet really, all he'd done was make a mess of it. He could have bought almost anything he wanted—and pretty much had. Yet it hadn't been enough. Despite all the stuff, all the renown he'd accumulated, something was missing. And he'd come back to the place where life had first begun to see if he could find that meaning again.

The band struck up a new song as couples filled the dance floor.

Their conversation had been polite, shallow, since he'd made that comment in the car. He hadn't intended to upset her. But ignoring her mother's death would have been worse, like that proverbial elephant in the room that everyone pretended didn't exist.

She looked up from her plate and smiled. "Just as delicious as I remembered. Thanks for the suggestion, Sam."

"I'm glad you enjoyed it. But I'm somewhat disappointed that I didn't get to try sushi again. Maybe next time." He smiled.

First her eyebrows raised, and then her forehead wrinkled in response. "Maybe." She turned to watch the couples moving around the old concrete floor. Her sable eyes warmed as a slight smile rested on her face. "Wow, that couple in the straw hats is really good."

Ah-ha! He stood and moved in front of her. "Would you like to dance?" he asked, holding out his right hand.

Her eyes opened wide. "Oh, I couldn't. I don't know how."

He left his hand extended. "I don't believe that was the question. Would you like to dance?"

She shook her head in response. "I mean, I might like to if I knew how, but I don't. So I can't."

Maybe dancing would break the ice. The date had been going downhill anyway. What did he have to lose? "Give me your hand. Let's just go watch."

She bit her lip. "I don't think so, Sam."

"OK, we'll watch from here." He sat back down. "They're doing the Texas Two Step. I'm not the best dancer, but the basics are really pretty easy. Just ignore all those fancy turns and stuff. The couples move in a counter-clockwise direction around the floor, the man facing forward and the woman moving backward. Can you see?"

She nodded.

"Now the steps. The guy begins by stepping forward on his left foot while his partner steps back on her right. There are four steps, like this. Quick, quick, slow...slow. Quick, quick, slow...slow. Got it?" He repeated the sequence of steps while the couple in the hats continued and she watched. Her head nodded in time with his words.

She turned toward him and smiled. "I see. It's easier than I thought. All those other moves distracted me."

"Don't get me wrong. Some of the steps can get pretty complicated. But the basics? They're easy." He stood up and faced her again. "So, Katherine, would you like to dance?" The music stopped as the band retuned for the next song. "Perfect timing."

"But what about your knee?" Her eyes opened wide as she bit her bottom lip again.

His heart pounded. *Nice!* "My physical therapist will be extremely pleased."

"I don't know. I hadn't planned on dancing tonight." Her face turned bright red.

"Neither had I. Didn't know we'd have the chance. Last time I was here, a Mariachi band played. Now trying to dance to that might hurt the knee." As he moved his hand closer, she sighed.

"I, uh, guess so." She stood without giving him her hand. "Lead on."

When they reached the dance floor, he led her to the outer perimeter, turned, and held out both hands. "We can start by holding hands instead of in the traditional dance position. That way you can see your feet if you need to."

As she faced him, he grasped her hands. They were clammy. He squeezed them and then gently shook them up and down. "Relax. It'll be fun. Just remember to start by stepping back with your right foot."

As the music began, he moved her hands in time to the cadence of the steps. "Quick, quick, slow...slow. Quick, quick, slow...slow."

As she repeated his words, she looked into his eyes, and he saw fear. "Quick, quick, slow...slow. Quick, quick, slow...slow."

"OK, here we go." As he stepped forward, she stepped back, and they began moving around the floor. Her brow wrinkled as she continued to repeat the cadence under her breath.

He remained quiet so he wouldn't interrupt her concentration.

About halfway through the song, her face relaxed as she looked into his eyes and smiled. "I think I got it," she said. "You were right. It's really pretty easy."

He winked. "Told you. I wouldn't steer you wrong." She was ready, so he let go of her left hand, placed his right hand high on her back, and gently pulled her into a more traditional Two Step posture. When she widened her eyes, he leaned close to speak into her ear. She smelled great. Even better than that night in high school. Hard to believe he still remembered. "Now, no one will think I'm a beginner."

She rolled her eyes. Her movements were more wooden than when they'd been holding hands earlier. Plus, she was pulling him. He moved his right hand from her back and grasped her left hand. "Let's go back to this. I think it's better."

After a few more passes around the dance floor, the band transitioned into a slower song and the dancers moved into slow-dance position. She stepped away, but he held her hand tight. "How about one more? Nothing complicated about a slow dance."

"Thanks, but I need to pass. I'm kind of tired. In fact, I think I'm getting a headache." She looked down at her watch and then back up into his face. "It's later than I thought. I probably should be getting home soon. I've got an early day tomorrow." She looked away.

Although it had rarely happened, he knew a brush-off when he got one. He'd definitely broken the ice—and gotten sucked all the way down to the bottom in the process. Yep, he was drowning in frigid water. "Sure. Me, too. You're probably right. We should head home."

~*~

Katherine waited while Sam opened her car door. Her breathing quickened as she stepped onto the driveway and he followed her to the kitchen steps. Time for the awkward good night. He'd better not try to kiss her. Turning to face him, she took a deep breath. "I had a nice time, Sam. Thanks so much for dinner...and the Two Step lesson."

Only his thumbs showed as he jammed his hands into his front pockets and smiled. "Sure. I needed the practice. It's been awhile. You did great, by the way." The porch light reflected off his bald head. "Oh, and thanks for choosing Tex-Mex instead of sushi."

She climbed the first step and then turned back to look at him. "You're welcome. Good night, Sam. Thanks again."

He hadn't moved. "Good night, Katherine."

She moved up one more step. "Bye. I, uh, guess I'll see you around."

He nodded. "I would imagine so. Crescent Bluff's a small town." He still didn't move.

She smiled, but he remained motionless. "Is there something you need?"

"Only for you to go inside. Can't leave a lady on the doorstep." He crossed his arms over his chest and grinned.

Her face and neck burned. "Oh, sure. Of course. Good night. Again." He probably thought she was some sort of socially inept idiot.

As Katherine stepped into the kitchen and closed the door, the rich aroma of freshly baked chocolate chip cookies greeted her. She looked toward the overstuffed, blue toile chair in the family room where Mom should have been sitting, but it was empty. The cookies had to be slice and bake.

A deep-throated hum signaled Sam's departure, and Dad walked into the kitchen from the dining room. "Hi, sweetie."

She moved close, pulled him into a hug, and placed her head on his chest. "Daddy, you didn't have to make cookies." A lump formed in her throat as she looked up into his face.

His eyes reddened. He was trying so hard to soften the blow of their loss. Breathing deeply, he kissed her on the top of her head. His words were whispered. "Your mother loved the postdate recap. No way am I breaking the tradition." He pulled out a stool and sat at the island.

"I'll get the milk." She couldn't remember a time when she'd come in from a date that Mom hadn't met her with freshly baked cookies and cold milk. One of the few areas of life in which she'd been consistent.

The summer after her freshman year in college, Katherine had finally figured out that the after-date cookies were Mom's way of snooping. And it had always worked. If it hadn't been for chocolate chips, she'd have gone straight to bed, and by the morning, the excitement would have waned, and the shared facts would have been edited down.

Mom had been a smart woman.

Katherine set the glasses of milk down and perched on the stool next to Dad.

He popped a cookie into his mouth. "So how was the evening with James?" He smiled.

"What? Dad, his name is—"

"Bond...James Bond." He raised his eyebrows and cocked his head to the side.

Sam looked absolutely nothing like James Bond—any of them.

He slowly shook his head. "The car, Katherine, the car. He's driving the same kind of car 007 drives. Nice set of wheels." His eyes suddenly widened. "I wasn't spying or anything. I, uh, just had to look out the window when I heard the sound of that engine." He'd always liked expensive, exotic, foreign cars, although he'd never owned one.

"The date was fine, Dad. We went to dinner at The Cantina." She nibbled on a cookie. Two was all she'd allow herself. When she was younger, she hadn't had to watch her weight. But now she needed to be careful. She couldn't hurt her father's feelings, though. "The cookies are delicious."

"So, did you like him? James Bond? What did you think?"

Be gentle. "It's hard to tell much from one date, Dad. He seems to be a nice man. I'm just not sure how much we have in common. And in all honesty, he's really not my type."

"Give him a chance, Katherine. Give him a chance." He placed a stack of cookies on his napkin. "So tell me about the car. Any machine guns or heat-seeking missiles behind the grill?"

"Oh, Dad," she laughed. "It was fast."

Minutes later, Katherine picked up the black embossed notebook from her nightstand that Dad had given her for Christmas and opened it to today's list. She put a check mark beside the final entry—Blind Date. Done. Turning the page, she read over tomorrow's list. Devotion; Snacks and Drinks; Soccer Game; Store; Revise Resume; Gym; Unpack. After Store she inserted Plastic Tubs and Organize Closet.

Somebody—probably Cassie—had moved the vase of tulips from the kitchen to her dresser. Tulips had always been one of her favorite flowers. Interesting that Sam chose them over roses or a more traditional "date" flower. Maybe someone had told him. Or maybe they were on sale at the grocery store.

She turned off the lamp and waited for her eyes to adjust to the dark. Her body begged to sleep, but her mind replayed tonight's date. Something about it really weighed on her, but she couldn't quite pinpoint what. After all, it hadn't been so bad...for a blind date, especially. Sam seemed like a nice enough guy, and he would have been OK looking if he'd had some hair.

But he didn't match her ideal man. The One. Maybe that was it.

Yes. She breathed slowly to calm herself.

No. He hadn't even tried to kiss her good night. Hadn't even acted as if he'd wanted to. While she wouldn't have let him, of course, just knowing he'd wanted to, that he was attracted to her, would have been flattering.

But then, maybe he hadn't wanted to go out on the date any more than she had. Maybe he'd gone out of respect for his aunt as she had for her father. Her eyes burned with tears of disappointment. As she rolled over onto her side, she snuggled into the familiar cocoon of Nana Herrington's lone star quilt and pulled her knees up. Why did she even care?

As a tear escaped down her cheek, she grabbed a tissue from the box on the nightstand and dabbed her cheeks. Well, tonight she and Sam had both fulfilled their responsibilities. The date was over, and she could get on with her life. She'd never have to see, much less go out with, him again.

At least one thing about tonight was certain.

He absolutely wasn't The One.

3

Katherine walked the entire length of the soccer complex from the concession stand to the far field. How could Cassie have forgotten something as basic as her water bottle? She was just like Mom had been— disorganized and distracted. Well, at least water could be bought here at the field. Last week they'd had to turn around and go back home for her cleats. Her cleats, of all things!

She'd been Cassie's age when she'd started keeping lists, and that had changed her life. When she went to the store today, she'd buy Cassie a notebook and help her get organized.

The team ran warm-up drills as Katherine set the water by Cassie's gym bag and walked over to Dad. Flopping down into the folding chair next to his, she sighed, "I hope four bottles is enough."

"I'm sure it will be, Katherine. Thanks. You're a good big sister." He reached over and patted her on the knee.

She should be more patient with Cassie.

"Hey," he continued, "I hear Brad Thompson's brought on some new consultant to help finish out the year. Rumor has it he's a pro from England."

Katherine looked across the field to the far end. A third man had joined Brad and John on the sidelines.

He was dressed in black soccer shorts, socks and cleats, and a black and red warm-up jacket with a white crest on the back embellished with red letters—FFC. His hood covered his head.

"Dad, I can't imagine that's true. They may have gotten someone to help, but what professional soccer player would come half way around the world to a little town like Crescent Bluff to help coach a girls' soccer team?"

He nodded his head across the field and chuckled. "Either way, your sister seems excited."

Facing their direction, Cassie waved both hands above her head, pointed toward the black-hooded coach, and gave two thumbs up. When she poked him in the middle of the crest, he turned around to face across the field. Cassie pointed in their direction.

The guest coach pulled his hood down to reveal a hairless head. He smiled and waved.

Heart pounding, Katherine gasped.

"What is it?" Dad leaned forward and stared at her. "Are you OK?"

"It's him."

"Who?"

She pointed and responded with an obligatory wave. "Him...James Bond."

~*~

For the next few minutes, as much as Katherine tried, concentrating on the game proved almost impossible. Her eyes continually strayed from the players...to the sidelines...to Sam.

Standing with his arms crossed, he appeared to be

a casual observer with no more, maybe even less, interest than she or her father had. While Brad and John coached from the sidelines, Sam watched, offering no comments. A fan, no doubt, but certainly not a professional soccer player. He was in public relations, or so he'd said last night. Oh, well, that's how rumors got started.

At the end of the first half, their best defender turned her ankle when she tried to stop an attack.

As she hobbled to the sidelines, it didn't take a medical license to know she was finished for the day.

After Brad, John, and even Sam had a brief meeting, Sam pulled Cassie aside and talked with her.

When the team returned to the field, Cassie was in the back in the place of the injured player. Cassie had always played midfield because that was, as Brad said, "the most forgiving position." She was a good player when she concentrated on the game, she just wasn't as intense as most of the other girls. She played for fun, not blood. Past coaches had always said she had great potential if she'd only apply herself.

The last half of the game would not be good.

"Hey, look at your sister. They've moved her to fullback. This should be interesting." Dad raised his eyebrows and chuckled.

Disastrous was a better word. Cassie was too easily distracted to be the last person before the goalkeeper.

As Cassie turned toward Katherine and her father, her face was red and her eyes as big as saucers. She clenched her jaw and raised her eyebrows. Her mouth formed a word. *Yikes.* Then she turned in Sam's direction.

He held up a "you-can-do-it" fist, smiled, and

nodded.

Forty-five minutes later when the ref blew the final whistle and the teams lined up for the routine "good game" high fives, the opposing team's score was the same as it had been at the half. They'd scored no more goals. Cassie's team had won, and she'd had been a wild woman.

Katherine had never seen her play like that in all ten years of her soccer life.

Congratulations complete, Cassie ran over to Sam and chest-bumped him. *Oh, dear.* They'd have a talk about that later. Sam was a man, not one of Cassie's contemporaries or friends. Next Cassie held her hand up for a high five, and he responded by slapping her hand and then momentarily closing his fingers around hers.

Katherine's right hand tingled as the memories of last night's Two Step and Sam's continuing to hold her hand as he'd invited her to slow dance suddenly replaced the scene across the field. On the dance floor, she'd been so worried about counting steps to avoid making a fool of herself, she really hadn't relaxed and enjoyed their dance. She'd wanted to leave as a victor over the Two Step. But now that she was out of the moment, the remembrance flooded her with warmth. An involuntary giggle escaped.

"What's so funny, Katherine?" Dad smiled, his eyes sparkling in anticipation.

She cleared her throat. "Nothing."

~*~

"Great playing, young lady." Sam dropped

Cassie's hand. "Knew you could do it." What a surprise to see her this morning. He hadn't thought to ask her what team she'd played for when they were talking last night before Katherine came out.

"Thanks, Sam. C'mon, I want you to meet my dad. And I'm sure Beth would like to see you." She winked and then trotted off across the field.

Probably not. Meeting her dad was fine, but Sam was most likely the last person Katherine would want to see. He'd embarrassed her last night. She'd expected him to try to kiss her, and everything in him had wanted to, but he hadn't. He wouldn't mess that up twice. Although, maybe the first time didn't really count. They'd only been kids. Plus that attempt had been more like a hit-and-run than a kiss.

Half way across the field, Cassie stopped, placed her hands on her hips, and yelled back in his direction. "Sam? You coming?"

Let the good times roll. "You bet." He grabbed his bag and jogged over to meet Mr. Herrington.

Cassie hugged her father as he spoke. "Great game, Cass. I've never seen you play like that."

"Thanks! Daddy, this is Sam. He was Beth's date last night."

Sam extended his hand. "Hello, Mr. Herrington. Sam Tucker."

"Call me Jim. Nice to meet you, Sam."

"The same, sir." He dropped Jim's hand and turned toward Katherine. "Good morning, Katherine."

Her face reddened. "Hello, Sam. This is quite a surprise."

"Same here." In the bright morning light, she was even more beautiful than she'd been last night. Clean and fresh looking. He was staring.

As she looked away and focused on the ground, Sam looked back at her dad.

Jim cleared his throat and briefly glanced sideways toward Katherine. "So, I'd heard the team was bringing on a professional soccer player to help coach Cassie's team for the rest of the season. I'm guessing you're the guy."

Katherine's eyes were still downward as Sam answered. "Well, sir, it's more of an advisory position. Brad and I were college roommates, and when he found out I was coming to Crescent Bluff on medical leave, he asked if I'd be willing to help. So, Brad and John are still the coaches. But, yeah, I'm the one."

Jim nodded. "I see. Well, I already respect your advice. I've never seen Miss Cassandra play quite like that." He pulled Cassie close and kissed her on the top of her head. "Well done, sweetie."

Sam held out a fist toward Cassie, and she bumped it back. "I knew she could do it, and she didn't let me down."

"It was fun. Scary, but fun." Cassie grinned.

"So, who do you play for, Sam?"

"Fulham Football Club in the UK."

Katherine turned and stepped away.

"Glad to have you on board, son." Jim shook his hand again. "Cassie, let's go across the field and get the cooler."

"But Dad, do I have to? It's not that heavy."

"Cassie, I'd like your help, please." Jim smiled at him. "Nice to meet you, Sam."

"Same here, sir."

As Cassie and Jim headed across the field, Sam turned toward Katherine.

She had one camp chair folded up under her arm

and was trying to pull the carrying bag up around it.

He stepped toward her. "Here, let me help you with that."

Her eyes never left the chair. "It's OK. I've got it." Her words were short, cool.

"I'll just get this one then." He collapsed her father's chair, pulled the bag around it, tightened the cord at the top, and laid it on the ground. "Sure I can't give you a hand with that one?"

"No." She exhaled out loud and flipped her chair upside down. Struggling to slip the bag on over the chair feet, she muttered under her breath, "Stupid chair."

Something had upset her, and most likely, not the chair. As amusing as the scene was, he wouldn't laugh. She was frustrated enough without making it worse, and besides, she was particularly cute when she was angry.

Her face was a little redder this time, her voice a bit louder. "What in the world is wrong with this thing?"

The question was obviously rhetorical, but he'd answer anyway. "I'm guessing the feet are caught on the cord or something inside the bag."

As she jerked the bag off the chair, it fell over.

He'd watched long enough. This was his chance. He reached down and picked it up. "Come on, Katherine. Hand me the bag, please."

"Sam, I said I could do this." Her face was scarlet.

"I'm not doubting your abilities. It's not about you. The least you can do is help me feel useful by humoring me. Besides, I minored in chair-folding in college, you know."

As she looked over at him, he grinned. Uh-oh, no

corresponding smile.

Lips pursed, she handed him the bag. "Whatever."

Opening the bag all the way, he slowly slipped it down over the chair. Then he flipped the chair upright and tightened the cord. "There you go. See, as I said, I'm a trained professional."

"Yeah, so I heard." She spat out the words as she glared at him.

Something more than chair-folding was going on here. He reached down and picked up both chairs and then looked straight into her eyes. "What's that supposed to mean?" All he'd done was help fold up a couple of chairs.

"Never mind. I don't think this is the time or place to go into it." She crossed her arms and looked away.

The sidelines were filling up with onlookers for the following game.

She was right. He stepped closer and lowered his voice. "When, then?"

"Hey, Sam." Cassie's voice broke through the tension as she and Jim set the cooler on the ground. "My dad's grilling out tonight. Can you come eat dinner with us?"

"Yeah, we'd love to have you, son."

Cassie's eyes sparkled, Jim's were warm, Katherine's...icy. "Sounds great. Thank you, sir." He stepped away from Katherine. "Let me carry the chairs to the car for you."

She grabbed them out of his hands. "No, thanks. We got them here without your help, and we can get them back just fine." She turned and marched away, one bag hung on each shoulder.

Jim flashed his palms up in the hands-off position, and shook his head.

The two read each other's mind. *Women...*
Sam called out, "Tonight, then, Katherine."

~*~

She sank back into the wicker rocker in the upper seating area of her mother's garden. She hadn't come close to getting everything on her list done today, especially since she'd had to run to the grocery store and then prepare all the side dishes for tonight. The make-believe headache she'd used as an excuse last night had blossomed into a full-blown reality. Enveloping herself in the dark womb of her bedroom and the silkiness of the chenille throw at the foot of her bed sounded like heaven. But no. Time instead to put on a happy face for company.

The mockingbirds echoed the cheerful call of the cardinals, and somewhere in the distance a couple of squirrels gossiped back and forth. Before long, the grating summer music of cicadas would be all she could hear in the evenings. She closed her eyes, leaned her head back, and breathed deeply. The soft scent of jasmine and roses flowed over her. Mom had poured so much of herself into this haven.

When she'd been a child and the Sunday School Bible story had been about the Garden of Eden, Katherine had always envisioned this spot. Truly, she couldn't imagine how paradise could be any more wonderful. Except for the weeds...surely there they would be nonexistent.

Before long, everything would be in bloom, and then she'd have her hands full. She'd never been interested in gardening, but out of love for her mother she'd do all she could to keep the yard in shape while she was home.

Today had been a disaster, starting with seeing Sam at the soccer game. She'd acted like a spoiled child at the field this morning. But she'd been, and still was, angry with him. He'd lied to her. Just one more in the list of traits she wasn't looking for—short, bald, and dishonest. Neither was smug, as far as she could remember.

Yet, she hadn't exactly earned the kindness award today. For some reason, he seemed to bring out the worst in her. But no matter how he'd behaved or what his character was or wasn't, she owed him an apology.

From around the front of the house came a deep-throated rumble. James Bond had arrived.

Normally, she would have gotten up and let him in the house, but Cassie would take care of that. Young girls always seemed to have crushes and dreamed of relationships that could never be. Maybe they saw a maturity in older men that boys their age lacked. Or maybe Cassie saw some of the characteristics in him that she wanted in her future husband. Plus, knowing the relationship could never develop made it safe. She could love from afar without the strain of commitment or the mess of a breakup when she found out he wasn't The One.

She'd have to talk with Cassie and set her straight.

The fresh scent of his cologne blended in with the garden potpourri. He came out the patio door and down the steps from the deck behind her. His deep voice sounded. "Hello, Katherine. Lovely evening."

British. A mixture of British and Texan. No wonder she hadn't been able to place his accent last night. She turned and looked up at him. "Hi, Sam."

He was dressed in long, baggy shorts, a formfitting royal blue t-shirt, and flip flops, a glass of ice tea in his hand. The color of the shirt only enhanced the rich blue of his eyes.

As her stomach fluttered, she gestured toward the chair next to hers. "Please, have a seat."

"Thanks." He dropped down in the companion rocker.

"Where's your shadow?"

"Pardon?"

"Cassie."

"Oh, my biggest fan?"

When he grinned, her heart jumped.

"Your father has her busy helping him." He sat up and turned toward her. "He's a nice man, your dad."

Katherine smiled. "Yes, he is. My mom was a nice lady, too."

"I imagine she was." He leaned back in the chair and focused toward the trellis across the way. The rocker creaked against the stone patio as his feet pushed it back and forth. "Is this the time and place?"

He certainly jumped right to the point. No easing his way in.

The rocking stopped as he looked into her eyes. "I've obviously done something to offend you, and I'd like to apologize for whatever it is."

She took a deep breath. "No, Sam. I'm the one who needs to apologize for this morning. What you did shouldn't have had any bearing on my behavior. I'm responsible for my actions, and I let them get out of control."

"I didn't realize helping you fold up some chairs was off limits."

"It wasn't that."

"If you'll tell me exactly what I did, I'll see if I can fix it." His eyes were warm.

Her heart beat faster. *Here we go.* "You lied to me."

"What?" His eyebrows knit together as if she'd spoken Greek.

"Last night you told me you were in PR, and then this morning you tell my dad you're a professional soccer player. And from what I observed at the field today, that's the truth. Why would you lie to me?" Her heart pounded even faster, and a lump formed in her throat. She hardly knew him, and his actions shouldn't affect her like this, shouldn't even matter.

He ran a hand across the top of his head as if smoothing his hair...if he'd had hair to smooth. "That's it?" he asked, a smile spreading across his face. And then he chuckled.

So, he thought this was funny. Not to her.

His words were gentle. "I didn't lie to you."

"Oh, so you lied to my dad, then." Either way he was dishonest.

"Whoa, there. Don't go deciding guilt or innocence without all the facts." The smile was gone. In silence, he stared again at the trellis and then turned back toward her. "May I approach the bench, Your Honor?" The smile was back.

How could he be so flippant? "I'm serious. Honesty is important to me."

"Me, too." He cleared his throat. "May I approach the bench?" This time the words were spoken slowly, stressed as if they'd not been understood the first time.

So now he was making fun of her. "I guess. Something tells me it wouldn't really matter how I answered."

"Probably not." He paused. "I'm under contract to

play football for Fulham through the end of next year. Instead of breaking the contract when I destroyed my knee, management moved me to PR until I could return to the field. Right now, I'm on a six month leave to recuperate. And I came here because I needed some time away and thought a change of scenery would be good." His eyes reached deep into hers.

Her face was on fire. Not only had she insulted him, she'd made a fool of herself.

He took a long drink of his tea. "The verdict, Your Honor?"

"Not guilty, Mr. Tucker. I'm really sorry. I shouldn't have been so judgmental." If only she could hit the rewind button. "I hope you'll forgive me."

"I don't know, Katherine," he replied, looking down at his feet. "Having one's integrity called into question can be quite insulting." When he looked back into her face, his eyes twinkled. "Maybe some penance would be appropriate here."

"Penance?"

"Yeah, penance." His forehead wrinkled and he pursed his lips. "Another Two Step lesson ought to do it. I may never be able to forgive you, otherwise."

The breath she'd been unconsciously holding escaped as she relaxed back against the chair cushion. If he'd been Clark, she'd never have heard the end of it. But he wasn't. Sam seemed to have a good heart, even though he wasn't her type. Having romantic feelings toward him was out of the question, but maybe they could become friends. Seemed as if they both needed one right now.

"I don't see how I could go on if you were unable to forgive me." She smiled. "Penance, it is."

He grinned as he stood, held up his left hand, and

opened his right in invitation.

"Now? Here?" Her palms became clammy just as they had yesterday evening.

"Sure. Why not? Or is this not the time or place again?"

"Well, I just...I mean, I hadn't planned on this tonight."

"Oh, I see. So your penance needs to be planned. OK, how about if we plan on next Friday night? Say about five o'clock? With some dinner afterward? Is that planned enough?"

4

Katherine leaned back against the smooth porcelain of the bathtub and closed her eyes while the steamy water blanketed in citrus and vanilla scented bubbles rose up to her chin. What a week. Thank goodness it was over. Dad had left for Southeast Asia last night, so maybe things would be calmer now that she'd gotten him out the door. Sam should be here in about an hour, and she was soaking in this tub until the last possible minute.

She hadn't seen him since Saturday night when she'd apologized, and he'd arranged her "penance." That evening's headache had grown so intense she'd ended up excusing herself from dinner, leaving Dad and Cassie to entertain him for the rest of the evening. But that was OK. After all, he'd been their guest. Not hers.

She'd figured he'd call the house sometime this week to confirm tonight, but he hadn't. Maybe he'd forgotten and wasn't coming. If so, that would be absolutely fine. Displaying her fledgling dance skills in the middle of the sea of people at The Cantina again wasn't really her idea of a fun time.

"Beth?" Cassie's voice squeezed under the bathroom door.

"Yes, sweetie."

"You just got a text. Want me to bring your phone in?"

It had to be someone in Dallas. She hadn't given her number to anyone here in Crescent Bluff. Well, except Brad. Maybe it was something about soccer. Or it might be from Clark. He'd promised he'd contact her if business picked back up.

When she'd turned down his proposal and suggested they take some time apart, he'd granted her wish by laying her off. Although he'd assured her the temporary layoff was simply a business decision and nothing personal, the dismissal had been very personal to her. The message certainly could be from him.

"Beth? Did you hear me?"

"Sorry, Cassie. Can you see who it's from?"

Cassie's voice rang with excitement. "It's from Sam."

"Sam? How did he get my number?"

"He asked for it last night at soccer practice, and I gave it to him. I meant to tell you, but I forgot."

"Cass, I'd prefer that you not give out my phone number to just anyone."

"Sam's not just anyone. He's your boyfriend."

"He's not my boyfriend."

"You're dating, aren't you? Want me to bring your phone in?"

Katherine sighed. Cassie would continue to argue any reply she could offer. "Why don't you read it to me, please?" Maybe he'd texted to say he'd forgotten or was canceling. She crossed her fingers and would have crossed her toes if she was capable of that feat.

"It says, 'Planning on our plan for your planned penance.' What's that supposed to mean?"

"Just that he's coming at five. That's all. Thanks,

sweetie. I'll be out in a few minutes." Katherine ran a little more hot water into the tub and grabbed her loofah. No more relaxing.

~*~

Katherine glanced sideways at Sam as he pulled up to the intersection where the truck had honked at them last Friday. Tonight, he didn't ask which way she wanted to go.

He simply turned left toward The Cantina. He looked really nice in khakis and a light blue, button-down shirt. In the soft evening light, his eyes were more the icy turquoise of those glaciers on television's nature channel than the deep blue of the Caribbean. He must know what blue did for his eyes. He'd worn it three of the four times she'd seen him. When he looked her way and smiled, electricity coursed through her body, causing an involuntary shiver.

Raising his eyebrows, he reached to turn down the air conditioning. "Too cold?"

She was anything but cold. "No," she replied. "I'm fine."

They sped by the cutoff for The Cantina. "Sam, you missed the turn."

"No, I didn't," he said, grinning.

"But what about my penance?"

As he reached over and squeezed her hand, the warmth from his touch flooded though her. "No worries. Planned is what you wanted. Planned is what you'll get."

She pulled her hand away. "Where are we going?"

"It's a surprise. Now settle back and relax. We've

got a bit of a ride ahead." The British-ness of his accent was back.

"Couldn't you give me a hint?" Her heart rate increased.

"I just did."

She turned toward him. "Sam, that was no hint."

"Well, it's all you're getting." He winked.

"I'm a little uncomfortable with this. My dad's out of the country, and Cassie's by herself. I told her we'd be at The Cantina."

"Cassie knows where we'll be. She has your cell number, and I gave her mine...and my aunt's. Aunt Ginny's only five minutes away. Plus, she'll call Cassie and check on her later tonight." As he smiled gently, he turned toward her. "Planned well enough for you?"

Having dropped some in the sky, the sun now shined in through the window behind him. Fine, light-colored stubble covered his entire head. Hair!

"Katherine? Are you OK with that?"

"Yes." She'd been staring.

"What's up then?"

She cleared her throat. "Your head. You're not bald." She pulled her mouth shut.

"Well, not permanently, I hope." He chuckled. "Just showing support for my teammates." He ran his hand across the top of his head as he'd done in the garden last Saturday. "You know how some athletes have weird superstitions? Well, five years ago, one of the team captains shaved his head in January, and the club had the best record in their history. So, ever since then, the captains shave their heads for the spring. And even though I wasn't playing due to my knee, I still wanted to encourage the guys."

All those weird habits and behaviors that some

athletes practiced often became obsessive-compulsive. And then for them to think that they really had some effect on the outcome. "You don't mean to tell me you believe that stuff, do you?"

"Me? Heck, no. Winning's like everything else in life. It's mostly about hard work and doing your best with what you've been given. Anyway, the season's almost over, and I'm far away. Time to grow the hair back."

She leaned her head back against the leather seat. So, he wasn't bald...or dishonest. But he was still short—well, less tall—and nothing he could do or undo would change that.

They drove all the way across Fort Worth to the north side and pulled up in front of Cattlemen's Hotel. Every time she'd come to the Stockyards, this historic, old hotel had fascinated her. She'd passed by the patrons rocking in chairs on its front sidewalks many times but never gone inside. Eating here, staying here, was something she'd always wanted to do. Tonight could be fun after all.

The last time she'd been to the Stockyards was this past summer when she'd thought Clark was The One, and they'd met her parents for dinner and the rodeo. She was sure she'd loved Clark. He was the man she'd dreamed about for years, but their relationship was not exactly the picture of what she'd thought love would be. Sometimes it felt more like a business arrangement than a romance. Predictable, respectful, guarded.

Sam hit the unlock button.

A young man dressed in black opened her door. "Good evening, ma'am. Welcome to Cattlemen's." He offered his hand and helped her onto the sidewalk.

Sam jumped out of the other side. "Hi, Kyle."

"Hello, Mr. Tucker. Nice ride. New?" Kyle walked around the front of the car.

"Yeah. Picked it up in Dallas a few days ago. Thanks." Sam handed the valet the keys.

"We'll take good care of her, sir." Kyle touched the tips of his fingers to his forehead in a casual salute.

"Appreciate it."

As Sam made his way to the sidewalk beside her, Kyle stepped into the crack of the open driver's door. "Sorry to hear about your knee. The team sure did miss you."

"Well, I should be back on the field in a few months after rehab." Sam's hand rested gently on the small of her back as he leaned close and whispered in her ear. "Surprise! We're here. Ready?"

"This is great. Every time I've come to the Stockyards, I've always wondered what it would be like to stay here."

"You have, have you? Well, you can just keep wondering because you won't be staying here tonight either."

Her whole body was on fire. Her words had popped out before she'd considered their possible implication. "Don't be so middle school. That's not what I meant."

He laughed as he reached forward and opened the heavy wooden door. "After you, Katherine."

Stepping into the hotel lobby transported her back a hundred years—high ceilings, antique oak and cowhide furniture flanked by large green palms, planked hardwood floors that were rutted in places by the thousands of feet that had trodden them over the years. Dark, red painted walls and pine bead board wainscoting gave the cavernous room a warm, intimate feel. She could sit here for hours and people-watch.

As they approached the front desk, the young clerk smiled.

Sam stepped up to the window, folded his hands, and placed them on the countertop. "Hi, Tanya."

Tanya turned her head a bit to the side and looked out of the corner of her eye. "Mr. Tucker," she said, "so good to have you back. Everything's ready. You're in the Longhorn Suite. Down the hall, fourth door on the right. Juanita's already there." She placed her hand on top of his. "Just let us know if you need anything else...anything, you understand?" As she turned toward Katherine, her smile was polite. "Ma'am, welcome to Cattlemen's Hotel."

Sam placed his hand on Katherine's back again, more firmly this time, and guided her toward the hallway.

She pulled away and spoke quietly. "Well, that was a pretty blatant invitation, I'd say."

"Who's the middle-schooler now, Katherine?" He stopped and stared straight into her eyes.

Her face had to be the color of the walls in the lobby. "I've just never been out with a guy and had that happen."

"That's 'cause you've never dated me. Except for last Friday, that is." He laughed. "A bit jealous, are we?"

"I won't even answer that question." He'd only twist her words into something she didn't mean. Or worse—into something she did mean but didn't want him to know. The less said the better.

As a smirk covered his face, he shrugged his shoulders. "Seriously, it's much worse in the UK than here. But you get used to it."

So now he seemed to think he was some sort of celebrity. Smug, for sure.

"Here we are." Sam grabbed the handle on one of the double doors on the right side of the hall and held it open for her.

The Longhorn Suite was a large room with a painted, brown tin ceiling, white stucco walls, and dark wooden floors. Giving the room a warm ambiance, glass-globed lanterns that had been converted from gas to electricity decades ago were mounted on the walls at regular intervals around the room. The area to her left was empty except for a heavy wooden console table against the side wall. An electronic music player was docked on the top. A huge set of horns were mounted on the wall at the far end.

A stone fireplace with an enormous metal star hanging above the rustic mantel dominated the other end of the room. On one of the two leather loveseats flanking its hearth sat a sixty-something woman with a massive amount of bleached, blonde hair. "Hi, y'all." She was dressed in a fringed and sequined western shirt and tight jeans crammed into cowboy boots with peacocks tooled into them. Expensive and custom made, no doubt. She stood, walked toward them, and stuck out her hand. "I'm Juanita. You must be Sam."

So not everyone in Fort Worth knew Sam.

He extended his hand. "Nice to meet you, Juanita. Thanks for coming." He placed his left hand on Katherine's back again. His touch was starting to feel routine. "I'd like you to meet Katherine."

"Hi, sugar." Juanita stepped forward and hugged her. "Nice to meet you."

"Thank you. Nice to meet you, as well."

Juanita rubbed her hands together and then clapped them once. "OK," she said, "let's see what I'm working with here. You two face each other and hold hands."

As they did what she asked, she began rubbing her chin, and with her eyebrows knit together, circled them like a predator sizing up its prey. "Um-hmmm. You two are gonna be fine. Just the right height difference. When the man's too tall or the woman's too short it can be hard. Imagine a Chihuahua trying to dance with a Great Dane. Ain't a pretty sight. But you two are gonna be perfect partners. Yes, sir, perfect."

As Katherine looked up at Sam, she bit the inside of her cheeks to keep from smiling.

He winked in response.

"All right. Time to show me what you got." The heels from Juanita's boots pounded the floor as she strutted over to the console table. She pushed a button, and some country song blasted out. Juanita yelled over the music, "Quick, quick, slow...slow. Quick, quick, slow...slow."

Not only Katherine's hands but her entire body was clammy.

Sam smiled. "Ready?"

As she nodded, her stomach rolled. Whether she was ready didn't really matter.

Juanita wasn't about to wait.

They began their trip around the room while Juanita yelled the cadence and scrutinized their every move.

Katherine's knees wobbled like jelly as she moved backward. She trained her eyes on the top button of Sam's shirt to keep them from dropping down to watch her feet. She had to do better than last Friday.

Juanita's voice sounded over the music. "Not too bad for beginners. Now drop hands and move to the traditional position."

Sam dropped her left hand, placed his right hand high on her back, and pulled her closer. She stepped forward and placed her left hand high on his shoulder.

"Katherine, honey, move your left hand to the shoulder seam of his shirt and back away. You're way too close."

Sam smiled and whispered, "That's a matter of opinion."

Her breathing quickened, and her heart began to keep pace with the music.

"Katherine? You hear me? This ain't no slow dance."

"Oh, sorry." She moved her hand and took a deep breath. This hadn't gone well last week when they'd tried it at the Cantina. Maybe she'd been too close then, and moving backward made her afraid she would back into someone or something.

"One, two, three, go!"

They continued around the floor in a counterclockwise motion until the music suddenly stopped.

"Drop hands, and step away." Juanita sounded more like a drill sergeant than a dance instructor. She walked over and put her hands on Katherine's shoulders. "I see you trying to look back over your shoulder. My lands, honey. If you're ever gonna be a good Two-Stepper, you can't be in charge. You need to let this man lead. He can see where you're going, and he ain't gonna let you run into anything. Ain't that right, Sam?"

Sam's eyes were warm as he replied. "Absolutely."

The music began, and they started again.

Katherine tried really hard not to let her gaze stray to the sides, but trusting him was difficult.

"Stop, stop, stop. This calls for extreme measures." As Juanita neared them, she pulled a hot pink bandana from her back pocket and began rolling it into a blindfold. "We'll fix this little howdy-do." She stepped forward and tied the bandana around Katherine's head.

Katherine's mouth went dry. She couldn't see a thing.

Juanita's voice was gentle. "Now, honey, you just relax and feel the pressure from Sam's hands. You'll be able to tell what he's gonna do by how he moves 'em."

Jaunita must be crazy.

No one could be expected to relax under these conditions. Here Katherine was, blind and at the mercy of a Two-Step drill sargeant and a man she hardly knew. Not only was dancing blindfolded the most ridiculous idea she'd ever heard of, it was dangerous.

A hand patted her arm. "Everything's gonna be just fine, sweetie. You let Sam do all the work. OK, you two. Get into position."

A warm hand pulled her right hand upward, another placed pressure on her back, right below her arm, and gently guided her barely forward. She inched the fingers of her left hand up the Oxford cloth until she felt the seam at the top of the sleeve.

"My lands, that's perfect!"

She could feel Sam's hands, but he'd remained stonily quiet since she'd been blindfolded. What if this was one of those pranks where they substituted one man for another and she was dancing with some embarrassing person from her past? Her head prickled as nervousness flushed through her body. No. Sam wouldn't do that. He liked to joke around, but his heart seemed too kind for something as juvenile as that. Sam was there. Besides, she could smell his cologne. If only she could see his eyes, his face. "Sam?" Unbelievable...her voice shook.

"It's OK. I'm here, Beth—uh, Katherine. You'll be fine."

The music started and from somewhere behind her Juanita called out the cadence.

Katherine took a deep breath, and they began. The pressure from Sam's hands told her exactly how far to step. If her steps were too big, she'd feel too much pressure on her back, too small, not enough. After a few steps, her right arm was slightly pulled to her right, while the hand and arm on her back slightly pressed the same direction. They must be approaching the end of the room and beginning the turn to circle back around.

This was actually fun. All she had to think about was moving her feet and letting her body respond to Sam's leading.

"That's right. That's right. Beautiful, you two. Now kinda shuffle them two quick steps. You got it. My lands, you look almost like professionals. I knew you'd be the perfect couple."

Sam's left hand squeezed her right.

In her mind, she could see him smiling, and she smiled back.

The song ended, and they stopped.

Sam untied the blindfold. She'd been right. His eyes twinkled as he grinned.

"See what happens when you trust your partner?" Juanita rubbed her hands together as she had when they'd first begun. "OK, now for some fancier stuff."

~*~

"Thanks so much, Juanita." Sam hugged her and handed her four one hundred dollar bills. Not bad wages for a couple of hours' work.

"Any time, honey." She smiled as she stepped out into the hallway. "Y'all done good."

He pulled his phone out of his pocket to check the time. Dinner would be here any minute. As he closed the door, he turned toward the open end of the room. Katherine was spinning and twirling as she shuffled along, her hands encasing the open space he'd occupied minutes earlier. Her eyes were closed, and she was humming the last song they'd danced to. He could have stood there all night watching. She was gorgeous. Rather than interrupt, he walked toward the fireplace and sat down on one of the loveseats.

Katherine opened her eyes and looked toward him. She glowed. Stopping her dancing, she practically skipped toward him. "Oh, Sam. That was so much fun!"

"I'm glad you had a good time." An hour and a half ago when she'd been blindfolded, he'd thought this date would be a bust like the first one. But Juanita hadn't let him down. "I couldn't have taught you any more than I did last Friday, and I figured we'd both get more out of a private rather than public lesson. I must say, it was a bit intense at first."

Katherine dropped down on the other end of his loveseat. "She was wonderful. Where in the world did you find her?"

"Billy Bob's. She's taught lessons there every Tuesday night for about twenty years. Everybody says she's the best."

"I'd have to agree with that." As Katherine ran her hand through her hair, his blood pressure must have jumped about twenty points. "I'm starving."

A tap sounded on the door. "Right on time." Everything was going according to plan. A plan that had taken him a whole week to finalize. "Come in."

As the heavy oak door swung open, two waiters pushing carts approached the loveseats. The first one spoke. "Your dinner's ready, Mr. Tucker."

They transformed the square, primitive wooden coffee table into a low dining table, complete with candles, linens, tableware, and yellow roses. Eight to ten plates with metal covers sat on the top of the two carts. The second waiter handed Sam an insulated bag. "Your special order, sir. Can we do anything else before we leave?"

"Everything looks great. Thanks, guys." Sam stood and handed them each a hundred.

"Thank you very much, sir. Press the button to the right of the fireplace if you need anything else." They closed the door.

"I wasn't sure what you like to eat, so I ordered a bunch of appetizers and this." He held out the bag to her.

"What is it?" she asked.

"Open it and find out." Sam walked over to the hearth, picked up two Indian blanket pillows, returned, and drop them on the floor beside the table.

"Sushi! But you don't like sushi." As she leaned her head to the side, she questioned with a look.

"Yeah, but you do. Anyway, I don't plan to eat it.

I'm going for the wings." He held out his hand. "Let me help you down to the pillow."

Her eyes reddened. He'd unintentionally done something to upset her. "Thank you, Sam. This is so thoughtful."

"Sure, now for some dinner." He lifted up the covers of the plates, served them to her one at a time, then filled his plate. "How about some music without anyone yelling steps?"

She grinned as he walked over and set the player on a contemporary country station. "That's nice."

He dropped down onto the cushion across from hers.

She was staring at him. She cleared her throat. "So, will you, uh, be at Cassie's game tomorrow?"

"Yep."

"Good. I mean, I think your experience can be a real asset to the team." Katherine drew her gaze away from his and glanced toward her lap for a moment. The lights were low and painted golden highlights in her hair. She looked back up at him and smiled.

The last thing he wanted to talk about right now was Cassie, but… "She's got good instincts. She needed someone to put her in a position where she was the only chance to stop the ball before the goalkeeper. She had to know that when the ball got to her, it had passed all her teammates, and she was the last hope." He popped a stuffed mushroom into his mouth. "When I was about twelve, my coach moved me to sweeper, and it changed my game forever. Teams don't use a sweeper defense much anymore, but it's good for certain situations."

She nodded. "By the way, the sushi's outstanding. Thanks again." She grinned and lifted her eyebrows as she held out the container. "Sure you don't want some?

"Tempted, but I'll stick with the wings right now. I'd hate to deprive you of something you love so much."

"Chick-en!"

He couldn't help but smile. "Exactly...wings, that is."

She pursed her lips and cocked her head. "So, did you always want to be a soccer player?"

"Since I was four. But I got really serious when I was about Cassie's age, and my family moved to North Carolina." No bells seemed to be going off in her head. No recognition. "I played on my high school and college teams. Traveled a bit during the summers. That's when a scout from the UK spotted me." He'd rather be talking about her, but as he took a drink of his tea, she spoke again.

"Do you like it? Being a professional athlete? Living out of the country? I think I'd miss my family and friends." She set down her chopsticks, placed both elbows on the table, and wove her fingertips together. Resting her chin on the fingers, she stared into his eyes, waiting for his response.

"You know, I was young—straight out of college. I thought life was all about fame, fortune, and fun." He set down his glass and picked up a deviled egg. "Let me just say, after years of that, it's not exactly what I thought it'd be. There's gotta be more."

"I know. I think I understand what you mean. Not the fame and fortune part, but the unfulfilled expectations. Reality doesn't always coincide with our hopes and dreams."

The song on the radio transitioned to one they'd danced to earlier. She sprang up. "Hey, want to see if we can still remember the steps?" She held out her hand.

Absolutely. "Sure." He grasped her hand and stood.

They walked over to the empty end of the room, faced each other, and began. She was so relaxed now, leading her was easy. *Thank you, Juanita!*

A smile covered Katherine's face. She was having a great time, and so was he. Too soon the song ended, and an old ballad began. Definitely not a Two Step song.

As he dropped his right hand, she entwined her fingers with those on his left, bit her bottom lip, and looked into his eyes. "Still want that slow dance you requested last Friday?"

He grinned and pulled her close. "I think I could stand it."

She slowly placed her head on his shoulder. She smelled great, kind of like lemonade and sugar cookies. They moved in time to the music. Tonight, when he got her home, she'd want him to kiss her. And he'd want to. Shoot, he already did. But he wouldn't. Not unless she asked. She liked to know what to expect, so he'd promised himself last week that he'd wait until he knew beyond the shadow of a doubt she was ready.

She turned her face upward. "You're a good dancer." Her eyes locked on his. "Thank you for a wonderful evening."

Kissing her right now would be so easy, so natural. He leaned forward and brushed his cheek against hers, placing his lips near her ear. "I need to tell you something," he whispered. "You're forgiven. Your penance is complete."

~*~

Katherine set the notebook on the nightstand and turned off the lamp. Today's entries were all checked off and tomorrow's reviewed. Tonight's date was the best one she'd had in a long time—no—ever. She'd never dated a man like Sam. In fact, she'd never even known a man like him.

Even though he'd tried to be discreet, she'd seen the money he'd given Juanita, the waiters, and the valet. Plus, he'd had to rent the room. He must have spent a fortune tonight.

But the money wasn't what made the date so special. While the evening had been full of surprises, everything about it was as well-planned as if she'd done it herself. He'd been considerate of her feelings and done everything possible to make her feel comfortable. And special. Sushi from Dallas, for goodness' sake!

But then came the good night. Just like last weekend, he'd stood at the bottom of the steps with his hands in his pockets waiting for her to go inside. However, unlike last weekend, if he'd tried to kiss her tonight, she'd have let him. Giving him as much opportunity as possible, she'd dawdled until the delay became embarrassing. Most of the men she'd dated before Clark would have expected some kind of return after having invested a pile of money on a date. Yet, Sam had just stood there grinning.

Last Friday night, she'd thought lack of attraction might be the reason he hadn't tried to kiss her. But tonight, the warmth in his eyes had disproven that theory. When they'd slow-danced after dinner, she'd been sure he would kiss her. She'd hoped so, anyway. As his cheek had brushed hers, her entire body had tingled, but all he'd done was "forgive" her.

As the melody from that song played through her mind, she smiled. Sam was shorter than any other man she'd dated before, but he was taller than she was. And Juanita had been right, he was the perfect height to be her partner. When she'd placed her head on his shoulder against the crook of his neck, and he'd pulled her close, their bodies were like two adjacent puzzle pieces—a perfect fit, as if they were made to go together. His nearness had felt so right.

As she turned over on her side, the smile faded and unwanted tears filled her eyes. Meeting Sam was so unfair. She liked this man a lot. So why couldn't he be The One instead of Clark?

Because Sam wasn't at all the man she'd prayed for these many years. She'd consistently asked God to bring the man on her list into her life, the man who possessed the qualities that would fulfill the deepest desires of her heart, that would make her happy. She'd judged every man she'd dated since high school by those standards, but no one had even come close to measuring up...until Clark.

But if he was the one she'd asked for, she should have been able to say "yes" to him. Yet, she'd been afraid to accept his proposal. Afraid because their relationship lacked one important quality she'd never even thought to put on the list.

Passion. Being trapped in a relationship devoid of passion scared her.

And now, after she'd done everything she could to convince herself that Clark was her Prince Charming,

Sam had shown up to the ball, and she'd felt more passion in the three, no four, times she'd been with him than she'd felt in the years with Clark. Something about Sam ignited her emotions, both good and bad, like sparklers suddenly exploding to life when the flame is held to them the perfect length of time.

Her heart had meandered off course, but her mind pulled it back onto the well-trampled path. She shouldn't have gone tonight. She shouldn't have let her feelings get so far out of control, because no matter what she felt, continuing to date Sam would be a waste of time. They would never be anything more than friends.

5

Eyes closed, Katherine sat on the redwood bench under the arch of sweet jasmine in the backyard while an entire chorus of birds echoed their songs from live oak to live oak. When Sarah's mom had called and volunteered to drive Cassie to the game and then to pizza lunch afterward, Katherine had wimped out of going. The last person she wanted to see today was Sam. Thanks to him, she hadn't slept well last night, and she needed some time to work through all the confusion in the light of day.

The faint dinging of the doorbell drifted out through the open family room windows. Cassie had forgotten her key—again. That girl. She could have just let herself in through the back gate. Katherine walked to the side of the yard, lifted up the wrought-iron latch, and pulled open the gate of the tall wooden privacy fence. "Cassie, you have got to..."

Sam turned to look at her. "Hi." Today he wore black soccer shorts, a jersey from Cassie's team, and soccer slides. His sprouting hair was actually shining in the sun. It couldn't have possibly grown that much overnight. He held up a pink water bottle. "Cassie left this at the field. Is she back yet?"

Katherine must have been so lost in thought she hadn't heard his car. "Uh, no." As he smiled and walked toward her, she ran her fingers through her hair to tame it. If she'd known she would see him, she'd have combed it and put on makeup. At least she had brushed her teeth.

Leaning nonchalantly against the fence, he held out the plastic bottle with his right hand. "Would you mind giving this to her for me?"

"Sure." His nearness alone made her heart rate skyrocket. "Sorry you had to bring it over."

"Oh, I wanted to. I volunteered." He didn't move. He looked over her shoulder into the yard and then back into her eyes. "I had fun last night. Thanks for being such a good sport."

"Sure." She grasped the bottle, but he held on to it.

"Missed you at the game this morning." His eyes were Caribbean again today, even in the red jersey.

If she held his gaze any longer, she wouldn't be able to breathe. She looked at her feet. "I was kind of tired, and when Cassie said Sarah's mom had offered to drive her, I agreed." She looked back up.

His smirk said he wasn't buying her excuse. "Oh well, that's good to know. I thought you might be avoiding something...or someone." He let go of the water bottle and then lifted his eyebrows and waited.

"Sam, I had a really great time last night. In fact, I can't remember ever having a better date. I could tell you'd really put a lot of effort into planning it. I couldn't have done better myself. You'll never know how much I appreciate your efforts."

The smirk softened to a warm smile. "Good. I'm glad. I hoped you'd be able to relax and feel comfortable. That was my goal. But then for a minute, I thought Juanita might ruin everything."

Katherine couldn't help but grin. "I thought so,

too, especially with that blindfold deal. But she was wonderful." Everything inside her screamed, No. She shouldn't do this. "I've been sitting in the back, trying to get in all the garden time I can before the summer heat sets in. Would you like to stay for a few minutes? Cassie should be back any time. I'm sure she'd love to see you."

"Sounds great." He closed the gate behind them and followed her back to the bench.

As she sat on one end, he dropped down onto the other. Placing his elbows on his thighs, he leaned forward. Several pink scars dotted his left knee. "How did your knee hold up after all that dancing last night?"

"Good. I'm thinking about making it my new form of physical therapy. Say, once a week. But I'd need a partner willing to help me out." He turned toward her and smiled. "Know anyone who might be interested in rehabbing an old, broken-down soccer player?"

Her stomach rolled. This conversation was headed in the absolutely wrong direction. She couldn't tell him the truth. She couldn't explain that as wonderful a job as he'd done planning the date and as much fun as they'd had last night, she couldn't go out with him again. He'd never understand.

The door on the deck opened. "I'm back. Sam." Cassie came bounding down the steps.

"Here's the team's star player." Sam stood and high-fived Cassie. "Spectacular job today, young lady."

Cassie's face flushed as she grinned. "Thanks." She crossed her arms and smiled. "What're you guys doing? I didn't interrupt anything, did I?" Her eyes twinkled as she leaned her head to one side.

"No." Katherine held up the water bottle. "Sam

had to make a special delivery because you forgot this. Sweetie, you really need to work on being responsible for your things. If you'd use that notebook I bought you, it would help."

Cassie shrugged her shoulders. "When I forgot my water bottles, Mom would either get me another one or get the old one when we returned to the place I'd left it. It's not that big a deal, Beth. I'll bet Sam didn't mind bringing it by, did you, Sam?"

"Not at all. I wanted to talk to your sister about something, anyway."

Cassie lifted her eyebrows and grinned. "Really? Well, I'll just go into the house and do the dishes."

There were no dishes to do. Katherine had thoroughly cleaned the kitchen after breakfast, so the dishwasher was already loaded and ready to go after she'd put her lunch dishes in. Besides, Cassie had never in her life done dishes or any other household chores as far as Katherine could remember.

When she reached the top step, Cassie turned around and made circular movements with her hands. "Talk amongst yourselves."

As the back door slammed, Sam chuckled. "She's a mess." He sat down and placed an arm on the back of the bench. "Now, where were we? Oh, yeah, my new plan for PT. Any volunteers?"

In a perfect world, she would have had enough time to have carefully considered her answer. But, nothing about life was perfect. Katherine took a deep breath, "Sam..."

"Help! Come quick! Water—"Cassie shrieked as she ran back out.

Sam jumped up, scaled the stairs onto the deck in one step and rushed inside.

Katherine couldn't keep up with him.

A small geyser gushed sideways from under the dishwasher and had covered the floor with hot water.

Cassie jumped up onto a barstool, horrified.

"Katherine, where's the shutoff valve?" Sam asked.

Water flowed toward the family room. They needed to stop it before the whole house was flooded.

"Katherine, the shutoff valve."

"The what? I don't know." Her feet were cemented to the floor.

Water just kept pouring across the floor.

"I didn't mean to break it. It was already loaded. All I did was hit the start button." Cassie wailed.

Sam turned toward her and spoke calmly. "You didn't cause this." He took hold of Katherine's shoulders and looked into her eyes, his voice still calm. "Where's the hot water heater?"

Katherine pointed to her left. "The garage."

Sam disappeared. The gushing stopped.

"All right, Katherine," Sam reappeared. "You and Cassie get some brooms and start sweeping water out the kitchen door. I saw a wet-dry vac in the garage. OK if I use it?"

"That's so kind, Sam. But I don't expect you to help. We can get it."

"Now what kind of a man would I be if I left two of my favorite ladies alone to clean up this mess?" He raised his eyebrows and then turned back toward the garage. "Besides the three of us should be able to knock this out in no time."

After thirty minutes of sweeping, vacuuming, and sopping with the dozen or so towels now piled on the garage floor, everything was dry and as good as new.

Sam put the vacuum away.

Katherine sat down at the kitchen island with the laptop. "Cassie, does Mom, I mean, Dad have a regular appliance repair person he uses?"

Cassie shook her head. "I don't know."

Katherine sighed and opened the computer. "I guess I'll look online. Don't know if I'll be able to get anyone out here today since it's a Saturday. But a dishwasher's not a necessity of life. It can wait until Monday."

"What can wait 'til Monday?" Sam stepped back into the kitchen, holding her Dad's tool chest.

"Repairing the dishwasher."

"If you think your dad would be OK with me borrowing his tools, I should be able to get it fixed for you. I'm pretty sure I know what the problem is. Just need to run to the store for some parts." He set the tool chest on the counter.

"I can't ask you to do that, Sam. You've already helped enough. Besides, we can live without a dishwasher for a few days."

"You didn't ask. But you need to get it repaired today unless you like cold showers. I turned off the hot water, remember?" He lifted his eyebrows and extended his hands, palms up. "Your call."

~*~

Steam billowed up from the kitchen sink as Sam washed his hands under the faucet. "You're good to go." The dishwasher was repaired and back in place—no evidence of the miniature tsunami other than the towels tumbling in the dryer. The forgotten water bottle had ended up being a blessing.

Cassie jumped off the barstool and gave Sam a sideways hug. "Thanks, Sam. You're the best. If I had a brother, I'd want him to be just like you." She stared right at Katherine and grinned. "Isn't that right, Beth?"

Katherine couldn't look him in the eyes. "Well, I, uh..." After last night's final dance, "brother" was not what came to mind. She probably should hug him, too, but what she'd mean as a casual embrace wouldn't feel casual. "No—yes—what I mean is, we really appreciate your help. I don't know what we would have done if you hadn't been here. How much do I owe you?"

"I'd say some ice cream ought to just about do it."

Her resolve to end their relationship, if one could even call two dates that, weakened more every moment he was around. If she could last a couple more weeks, her dad would be back, and she'd have hopefully heard from work and Clark. Maybe by then she could move back to Dallas. Right now, she needed to stand by her decision. Positively no more dates with Sam.

He turned toward Cassie. "What do you think, Cass? Does ice cream sound good to you?"

"You bet." Cassie grinned. "Come on, Beth."

With Cassie along, getting ice cream would be more like a family outing than a date. Besides, Katherine couldn't refuse and let Cassie go out alone with him. It wouldn't be proper. She trusted Sam, but with her dad out of town, she was the responsible adult. "Sure. That's the least we can do after all the help you've given us today."

Smiling, Sam opened the kitchen door, and the three of them walked out toward his car. As he held open the passenger door and moved the front seat so

Cassie could climb in the back, she stepped away. "You know, I just remembered I was supposed to call Sophie. Beth, you'll have to go alone with Sam. Sorry."

The grin on Cassie's face said she was anything but sorry. Katherine had been trapped, and if she backed out now, Sam would know she was making an excuse. She shot Cassie a you're-in-big-trouble look as she pushed the seat back in place and climbed into the car. Maybe this would work out better anyway. Without Cassie along they could talk.

6

Sam backed his car out of the driveway. *Thank you, Cassie!* That girl must be a mind reader.

"A little gourmet ice cream shop recently opened on Main Street—The Scoop. My dad took Cassie and me there last week. Just go down two blocks and turn right."

"I kinda had someplace else in mind."

"Oh." She ran her fingers through her hair again and looked down at her tank top and shorts. "I'm not really in shape to go to any place too fancy."

She looked great—no makeup, tousled hair. He could wake up to this every morning. "You'll be fine. Trust me. I'm not exactly wearing a suit myself." He smiled at her, turned south toward Austin, and shifted through the gears until they reached driving speed.

"Doesn't this car come with an automatic transmission?"

"It does."

"Really? Why wouldn't you get it then? Was the dealership out of that model?"

He couldn't help but chuckle. "The car was made to my specifications. In this time when cars can drive, park, and stop themselves, I want something I can feel in control of. Driving a standard's fun."

"I wouldn't call it fun." She crossed her arms and

looked straight ahead.

He glanced down at the speedometer. Sixty. "I'm not speeding. Am I scaring you again?"

She looked over at him. "I'm not scared now, and I wasn't scared the other night either."

Yeah, right.

"I was remembering the time my grandfather tried to teach me to drive a standard in his old pickup. He laughed, I cried, and we both gave up." She sighed. "As I said, not fun."

"How many lessons did he give you?"

"Only one. Believe me. That was embarrassing enough."

"Most people need more than one." He moved his right hand up to the wheel. "Look down at the gearshift. See the 'H' markings? First is on the upper left, and then you shift straight down, up and over, down, up and over, down. But we probably won't get to that last one."

She pursed her lips together. "I know how to read the diagram on a gearshift, Sam."

"Good. Glad we got that out of the way." He pulled the car off onto the frontage road, stopped at the stop sign, and then he put the car back into first. "OK, put your hand on the knob." This should be fun.

"What?" She opened her eyes wide. "No, I'll ruin your new car."

"You're not gonna spoil—uh, ruin—my car. C'mon, take hold of the gearshift."

She leveled her eyes and shook her head as she grasped the gearshift knob. "Whatever."

As he gently cupped his hand over hers, his heart pounded as it did in the tunnel before the team took the field. He looked over at her to see if she felt the tension, too. Her face was scarlet. Yeah, she did. "Here we go. Just keep your hand on the gearshift."

He gave the car some gas and eased off the clutch. As the speed increased, he guided her hand back into second, then up into third, and finally back to fourth. He glanced right out of the corner of his eye. She was grinning. As he squeezed her hand, she laughed. Her skin felt soft and silky.

Still gripping the gearshift, she leaned forward. A couple of minutes passed before she turned and smiled, her eyes sparkling like chocolate diamonds. "When will we shift into fifth?"

"We're not. I just needed a good excuse to hold your hand."

Her fingers tensed, and she slipped them out from under his. "Oh." She cleared her throat and opened her mouth to speak but then looked out the window.

He drove to the off-ramp at exit ninety-seven.

A smile covered her face. "The Dairy Delite. I didn't know the place was still in business. I haven't been here since the summer after I graduated from high school." She leaned her head to the side and lifted her eyebrows. "How did you know about this place?"

"Doesn't everybody?" He pulled into a space up under the red and blue metal awning, rolled down his window, and pushed the order button.

A young woman's voice cracked over the speaker. "It's a Dee-lightful Day at Dairy Delite. What can I get you?"

Sam leaned toward the speaker. "Two large root beer floats, please. That's all."

The faceless voice rattled off the price. "We'll have your order right out, sir."

He turned back to see Katherine staring at him

open-mouthed. "You didn't even ask me what I wanted."

Whoops!

"How did you know I love root beer floats?" Her forehead wrinkled.

She was so cute when she was puzzled and not in control.

"Doesn't everybody?"

~*~

She dipped her spoon down through the ivory froth and brought up a perfectly proportioned bite of ice cream and root beer. No place in Dallas made floats like this. A Little Bit of Heaven at Exit 97. But a drink wasn't enough payment for what he'd done. "Sam, I'd really like to pay you for fixing the dishwasher."

He lowered his head and looked into her eyes. "Can't a friend help a friend? A 'thank you' is more than sufficient."

The last bite he'd taken had left a small droplet of white foam on his upper lip. As he wiped it away with the tip of his tongue, an unexpected question popped into her mind. What kind of a kisser was he? Probably a pretty good one. Confirming her suspicions would be easy enough. She could lean over and find out right now. In spite of the cold ice cream, fire radiated throughout her body as her mind wandered into forbidden territory again. What was wrong with her? She barely knew him, and what she knew was certainly far from her ideal man—The One. "Thank you, then." She took another bite. "How'd you know what to do, anyway?"

"Just a lucky guess. My dad was a contractor, and I helped him fix things around the house as far back as I can remember. Before I was old enough to really help, I'd hold his tools." A soft warmth settled in his eyes.

"Then in high school and college when I wasn't studying or on the soccer field, I was on the job site with him. Construction work was the only job I had until I signed to play professional football, uh, soccer. My dad never viewed soccer as a career. He wanted me to have real job experience to fall back on when I was tired of playing around." His empty cup rattled as he sucked the last few drops of root beer and air up his straw and then smiled. "He changed his mind." He set his cup on the ledge under the menu board outside his window, and when he turned back the smile was gone. "You go to church?"

Pretty much everyone in Crescent Bluff went to church, out of habit if for no other reason. "Why?"

He rubbed his hand across the top of his head. "I got invited to go tomorrow."

"Invited? By whom?" As if she didn't know.

"Cassie...and Brad. It's been awhile since I've gone, and I just wondered if you'd be there. It would be nice to have someone to sit with, besides Aunt Ginny and Uncle Jess, that is." His eyes were big and soft, searching hers for some sort of acceptance.

"I haven't gone to my church in Dallas for a few months, since right after my Mom..." Her voice caught, and she breathed deeply to steady herself before continuing. "But I'm going with Cassie tomorrow. I guess we could save you a place. I have to warn you, though, get there early. The seats fill up quickly, or at least they did when I was here around Christmas." She handed him her empty cup. "Would you set this on the tray, please?"

He took her cup and set it outside. "Great! Thanks." Putting up the window, he cranked the car. "Ready to head home?" When they reached the entrance to the frontage road, he grinned at her. "The gearshift is all yours, Katherine."

"What?" Her heartbeat increased in proportion to the revving of the engine.

He placed both of his hands firmly on the wheel. "I'm not touching that thing. It's up to you to get us home. Ready?"

"No, I can't do it." Dad had looked this car up online and told her its average price. She wouldn't take any chance at ruining the transmission on a car that to replace would cost more than her entire 401K, and then some of Dad's, too.

His gaze challenged her. "Have it your way." He accelerated out of the parking lot and then said, "Shift."

"No." She wouldn't be manipulated into playing his juvenile game.

The speed of the car grew slower and slower until it finally rolled to a stop in the middle of the road and the engine died. He just sat there with both hands on the steering wheel.

What was he doing? "Sam, go. We might get rear-ended sitting out here like this." She looked over her shoulder. The road was clear, no one behind them.

He flipped on the emergency flashers. "And who's fault would that be?"

The memory of sitting at the intersection to the highway on the blind date when the truck had honked at them popped into her mind. She wouldn't win this battle. He could be so unbelievably infuriating. She grasped the gearshift. "OK. But I'm not taking any responsibility for what might happen to your car."

"Fair enough. I don't believe I asked you to." He restarted the car and accelerated down the road. The revving of the engine stopped. "Shift."

Her heart hammered in her chest as she pulled the gearshift straight back. The car kicked into gear, and the speed increased. She giggled.

"Shift."

Following the H diagram on the knob, she pushed the lever upward and to the right. The car sprang forward as the needle on the tachometer climbed toward the right. They were accelerating onto the highway.

"Shift."

An involuntary squeal popped out as she put the car into fourth. She'd never felt so connected to a car before, and she wasn't even driving it. Something about this seemed totally unsafe...and completely fun. Her hand gripped the gearshift like a vise.

Sam's voice broke into her thoughts. "You can let go, now. Your job's done for a while."

A few minutes later they pulled into her driveway. A part of her wanted to invite him in, but she shouldn't. She'd never had this much trouble reading a man. He didn't ever seem to want to kiss her good-bye, but then he'd admitted earlier he'd wanted an excuse to hold her hand. Maybe he'd been joking. Maybe she was just another of his ridiculous games.

Time spent with Sam was unpredictable. She did things she'd never done before—felt things she'd never felt before. He was turning her plans upside down, which was the very reason she'd vowed just a few hours ago not to go out with him again. Sure, making that choice was easy when he wasn't around. But whenever she was with him, her heart overrode her mind, and all sanity disappeared. She needed to stick by her original decision. No, she wouldn't invite him in.

He opened the car door and offered her his hand to help her out. As she stepped toward the kitchen door, he held her hand tighter and pulled her close. "Hey." The nearer she came to him, the more her resolve ebbed away. Her stomach fluttered. Would he finally kiss her?

His voice was low and hushed. "I've thought of another way you could pay me for repairing the dishwasher."

As his gaze locked on hers, she floated weightlessly in the Caribbean. So much for the discussion she'd just had with herself.

Putting his arm around her, he pulled her closer. Her heart raced as she lifted her head and he leaned nearer. She shouldn't do this, but she wanted to. Stopping, he waited. As she closed the minute gap between them, he turned away at the last second. She kissed his cheek, not his lips.

Eyes twinkling, he drew back just enough to look into her face. As he moved forward, she closed her eyes, and his whisper brushed her ear, making her tingle to the tips of her toes. "I meant going dancing together to rehab my knee."

He'd deliberately embarrassed her, and worse than that, she'd let him, even helped him, put her in that position. She jerked away, tramped up the steps, and pushed open the kitchen door.

His voice laughed behind her. "See you tomorrow morning at church."

Slamming the door, she breathed deeply and steadily to keep from screaming her frustration. So, so, so smug. And no way, no how, was that...or would that ever be...on The List.

7

A contemporary worship song played in the auditorium as people found seats for the morning service. If only she hadn't agreed to save a place for him. Coming to church again after all these weeks made her feel uncomfortable enough. Throwing Sam into the mix, especially after yesterday, just complicated the whole situation. A good person would have wanted him to show, but she didn't. She was a bad person, or at the least, a self-centered one.

Brad stepped into the row of chairs in front of hers. "I'm glad you agreed to go to Oklahoma in your mother's place, Katherine. I'm sure it means a lot to Cassie." If people had told her in high school that Brad Thompson, the man who should have been voted "Most Likely to Party," would be her baby sister's youth minister and soccer coach, she would have called 911 and had them committed. But something happened to him in college, and all that wild spirit had been channeled in a different direction.

"I'm glad it worked out so I could go," Katherine replied. The last mission trip she'd gone on had been to Mexico the summer after she and Clark had started dating. "I've really been looking forward to chaperoning. The only conflict I had was work, and now I don't have to worry about that."

"I found him." Cassie stepped into their row with Sam right behind her.

Katherine's stomach rolled as a lump swelled up into her throat. She breathed deeply and slowly to calm the lingering waves of last night's embarrassment.

Today he wore jeans and a brown and blue plaid western shirt. In the low lighting, his feet weren't visible, but his height indicated he was wearing boots. Cowboy boots, most likely.

"Hey, man." Brad stepped out into the aisle, and he and Sam did one of those guy hug-handshake things.

"Brad." Sam turned in her direction.

Katherine quickly locked her gaze onto the church bulletin so he wouldn't find her looking at him.

"So, this is what church is like nowadays," Sam said. "A lot's changed in fifteen years."

Brad grinned. "Only the way it's served. The meat's still the same. See you later, man."

"Excuse me, Beth." Even though Katherine had left two seats beside her on the aisle, Cassie tried to climb over her to the inner portion of the row.

Katherine gestured to the chair between hers and the one on the end. She kept her voice low. "I saved this seat for you. Sam can sit on the aisle."

"Good morning, Katherine," Sam said as he dropped down into the aisle seat and leaned forward. "I hope you slept well last night."

She cast him a cool grin. "Like a baby."

"Yeah, me, too." His eyes danced.

The lights in the auditorium dimmed as the band moved into their places. Even though Cassie was between them, Katherine could still see him out of the corner of her eye. She'd never be able to concentrate on the sermon today with Sam and his attitude only one chair away. And if the title in the bulletin meant anything, she really needed to hear this.

God's Will—Why Doesn't He Just Text Us?

~*~

Katherine pulled a lasagna Florentine from the freezer. She was glad Cassie had gone over to Sophie's for the afternoon. Now she had some time alone to process the sermon. As she opened the microwave, her gaze fell on the pottery spoon rest she and Mom had seen at the arts and crafts fair in Fort Worth last year.

The combination of the earthy sienna clay mixed with splashes of sky blue, swirls the soft green color of mesquite trees, and dots of pink and lavender had brought tears to Mom's eyes. Tears from a simple piece of pottery not much larger than the palm of Dad's hand.

"Oh, Katherine, isn't this lovely? It's a miniature representation of the beauty of God's creation." Mom had picked it up, and as she'd tilted it in different directions, the way the light reflected off the glaze made the pattern seem to shift. Almost like a kaleidoscope. "A clay garden in my hand. Kind of like that song about God holding the world."

"You should buy it, Mom," she'd suggested.

Mom had sighed and set it back down. "No, I'm trying to exercise self-control. I don't need it. Your father says I do way too much impulse buying, and he's right." She'd chuckled. "Besides, I have the real thing right outside my back door."

A few minutes later, when they'd walked far

enough down the lane that the pottery booth was no longer visible, Katherine had made an excuse about needing to find a restroom and went instead to purchase the spoon rest. She'd had a difficult time biting her tongue when her Mom had changed her mind and stopped back by the pottery booth on the way out, only to find the spoon rest was gone.

The guilt she'd felt the day of the fair was washed away by the glimmer in her mother's eyes when she'd pulled the clay 'garden' spoonrest out of the small gift bag on her birthday a few weeks later. The monetary value of the piece—it had been less than twenty dollars—hadn't brought tears to her mother's eyes, but the joy of obtaining something she'd wanted badly had. She'd gotten something she'd loved, something she'd thought she'd never have. Something that spoke to her soul.

Tears obscured the clay mini-creation, as the colors mixed together into that drab gray of nature, when the life of springtime is hidden by the death of winter. A commentary on Katherine's present life.

She threw the lasagna back into the freezer and grabbed her purse from the counter. She couldn't stay here. She'd leave a note for Cassie in case she got home from Sophie's before she returned.

~*~

The ride to The Perks was a blur. Katherine settled into one of the high back wooden booths near the door, placed her chai tea on the table, and pulled her notebook out of her purse. Any appetite she might have had earlier was gone. The warmth of the wood and stone decor mixed with the calm classical music and rich aroma of numerous blends of coffee wrapped her soul in a blanket of comfort. Going to a restaurant alone was generally unappealing, but not today. This was the perfect time and place to consider this morning's sermon.

Her gaze was drawn to movement in the far corner as a man stood and stepped out of the booth closest to the stone fireplace, cold and flameless in today's spring weather. Her heart pounded as Sam began to make his way toward the door behind her. Hiding was impossible. She'd attract more attention if she tried to slide under the table than if she just sat there. Maybe he wouldn't notice her. As his gaze fell on her, he briefly lifted up a hand in recognition. Too late.

He altered his course just enough to end up beside her table. "Hi." His voice was deep, his smile almost imperceptible. "You here alone?"

"Yes. Cassie's at Sophie's. What about you?"

His eyes were soft, the normal twinkle missing.

"Brad left about ten minutes ago. I've just been sitting here thinking. It's a good place for that. My aunt and uncle are keeping their three grandsons this weekend, so the house is a bit...uh, I mean...really chaotic." He leaned his head to the side. "I'm working hard to rid myself of the British expressions and accent I've picked up over the years."

"You mean to get rid of?"

"Exactly." He smiled. "When I think I've conquered them and relax, the accent and the expressions creep back in." He hooked his thumbs into his front pockets and rocked back and forth. He was wearing cowboy boots. He looked toward the exit door and then back at her. "Well..."

"Would you like to join me?" Her brain had lost all control of her mouth.

"Sure." He scooted into the booth across from her and rested his forearms on the table. His fingers reached out and gently traced the edges of her notebook. "What's this?"

She placed her fingers on the black embossed rectangle and gently drew it closer to her. "My notebook."

"Notebook?"

"Yes. I started doing this years ago as an organizational tool. I make a list of what I need to accomplish each day on the left-hand page, and then on the right side, I put notes from that day. Every night before I go to bed, I check off what I've accomplished and then review my list for the next day."

"I get it. Kind of like a calendar."

No, he didn't really get it. "Kind of, but not exactly. I write down thoughts, dreams, things I want to remember or that I'm praying about. Just kind of whatever's on my mind. That way I can look back over the pages and relive memories from my life."

He nodded. "More like a diary than a calendar."

"You're getting warmer."

"So how long have you been doing this?"

"Since middle school, and I've saved them all."

"And you write in it every day?"

"Probably seems kind of silly, I imagine. But I brought it because I made notes from the sermon today, and I wanted to go back over them and really take a few minutes to let the ideas sink in."

"I love the concept." His eyes warmed. "Speaking of the sermon, church was...interesting." The barely perceptible smile returned. "Maybe thought-provoking is a better description. I honestly can't remember the last time I went."

"Really? It's been that long?"

"Yeah. Once we moved to North Carolina, soccer became my universe. My games were on Sundays, so I never got plugged in to a church." A boyish vulnerability settled in his eyes as they focused over her shoulder. "Then in college, I was too busy. And after I graduated, I was too cool." His forehead wrinkled as he lowered his brow and fixed his gaze back on hers. "As I said the other night—fame, fortune, and football. I got everything I ever wanted."

Why was life like that? Some people who couldn't care less about God got what they wanted in spite of themselves, and others who tried to follow God, obey the rules, and live right didn't.

"What about you?"

"What?" Her situation, her life, what she had or didn't have was none of his business.

"I'll bet you're a church girl. I'll bet you go all the time." He winked.

"Oh, church. Well, I did until about a month after my mother's..." She paused.

"Passing?" The playfulness was gone.

"Look, Sam. Don't take this wrong. Why do people feel the need to use some ridiculous euphemism? It's not like she got a C+ on her report card. She was killed in a wreck. She died. Not saying the word doesn't make it any less real or less painful."

His only response was a nod.

She sighed. "When everybody at church started telling me that I should be comforted by the fact that her 'passing' was God's will and plan, I stopped going." As an unexpected lump rose in her throat, her eyes filled with tears. No, no—she couldn't cry in front of him.

Too late. While the tears spilled down her cheeks, she forced a whisper. "Sorry. I can't figure it all out. I don't know why it happened. I just don't see how going to buy a new pair of shoes in a rainstorm and then sliding into the rear end of a dump truck was the perfect plan of a loving God. No matter what anyone says. Couldn't she have just been careless or in the wrong place at the wrong time?" Her throat ached from the pain of speaking. "I have to believe that God loved my mother as much as, no, even more than we did, and that He loves us, too. His heart has to be broken for us. That's the only way I can make any sense of it."

Sam reached over and placed a hand on hers. His touch was warm. "Sometimes in trying to make sense of the senseless, people say stuff they shouldn't. They can't explain the unexplainable, but they want to make things better, to offer comfort and ease pain. And they don't think through their words. I imagine those words were spoken because they loved you."

"I guess." She'd only shared these feelings with one other person. "After the funeral, when I went back to Dallas, some days I'd forget she'd died." She paused to steady her voice. "My father and sister were home grieving, but I was going on with life as if nothing had changed. And then I'd pick up the phone to call her..." She bit her bottom lip as her chin quivered and then whispered the words buried deep in her heart, "I was such a bad daughter." Her sobs shook her shoulders.

Sam stood, moved to her side of the booth, and slid in next her. After pulling some napkins from the dispenser on the table, he placed his fingertips under her chin and turned her face toward him. He quieted her as if she were a baby and gently dabbed away her tears. "Sh-h-h-h. Sh-h-h-h, Beth. You are not a bad daughter." He slipped his arm around her and pulled her close.

She should push away, but she couldn't.

"You've given up a portion of your life to come help your father and sister. Your mother would be proud of you, I'm quite sure."

She leaned her head against his shoulder into the comfort of his embrace.

The deep bass of his voice vibrated his chest as he spoke. "My dad died about three years ago. I came home from the UK for the funeral, but since I saw him only a few times a year, resuming my regular life after I went back—feeling normal, forgetting—was easy. Until I'd sit down at the computer to send him an e-mail or, like you, pull my phone out of my pocket to call him. And then the sorrow would come. Just like you, I felt guilty that I could go on with life while my mom and sisters struggled back home. Their grief was concentrated—more compacted—because he was a part of their everyday lives. Mine was more sporadic and spread out."

He squeezed her shoulder, his words soft. "But my feelings, like yours, weren't any less real than those of the rest of my family. Just different because of our circumstances of life. In the end, we all suffered a terrible loss. We all hurt. We all grieved."

As his hand softly rubbed her upper arm, she looked up into his eyes. Clark had told her she was wrong to doubt God's will. He'd said she shouldn't question what happened. That she should trust God and accept that it was for their best. What comfort was she supposed to find in those words?

But Sam hadn't judged her—hadn't criticized her for feelings she couldn't control. He'd listened and shared his experience. She leaned back against him for a few seconds and then sat up. "Thanks, Sam."

As she sniffed he handed her a dry napkin, and she knew what she had to do. "Put me in, Coach."

His brow wrinkled. "What?"

"Now entering the game in the position of chief Two-Step-Rehabber—Katherine Herrington."

8

Katherine climbed into bed, her heart light. Tonight had been so much fun. No one at The Cantina would have guessed this was only their third time to dance together. Juanita would have been really proud if she'd seen them.

She opened her notebook and checked off the last entry on today's list. Her breathing caught as the words she'd jotted down earlier this week registered — Date with Sam. She'd called it a date even though he'd never referred to whatever they were doing as dating.

Certainly, the first time they'd gone out had been an official date, although not arranged by either of them. The times afterward, though, had been — according to Sam — "penance, payment, and rehab." Yet, no matter what names he'd given these times together, anyone else would have called them dates.

But dating involved attraction on some level. And as usual, he hadn't tried to kiss her good night. Just another hands-in-the-pockets good-bye on her doorstep. He was new in town and probably didn't have many friends, so maybe he wasn't really attracted to her but was simply lonely.

No, he was definitely attracted to her. She placed her fingers over her mouth to cover the involuntary smile. Tonight, during the last dance, his eyes had burned with desire. She knew that when she saw it.

And yet he still hadn't tried to kiss her. Mom used to say that when it came to dating, Katherine built clear glass walls around herself so that she was visible but not reachable. But if she truly did, it was only for protection. She'd been simply guarding herself until The One came along. Her face warmed. Even if she had put up walls with Sam at first, she'd pretty much smashed them down the other day after the Dairy Delite.

And still tonight, no kiss. Not even an attempt.

So, were they dating, or was this another of his crazy games? Her heart had no answer. She couldn't read him.

Whatever his intentions, his self-control was confusing, but also intriguing...very intriguing. Other men she'd dated would have kissed her on the first date—if she'd let them. Clark had.

But Sam was different, and her feelings for him were different. In the short time she'd known him, he'd already kindled more passion within her heart than she'd ever felt toward Clark.

She slipped out of bed and opened the closet door. Lifting the stack of notebooks in one hand, she scooted out the white box beneath them with the other and carried it to her grandmother's old wicker rocker in the corner. This box hadn't been opened since she and Clark had become serious.

Snuggling down into the old chair, she set the lid aside. Images of almost fifteen-year-younger versions of her mother, her father, and herself smiled up at her. The waiter had taken the photo on the night the three of them had gone out for dinner after the Passion and Purity conference in middle school. The envelope holding the silver band bearing a small cross engraving and the signed purity pledge was under the picture.

At the bottom of the thin box was her very first notebook—the one she'd begun at the conference. She opened it to the final page. She hadn't looked at the list in more than a year now. Over time it had undergone several revisions, the qualities she'd desired in a husband changing as she'd matured. Nice Car, Cute, and Captain of the Football Team, now amusingly shallow, had been crossed off the list over the years, and replaced by other more important requirements. But the number one quality had been and would always remain the same—A man who knows and loves God.

She glanced over the rest of the list. Like an illustration in an old dictionary at the library, a picture of Clark should have been sketched beside the numbered entries.

After all those years of praying for The One, Clark had walked into her singles' Bible study and her life. The attraction had been immediate. The better she'd gotten to know him, the more she realized he had all the qualities on the list. God had finally answered her prayer. Clark was The One.

She'd surely thought so. But then when he'd asked her to marry him, she hadn't been able to commit to him. Although he possessed every quality on her list, the thought of spending the rest of her life with him in a relationship devoid of passion left a panicky emptiness deep in her heart. She'd told herself she'd rather be alone. But that wasn't true. She wanted to be married more than anything—just not to him.

Tears crept into her eyes. The leaders at that conference had lied when they'd told her God would send her the man she desired if she prayed specifically and waited patiently for him. Maybe "lied" was too harsh a word, as it implied intent, and their intentions had been good. Besides, the list had worked for all of her girlfriends who had attended the conference with her. They were all married to their "Ones." No, they hadn't lied. The fault had to be with her and not the system.

Katherine closed the book and placed the items back into the box. She'd kept her promise of purity to her parents, to herself, and to her Heavenly Father, but where had that gotten her? Certainly not where she thought she'd be at this time in her life.

She reached up and wiped the tears off her cheeks. Nothing was turning out as she'd planned. Despite her desires and prayers all these years, she still hadn't found The One. She should give up and move on with her life instead of continuing to believe in some Cinderella-like fantasy that would never come true for her.

But she couldn't yet, because of this one not-so-little, confusing thing...Sam.

She hadn't turned down Clark's proposal because she'd wanted to pursue another relationship. She'd needed some time apart to think, and the loss of her job along with Dad's extended business trip had been good reasons to come home...to escape until she could get her thoughts together. And now Sam was complicating everything.

She'd never before felt passion such as Sam stirred within her. But while he possessed some of the qualities on the list, he lacked the most important one. She couldn't say he knew God. And the only thing worse than a passionless relationship would be a

Godless one.

So, no more obsessing about why he hadn't kissed her. His reasons no longer mattered because they'd never be more than friends, if one could even call them that. Once his knee was healed, he'd go back to his life in London, and hopefully by then she'd go back to Dallas. And that would be that.

~*~

Sam pulled his car into the garage behind Ginny's house and turned off the ignition. Closing his eyes, he pressed his head back against the headrest. He couldn't keep this up much longer. Not pulling Katherine into his arms and kissing her was more difficult every time they were together.

Their Two-Stepping tonight was much better than the last time they'd danced together at The Cantina. All the money spent on their evening with Juanita had been worth every penny. That night at the Cattlemen's Hotel was the most expensive date he'd ever had. Yet, for those hours with Beth, Katherine...whoever she was...he would have paid double or triple—shoot, maybe even ten times—as much.

Tonight, when the band had begun their last song, a slow dance, she hadn't even paused. She, not he, had closed the gap between them and then rested her head on his shoulder. As his arms had tightened around her, everyone else had disappeared, and they were alone. A couple of times he'd been jerked back to reality when they'd almost bumped into other couples.

He sat up and pulled his key out of the ignition. He couldn't stand that fancy keyless stuff. The silver band threaded onto the keyring reflected the moonlight. His parents had given the purity ring to him after that conference in middle school when he'd promised them he'd wait until after marriage. Purity...what a joke. That commitment had been willingly broken countless times with often nameless women between then and now. Or at least until about a year ago when he'd finally begun to realize how much of his life he'd wasted.

Katherine was the first woman he'd dated since college who hadn't thrown herself at him. All the partying, all the women, had failed to quench the yearnings deep in his soul. They'd given him nothing and had taken away the one thing he should have saved for his wife.

He couldn't change the past. Those mistakes were already made. He could only change his decisions in the present and thus the direction of his future. The old purity ring on the key chain was a physical reminder of the recommitment he'd made to himself, his future wife, and to God — if God would even have him back.

His life in the UK came with certain expectations — all of which he'd lived up to, unfortunately. Everything the world said would bring him happiness and contentment had only left him empty, craving for something he hadn't been able to find there.

But here, in Crescent Bluff, there were no expectations. That was one reason he'd pushed to spend his rehab time here, where no one really knew him anymore.

The other reasons? He'd needed to return to the last place he could remember life having any purpose beyond himself.

So, he'd come back searching for God...and for

Katherine.

9

Today had been a great day. Katherine had completely rearranged the kitchen. Dad would be so happy when he returned in a few days. The way Mom had set it up when they'd moved to this house before Cassie had been born had never made sense. But now, everything was as it should be. The dishes were close to the dishwasher, the pots, pans, and other cookware were under the oven or next to the stove. Items used rarely or only once a year were out of the way in the high upper cabinets. Everything was much more efficient now—the way Katherine's kitchen in Dallas had been.

So yes, today had been a productive day—until now. She backed her car down the driveway. They were late, and there was no excuse for consistent lateness. Cassie's inability to keep on schedule was nothing more than poor planning. It took Katherine exactly thirty-seven minutes to shower and wash her hair, dry and style it, put on makeup, and get dressed. She could get ready in twenty-nine if she really needed to, or take longer if she wanted, but she always allowed forty-two minutes, just to make sure she'd be on time. Proper planning was the key to punctuality.

"Cassie, are you using that notebook I gave you?"

Cassie sighed as she turned to look out the

passenger side window. "No."

Katherine would have been shocked if Cassie's answer had been "yes." "Honey, if you'd plan each day the night before when you went to bed, you'd be so much more organized and less forgetful."

"Beth, it's just too much trouble. Besides, I don't care about all that stuff. I don't want some notebook ruling my life." Cassie turned back.

"It wouldn't rule your life. A planned life is a successful life. Planning allows you to accomplish more with your time."

"Yeah, well not planning is more fun. I don't want to miss the good stuff because I've got my nose in some notebook only doing what's on the lists. You may get more done. But I have more fun. Life is about enjoying what comes along even if you didn't expect it. You know...being spontaneous."

Mom's mantra. Katherine had heard it more times than she could count, and apparently, Cassie was fully indoctrinated. "Cassie, you're missing the point. Planning allows you to have more fun."

"Yeah, like moving around everything in the kitchen cabinets. Whoo-hoo." Her voice dripped with sarcasm. Cassie was her mother's child.

Katherine pulled into the church parking lot. "Look, sweetie, I'm not trying to tell you how to run your life. There are lots of organizational systems that work. This one just works for me. All I ask is that you give it a try. For a week. I'll even help you at night."

As they opened their doors and stepped out onto the asphalt, heat waves shimmered up, hinting at the summer temperatures right around the corner. Cassie looked back over the top of the car at her and smiled. "Maybe." She slammed her door and ran toward the entrance to the fellowship hall. Glancing back over her shoulder, she yelled, "Move it, Beth. We're late."

Katherine jogged after her. And whose fault was that?

They slipped into two seats on the back row of folding chairs. Everyone around them had an envelope of what must have been information about the mission trip. They'd have to get one afterward if there were any left. Katherine did have that chaperone's information at home anyway.

Brad leaned on the podium while a woman stood in the audience. He was apparently introducing her. The woman sat down, and Brad looked their direction. "And our last female chaperone is Katherine Herrington. Stand up, Katherine."

As she stood, the group politely applauded. How embarrassing that they were so late. She smiled and nodded.

"Katherine is Cassie's older sister. We've known each other since elementary school. She's recently moved back to Crescent Bluff and will be a great asset to the team."

Katherine smiled and waved as obligatory applause rippled again through the audience. She dropped back down onto the cold plastic seat. At least they hadn't completely missed the introductions.

"And now for the male chaperones. Sam..."

Katherine bolted forward as a man stood in the front row.

"Sam Tucker..." Brad paused.

The audience exploded with applause—well, at least the boys. Woofing reverberated throughout the tile-floored room as most of them pounded their fists in the air. One young man jumped up, threw both arms into the air over his head and yelled, "Gooooooooooal!" just like on TV.

Cassie giggled, stood, and joined the mayhem.

Sam hadn't told Katherine he was helping chaperone this mission trip to Oklahoma. Of course, she hadn't told him she was either.

He stood, turned back toward the audience, and waved. His face was scarlet, and as the clamor died down, Brad continued, "For the one or two of you who may not know, Sam is a professional soccer player from England."

Brad's words faded into the background as Sam made eye contact with her and smiled. The deep blue of his eyes was visible even from the back of the room. Butterflies fluttered as she smiled back. His hair appeared to have grown even more. It seemed impossible that such a little bit of hair could make that much difference in a person's looks. But, obviously, it could, because if possible he was even more unbelievably attractive.

As Sam pulled his gaze away in the direction of the other attendees, Brad's words returned. "Sam and I go way back. A word of warning—he's a snipe hunter extraordinaire." Sam shook his head and then sat down as applause tore through the building again.

Snipe hunting. Of course he would be the type of guy that would have done that. Just another of his crazy games.

She'd had that cruel trick played on her in middle school. No, it was on that youth camping trip the first part of ninth grade. Some ridiculously immature little boy had lured her away from the rest of the group and tried to kiss her. She hadn't thought about snipe hunting—or him—in years.

What was his name, anyway? Seems like it was something to do with Texas history. Austin? Stephen Austin? No. Travis? William Travis? No. David? Davey Crockett? No, not that either. Houston! That was it. Sam Houston. A pile of bricks thudded in her stomach.

Sammy Houston Tucker!

~*~

Uh-oh, Katherine remembered, and she was really ticked. "Mind if I join you?" Unaffected by her silence, Sam set his plate of barbecue and cup of sweet tea on the table in the corner and sat down on the plastic folding chair across from her.

"I deliberately chose this spot, Sam, because I'm not feeling particularly social at the moment." Katherine paused as she stared straight into his eyes. "But would it really matter if I minded?"

He leaned both elbows on the table and returned her stare. "Maybe. But...probably not."

She looked away first.

They ate in silence for a few seconds. Or he did anyway. Katherine moved stuff around on her plate. She obviously wouldn't say anything, so he may as well take advantage of her quiet. This was his chance. "I had a nice time last night. Thanks for going out with me. A few more sessions like that and my knee should be in great shape."

Ice.

OK, time to change the topic. "Brad didn't tell me you were going on the mission trip when he called last week and asked me to go. He thinks my experience will be a real asset to the team."

Her gaze found his. Fire.

When she finally spoke, venom filled her response. "Oh, I had no idea we'd be doing any snipe hunting on this trip. Or maybe playing soccer. Yes, I'm sure those activities will be the focus of our mission trip."

"He meant my construction experience."

She was actually really cute when she was angry, but if he smiled now, he'd be dead meat. Sam looked down at his plate and crammed a bite of potato salad in his mouth.

Cassie slid into the seat next to Katherine. "I'm really glad you're going on the trip with us, Sam. It'll be so much fun. Aren't you glad, Beth?" Not waiting for a reply, Cassie continued, "I didn't know you liked to hunt. What's a snipe anyway?"

Katherine pushed her plate away and folded her hands on the table. "Yes, Sam, please tell us about your snipe hunting experience. I've never seen a picture of one, and I'd love to know what they look like. I've always imagined that they resemble a rat...or maybe a snake."

Cassie's forehead wrinkled as she turned toward her sister. "Beth, that's dumb. Rats and snakes don't look anything alike."

"Maybe not," Katherine snapped back, "but they're both nasty creatures, completely unappealing to mankind and especially womankind. Cassie, if anybody ever wants to take you snipe hunting, don't go."

The angrier she got, the cuter she became. But if he didn't do something to diffuse the situation soon, he'd be in way over his head. "Cassie, snipes are birds, but your sister's kind of right. Snipe hunting is just a fun game, a trick to play on people. You take somebody out into the country at night and give him a bag or a pillow case—something big enough to hold a small animal. Then you tell him to stay in one place while you supposedly go off and scare the snipes back toward him. The idea is to abandon him and see how long it takes him to figure out the trick."

Cassie shook her head. "That doesn't sound like much fun to me."

"Well, it is for the person playing the trick but sometimes, not for the person being tricked. In fact, there's one person in particular that I took snipe hunting when I was about your age, Cassie, and I'd like to have the chance to apologize to her. I don't think she enjoyed it too much." He moved his gaze from Cassie's to Katherine's and then back to Cassie's. "What do you think, Cassie? You think I should find her and apologize? You think she'd accept it after all these years?"

Cassie shrugged her shoulders. "Don't know," she replied, standing. "Hey, Beth, I'm going outside to play volleyball until you're ready to go. See you later, Sam."

"Bye, Cassie." Sam lifted up a hand in response and then turned back toward Katherine. "So what do you think I should do, Katherine? Do you think if I apologize to this person, she'd forgive me?"

"I wouldn't know, Sam." She stood and picked up her plate and cup. She turned sharply and headed first for the garbage can and then toward the door into the hallway.

He crammed some more brisket into his mouth and jumped up to follow her. When he reached the garbage can, he took one last bite and then tossed the almost-full plate. He should be arrested for throwing away such great barbecue. But she was definitely worth it.

~*~

Katherine made a beeline up the hall toward the back door. She'd suddenly been on the bottom of a swimming pool, and no matter how hard she kicked, the weight of the water prevented her from making it to the top to breathe. She needed to get outside into some wide-open space where the Texas wind could rush across her face. Sam's voice ran after her as she stepped through the door into the Saharan wind, "Beth, wait. Please."

So the few instances of his calling her Beth these last few weeks hadn't been simple cases of misspeaking as she'd assumed, but clues from her—their—past. He'd obviously remembered her from the beginning, but she'd had no idea who he was. He'd changed so much, she could have never connected the scrawny little boy to this grown, but oftentimes not-so-mature, man.

The door behind her opened as Sammy Houston Tucker followed her out. "Hey, can we talk?"

She turned her back to him. The last thing she wanted to do right now was talk. She just needed some time alone. "Sam, I..."

"I'm really sorry for that night in ninth grade. I didn't realize how mean it was. I mean, teenage boys can be pretty dumb sometimes. They have all these grown-up feelings and emotions, but their grade-school minds give them bad advice on how to communicate them. Especially when they have a crush on a girl."

So that's what he really thought was going on here. She turned to face him and looked up into his eyes. He was so much taller than he'd originally appeared, almost as if he'd grown some over the past few weeks. "Sam, I'm not one of those people who can't move past middle school angst. I'm not upset about snipe hunting that night."

"I know."

"You know?" she asked.

"Yes, I know. But I had to apologize for myself." He took her hand, drew her close, and spoke gently. "You're upset because you were caught by surprise. Beth, I've known who you were since before I held out that bouquet of tulips to you the night of our blind date. And it was wrong of me not to confess to you that very first night. I guess I was being selfish. I just wanted you to get to know me, Sam, now. I didn't want any future relationship we might have to be colored by that past boy."

His usual smugness had disappeared, replaced by the same caring spirit she'd seen that Sunday afternoon at The Perks. His words completely summed up her feelings. She couldn't have expressed herself any better.

His eyes were gentle as he took her other hand. "So, Katherine, do you think that young lady I was asking about a few minutes ago would accept my apology? As I said, guys can do some pretty dumb things when they have a crush on a girl."

If only Clark had been this understanding and compassionate. There was that word again—passion, com-passion-ate.

Heat that was no result of the Texas spring weather rushed through her body. Slowly withdrawing her hands from his, she stepped back. "Who knows? Maybe she'd accept it, or maybe she wouldn't." She may as well play his game and take advantage of his regret. After all, he'd set the precedent. She looked at him from the corner of her eye. "But if you threw in some penance, I'm sure she'd be more likely to forgive."

As he crossed his arms, his eyes danced. "Penance, you say. Fair enough. Just tell me when and where."

"Tomorrow morning, my house, nine o'clock. Oh, and we'll be outside, so dress cool in clothes that can be gotten dirty."

10

Sam pulled the Texas Ranger cap down onto his head. The fuzz covering his head wasn't enough to provide any real protection from sunburn, and they would be outside today. That was all she'd shared about his "penance." Other than they'd be getting dirty.

The rest of his clothing included flip-flops, one of Uncle Jess's old college T-shirts, and some soccer shorts. The cargo shorts he'd originally pulled out of the drawer were too tight. He'd picked up some weight with good eating and not enough exercise. But now that the physical therapist had released him, he'd work some of the extra pounds off on some of the local jogging trails. He could even start by running drills with Cassie's team. In a couple of months, he'd be back to his summer weight, and then by September, he'd be down to his playing weight. Coach would expect nothing less.

He glanced at his phone: eight thirty. No time for breakfast. If he was late, Katherine might require additional penance, but that might not be such a bad thing—as long as she was participating in it, too.

Grabbing his keys, he headed out the door to his car. Today would be really hot. The temperatures were already oppressive. And yet his heart was light. The burden he'd been carrying around since he'd tried to hand her those flowers on their blind date was gone. No more having to hide his past identity. She now knew, and that knowledge was very freeing.

As he stuck the key in the ignition and turned it, the car sprang to life. Last night's apology had scored one goal, and it was time to start setting up the next one.

~*~

Although her phone had never rung, two missed calls from Clark had come in while she was taking a shower this morning, but he'd left no messages. If he'd really wanted to talk with her, he should have left a message. She'd been home almost a month now, and this was his first attempt to contact her. Maybe she'd call him later. Maybe she wouldn't. Right now, she had other priorities.

Katherine rubbed sunscreen on her arms and legs. If her father hadn't been coming home tomorrow, she would have waited to work on the garden until the end of the week when cooler, cloudy weather was predicted. But weeding the flowerbeds was the last item that waited to be checked off her to-do list, and her tank top and shorts should be cool enough. Plus, they'd be done long before the sun was high overhead—that is, if Sam got here on time.

Sure, she'd taken advantage of his guilt when he'd asked for her forgiveness yesterday afternoon, and she wasn't sorry in the least. He deserved it—as much as he had teased her and made her feel uncomfortable over the past few weeks. Now that she'd finally gotten the upper hand, she intended to keep it as long as she could. A little manual labor in the hot sun was hardly a fair trade for the embarrassment and discomfort he'd caused her.

As the garage doorbell rang, she glanced at the kitchen clock—eight fifty-nine. Well, there were a lot of things on The List that he wasn't, but prompt he was.

She walked across the kitchen, grasped the doorknob, and pulled the door open. "Good Morn—" Her words stuck in her throat as she looked at the incredibly attractive man before her. The ball cap made him look younger while accentuating those Caribbean eyes. A model couldn't have done any better.

"Good Morn' to you, too. Speaking Shakespearean English today, are we, m'lady?"

She coughed softly. "Sorry. Something got caught in my throat. Hi, Sam."

"Hi." He grinned as he held up a bag in one hand and a cardboard beverage caddy in the other. "Stopped and picked us up some bagels and iced coffee. Figured we...I...could use a little fuel before beginning my penance. Hope that's OK."

He was such a thoughtful man. "Sure, that's great. Have a seat at the island while I get us some plates."

"Forget the plates. Why don't we eat outside on the swing? It's a gorgeous morning and the barista put plenty of napkins in the bag."

As they stepped out onto the back deck, the soft potpourri of jasmine and lilac floated over her. "Great idea, Sam."

He waited for her to sit on the swing and then took his place beside her. He handed her a Styrofoam cup and began doling out the contents of the bag. "I was surprised to see you at the meeting yesterday. You hadn't told me you were chaperoning the trip to Oklahoma."

"You hadn't asked, and for your information," she looked over at him. "I don't tell you everything that's happening in my life. Besides you didn't tell me you were going either."

"Well, I don't tell you everything that's happening in *my* life, either." He raised his eyebrows for emphasis as he spoke and then winked. "Seriously, it would have made my decision a lot easier if I'd known you were going."

She kept her tone light, playful. "It would have, would it? So, shall I take that as a compliment?"

As he turned and stared deeply into her eyes, her breathing caught. She shouldn't be leading him on like this.

He leaned closer and whispered, "I never said my answer would have been yes." Grinning, he drew away and took another bite of his bagel.

Positively infuriating—another quality that was not on The List.

As he looked back at her, the sparkle in his eyes was gone. "Seriously, there are probably lots of people out there who would have been a better choice to go than me. Like you, for instance. You're the perfect choice. From what I've observed, you're a great role model for those girls."

Sure, if they wanted to end up disappointed and confused in ten years. "What do you mean? I'd say you've made quite a success of yourself." She looked over at him, and saw a vulnerable ninth grade boy sharing her swing.

"Let's just say, my life hasn't been exactly imitation-worthy. I'm great with a soccer ball and pretty darn good with a hammer...but not so proficient with the Bible and all this church stuff." The chains creaked as he gently pushed the swing back and forth.

"Nobody's perfect." Nobody was perfect. Not Mom, not Dad, not her...not even Clark. She'd followed all the rules, all the steps. She'd planned as perfectly as she'd known how, but she must not have done a good enough job, because life hadn't turned out as she'd hoped.

He raised his hand. "Exhibit A for imperfection right here."

"Sam, that's not what I meant. You have a very successful life."

"Yes, I do. I worked really hard and achieved every goal I set for myself." The swing stopped. "And now that I'm where I am, I realize they were the wrong goals. Not that they were all bad, but they just weren't good enough. I mean, how can a teenage boy really know what a man will want or need?"

The swing began to move again as they finished their breakfast in silence.

She was still waiting because she hadn't reached her goals. He was still waiting because he had.

As he pushed his trash into the bag, the crackle of the paper broke into her world. "So, m'lady, what's the plan for today?"

Time to get back to reality. "My dad's coming home tomorrow, and I wanted everything to be perfect for him. The last thing on my list is cleaning up this backyard. I've let it get in horrible shape."

"What do you mean? Looks pretty good to me. Your mom's flowers are blooming, the grass is green."

She pushed her trash into the bag he offered. "My mother would have never let things get so far out of control. Can't you see all the weeds between the flowers?"

"Well, maybe if you give me a magnifying glass. The garden is gorgeous, and you're missing all the beauty because you're concentrating on a few rogue plants." He stood and held out his hand. "Stand up."

She placed her hand in his and did as he asked.

"Now close your eyes."

After she followed his instructions, he covered her eyes with one hand, and placed the other on her far shoulder. "OK, we'll walk slowly to your right. Keep those eyes closed."

The hand covering her eyes was warm and scented like a cinnamon raisin bagel mixed with the fresh fragrance of his cologne. Her right shoulder began to tingle where his other hand firmly rested as he guided her. Memories of dancing blindfolded in his arms raced back.

"Relax. You're all stiff. Now turn a little to the left, but keep your eyes closed until I say. No peeking."

His hands no longer touched her. "Now look."

As she opened her eyes, an uncontrollable gasp escaped. She had never seen the garden revealed like the unveiling of a new acquisition at an art museum. A riot of yellow, pink, purple, red, orange, white, and lavender assaulted her eyes while the morning light electrified each blossom until it seemed to sparkle.

"Oh, it's lovely, absolutely lovely. Like a life-sized painting at the Kimball." The colors began to wash together.

His arm encircled her shoulder as he drew her close. "Yes, and you've been concentrating on the individual brushstrokes instead of the whole painting. You've let a few weeds destroy the beauty of the whole garden."

"You're right." She leaned into him and placed her head against his shoulder as they lingered in silence a few moments more. "Thanks. I'll never see the garden the same again."

She would have stayed within the circle of his embrace much longer, but she couldn't. She wanted to, but she shouldn't. She shouldn't have let him hug her in the first place in case he misinterpreted her actions and thought they were more than friends. But, then, couldn't one friend hug another?

The sun was climbing high in the sky, and its heat had already chased away any early morning cool. She placed her hands against his chest and gently pushed away. "Well, you've certainly proven your point, but the truth is I can still see those weeds."

"Ah, yes, penance time."

~*~

Sam dragged the hose across the grass, pointed the nozzle toward the freshly weeded flower beds, and squeezed the trigger. Katherine should be satisfied. Not a weed was left, and the bushes were trimmed. The garden was immaculate.

The door on the deck closed, and her voice called behind him. "I brought us some water."

He ignored her and kept his back turned. He shouldn't do this, but he just had to. It would be good for her. She needed to chill.

The grass rustled as she neared. "Sam, did you hear me? I brought you some water."

Game time. Still squeezing the trigger, he whipped

around and shot her full force in the stomach. "What?"

She shrieked and ran far enough away to be out of range. "Sam! Stop it!"

He stood still. "Sorry. Seems the nozzle's stuck." He made a show of adjusting the trigger and released his grip so that the water flow stopped. "I'm not sure what happened. Some sort of malfunction."

She dropped the bottled water on the ground and moved toward him. "That's strange. My dad just bought that before he left. I guess I need to exchange it."

As she neared him, he held it out. "See?" When she was well within range, he squeezed it and got her again.

She squealed once more, but instead of running away this time, she ran toward him. "It wasn't a malfunction. It was a Sam-function. Samuel Houston Tucker, you give me that hose."

"No way, missy." He kicked off his flip-flops to run, but she dove, tackled him to the ground, and grabbed the nozzle. As they rolled back and forth in the grass laughing, water spewing, she somehow managed to wrestle the hose away and shot him in the face.

"Stop. My contacts. I think I lost one."

The water quit as she tossed the hose to the side. "Oh, Sam, I'm so sorry. Let me help you look." On hands and knees, they both carefully surveyed the wet grass while he inched closer to the hose. "Hey, I think I found it."

"You did?"

"No. Wait. I just remembered. I don't wear contacts." He grabbed the nozzle and shot her on her shoulders and then in the back as she turned and ran across the yard.

"You liar!"

Suddenly she froze, and he followed her line of sight to the deck.

A tall man in a navy business suit stood with his arms crossed. He looked like a mannequin from an upscale store window except for the scowl on his face. Not exactly an average intruder. His words were cool. "I hope you don't mind. I let myself in when no one answered the door. I could hear the noise all the way around front and thought you might be in danger. But I see I was wrong."

Katherine's smile vanished. "Clark..."

11

Katherine quickly pulled on some dry clothes, wrapped a towel around her head, and headed out to the den.

Clark stood staring out the French doors into the garden, his profile accented by pursed lips and a knit brow. She'd seen that look many times before. He was angry.

"This is certainly a surprise, Clark."

As he turned toward her, his accusatory tone matched his frown. "Yeah, apparently so. I tried to call to let you know I was coming through Crescent Bluff, but you didn't answer. So I decided to take a chance and stop by."

She took a deep breath and struggled to keep her voice even. "Well, if you'd left a message, I'd have called you back."

His response was short. "You know I don't like to leave messages."

It had been weeks since they'd seen each other or even spoken or texted, and she didn't want to spend this time arguing. But she wasn't a mind reader. "All I'm saying is that if you'd left a message, I would have called you back and then I'd have known you were coming."

"Who was the guy?"

So, the real issue had nothing to do with phone calls and messages. "Sam? An old school friend of mine. He's been visiting his aunt and uncle here while he's on medical leave from his job. Our paths just crossed." He didn't have to know how. "And since neither of us has many friends left in town, we started hanging out—you know, just for companionship."

A twinge of guilt pricked her heart. While her words were honest, her intent was deceit—no, not exactly deceit, more like camouflage. After she'd turned down Clark's proposal, they'd both agreed they needed some time apart to think and pray. So this season of their relationship was meant to be one of reevaluation. And while he had suggested that if either of them found someone they wanted to date, they could, he'd spoken out of hurt, and he hadn't really meant it.

Besides, her relationship with Sam was yet undefined, swirling around out there in the land of confusion. Nothing Sam had said or done indicated that they were anything more than friends. She and Sam weren't really dating, but Clark would never believe that.

"He must be a rich friend. That was some car." As he moved closer and took her hand, the furrows in his brow softened. "I'm sorry. I was just surprised, that's all. Seeing you soaking wet and running around like some grade school kid was not what I had pictured for our first time together in so long."

Soaking wet and running around having fun...As he pulled her to his chest, his nearness almost smothered her. She hadn't realized this when they were dating, but he was way too tall. Juanita's picture of a Great Dane and a Chihuahua flashed into her mind, and she bit the inside of her cheek to keep from giggling.

As his arms encircled her so tightly that she fought to breathe, his words vibrated in his chest. "I've missed you so much the past few weeks. I didn't try to contact you before now because I wanted to give you some space. I haven't been dating, or even looking, for that matter. There's no one else for me but you. I want you to know that. I'm willing to wait however long it takes you to work out your issues and come back. I'll be here."

She stood on her tiptoes, strained to place a quick kiss upon his cheek, and then pushed away. "Thanks."

"So, I have some good news, and since I was headed to Austin for a meeting, I decided to deliver it myself." As he took both her hands, he grinned, his earlier frown completely gone. He certainly was a handsome man when he smiled. "I heard from corporate, and I'll be able to hire you back in a few weeks. Isn't that great?"

Complicated was a more accurate adjective. "Oh..."

His smile regressed back into the stony frown. "Not exactly the response I expected. Underwhelming, to say the least. I thought you'd be excited to get your old job back. Surely, you haven't changed your mind about returning to Dallas."

"It's not that. Of course, I want my job back. I trained for that job for years, so I haven't been looking for anything else, just waiting and hoping I'd be able to return. But I've obligated to chaperone a youth mission trip at church this summer, and depending upon when the job opens up, I might not be available."

"I went to bat for you with John. This is a good

opportunity, and if you want to advance, you'll have to make some sacrifices."

"I want to be successful at work, but I also want to fulfill the commitment I made to the church."

His face softened again. "My responsible Katherine. I've always loved that about you. We'll just have to hope the timing works out right. And if it doesn't, I can probably come up with some excuse to buy you a few weeks." He pulled her close once more. "Well, I've got to hit the road if I want to make it to Austin in time for the evening session of the seminar." Suddenly he placed the crook of his finger under her chin and gently lifted her face toward his as he bent down and softly kissed her. He drew back and whispered, "I hope that was OK."

After these weeks apart if he was really The One, she certainly should have felt something—some longing, some desire, or passion. But her heart was empty.

"Katherine?"

"Yes, Clark, of course that was OK." And that was the problem. His kisses had always been just OK. She couldn't remember ever feeling passionate toward Clark, or any other man she'd dated, for that matter. Maybe she'd been too busy checking off the items on the list rather than allowing herself to feel. Or maybe there was something wrong with her. Maybe she was incapable of romantic passion.

No. Simply imagining Sam's kiss evoked more passionate feelings than any actual kiss from Clark. But then, maybe the anticipation of what a kiss from Sam might feel like was more exciting than the act itself would be. Kind of like seeing the newest fashion in the window at the department store and then being disappointed when she tried it on and looked nothing like the mannequin.

Well, she'd likely never know. Sam's agenda, whatever it was, didn't seem to include ever kissing her. Besides, attraction, not curiosity, should be the reason to kiss someone. Even though Sam was fun, she could never let herself be romantically involved with him. He was lightyears away from the man who was right for her—the man she'd sought all the years.

So, a kiss from Sam? She could never let that happen.

~*~

Finishing the fifth lap around the soccer field, Sam pulled his shirttail up and wiped the sweat from his face. Not only was the temperature in the high eighties, but he was ridiculously out of shape. Other than some short periods on the treadmill at physical therapy—inside, in air conditioning—he hadn't really run in the weeks since the surgery. His endurance wasn't as bad as he'd expected, but he still had a long way to go before he could get back in uniform on the field.

Things with Katherine hadn't exactly ended today as he'd thought they would. He'd had a "spontaneous" lunch and a car ride planned. Whoever Clark was, he definitely believed he had territorial rights over her. Although she'd never mentioned him, they had some sort of history together.

A part of Sam had wanted to stick around and see what happened, but Clark's demeanor let him know he wasn't welcome. And while he didn't care what Clark thought or wanted, hanging around might have made it harder on Katherine, so he'd left. She didn't need him there, anyway. She could handle herself.

At least now he knew one of the other competitors. Game on.

A whistle sounded on the sidelines as Brad waved the girls over for a brief meeting. The changes in positions Sam had suggested had improved the team, and today's practice had gone really well. In a couple more weeks, they'd be ready for the tournament.

Sam stood quietly in the back while Brad went over the team roster for Saturday's game and gave a brief review of the strengths and weaknesses of the opposition. As he finished up, Sam glanced toward the knot of parents waiting across the field to take their daughters home. No Katherine. He wanted to see her—just to know she was OK.

Cassie and Sophie had begun crossing the field and were heading toward the parking lot. Sophie's mom must be picking up today because if it had been Katherine's turn, she would have already been here.

"I'm stoked. The girls looked great today." Brad slapped him on the back. "Thanks for the suggestions, man. Amazing what some fresh eyes and professional advice can do. Any other ideas?"

"Nope. We'll just see how Saturday goes, but I think they'll win."

"Me, too. Man, you were really moving out there. Should have gotten my stopwatch out. Made me tired just watching you."

"I don't even want to know how slow I was. I've gotta get into shape before I return to the UK this fall."

Brad placed a hand on Sam's shoulder and looked him straight in the eyes. "Hey, man, aren't you about done with all that playing around? Time to grow up.

You should move back here."

Yes, he should. "All this 'playing around' is hard work. And I've been rewarded by getting to do things and go places I would have never been able to go without it. My life's been great. Everything I ever dreamed of." Yet less than he desired. "But there's no way I could move back right now even if I wanted to. I'm under contract until the end of the spring season next year. And besides, what would I do? All I know is soccer and construction. And the last thing I want to do is construction work."

Brad placed a hand on his shoulder. "Mind if I add that to my prayer list?"

What could it hurt? "Sure, man. Go for it. See you later."

A familiar pink water bottle sat on the ground at the end of the bench. No need to read the name marked on it. Cassie's forgetfulness could be his windfall. Any valid excuse to stop by and see Katherine. He scooped it up and threw it into his bag. He jogged over to the parking lot, opened the trunk of his car, and dropped his bag inside.

"Hey, Sam." Cassie sat on the curb across the parking lot.

"Well, hey, Cass. Didn't see you. What are you still doing here? I thought you were riding home with Sophie."

"No, Beth is supposed to pick me up. She's not here yet."

Something was up. Katherine was never late. She was always on time—usually early. "Did you try to call her?"

"I forgot my phone. I'm sure she'll be here soon."

Sam grabbed his phone from the side pouch of his

soccer bag and dropped down onto the curb beside her. "Here, use mine."

She pushed in the numbers, listened, and then handed it back after a few seconds. "No answer."

"How about I give you a ride home?" This would be a good excuse to see how Katherine was doing without looking as though he was stalking her. "Give me five seconds to put on a dry shirt."

Sam walked to his car, pulled off the sweat-soaked jersey, and threw it in the trunk. Then he rummaged around in the bag for the T-shirt that was in there someplace.

As Katherine's car pulled up in front of Cassie, her words tumbled out nonstop through the open windows. "Cassie, I am so, so sorry I'm late. I went to the store to buy a roast for Dad's dinner tomorrow, and the checkout lines were so long, and then there was a wreck blocking the highway, and my phone died so I couldn't even call you and let you know. I'm really sorry. I hope you're not upset."

"No worries." Cassie stood and walked toward Katherine and then gestured Sam's direction as she climbed into the car. "Sam would have given me a ride."

Katherine jerked around to face him, her mouth gaping open. She'd apparently been so distracted she hadn't even noticed him there.

"Hey, there. You OK?"

Her face flushed. "Sam, I, uh...I mean, thanks...um...I..."

With each syllable her face grew deeper crimson. She wouldn't even make eye contact with him. She just kept staring at his chest.

Oh...he recognized that look. He'd just never seen

it from Katherine. All that upper body work at the gym had paid off. "Just a second." He grabbed the dry shirt from his bag, pulled it over his head, and then turned back to the car. "Sorry, you caught me in the middle of changing."

She giggled.

"So, is everything OK?" Sam placed his forearms on the window ledge and leaned on the car.

"Yes. No. I don't know." She leaned her head back against the headrest and sighed. "Yes, it is now. I was just concerned about Cassie."

"Hey, it's OK. Cassie's a big girl. It didn't hurt her to wait a few minutes. Isn't that right, Cassie?"

Cassie nodded.

"Plus," he continued, "I'd never let anything happen to her. You should know that."

"I know. I just didn't want her to be upset." She turned her head toward him and smiled her relief. "Hey, thanks for all your help this morning. I can't wait for my dad to see the garden."

"So, my penance is paid?"

"Yes, and then some. I've never had more fun weeding a garden."

"Me, neither. Sorry I left so quickly when that guy showed up. Did everything turn out OK?"

For the first time since she'd gotten seated in the car, Cassie spoke. "What guy?"

"Clark," Katherine replied.

"Clark? What was Mr. Plastic doing here?" Cassie asked.

"Cassie, that's not very nice." Katherine's response was soft.

"Well, neither is he."

"That's not true."

Sam had listened enough. "Who's Clark?"

"My boss." Katherine kept her gaze on Cassie.

"Ex-boss. He fired her after she refused to marry him."

~*~

Katherine placed a checkmark by the last entry on today's list and turned the page in her notebook to review tomorrow's plan. Everything was pretty much ready for Dad's homecoming. She would spend most of tomorrow straightening the house, putting fresh linens on his bed, hanging clean towels in his bathroom, and cooking. Her goal was to have everything done by the time Cassie got home from school so Dad would come home to a calm house.

Katherine had managed everything quite well in his absence these last few weeks, and she wanted him to be proud of her.

She placed the notebook on her nightstand and turned off the lamp. The room was silent except for the metronome ticking of the antique wall clock above the chest of drawers—every regular "tick-tock" a thief stealing moments of her life. Seconds, minutes, hours that could never be regained.

She'd always been taught that God had a perfect plan for her life, and she had done her best to figure out what it was. When she'd graduated from college, she'd had so many dreams and aspirations, but more than anything she'd wanted what her parents had—a loving marriage and a family.

And so, she'd waited. She'd pursued her career goals, and prayed, and waited. She'd been so sure that

God would bring her the man who was right for her, so certain "he" would come, the one who matched the numbered attributes on her list. And then Clark had, but when he'd proposed, she'd frozen. Everything she'd prayed for in a husband had been kneeling right in front of her, offering himself, and she couldn't reach out and take it.

She should have been happy—no, elated—to see Clark today after all these weeks. But she hadn't been. She and Sam had been having so much fun, and then Clark showed up and ruined it all. His presence had been an interruption.

Why couldn't she find a man with Clark's faith and Sam's passion? Heat prickled her entire body. When she'd seen Sam shirtless at the soccer field today, she'd been filled with a longing she'd never before experienced. She'd wanted nothing more than to throw open the car door and grab him—sweaty or not—into her arms. But, thankfully, her seatbelt had saved her from that embarrassment.

So, if Clark was supposedly everything she'd ever dreamed of, everything she'd ever desired—why had she never felt that same attraction toward him?

12

She'd made her father cry. Unintentionally, certainly, but she'd still done it.

As he'd opened the door of what was now the spice cabinet to get a water glass, she'd stood quietly leaning against the opposite cabinet, smiling, anticipating his words of praise as he realized that—thanks to her hard work—the kitchen was now properly organized. But the words had never come—only a leaden moan as he'd burst red-faced from the kitchen and escaped through the back door into the privacy of Mom's garden.

The only other time Katherine had seen him cry was at the funeral. All her life this man had been her comfort—his shoulder her solace, his arms her fortress. And now her childhood superhero sat alone, a heartbroken mortal. And it was all her fault.

If only she had never reorganized the cabinets. She'd managed to convince herself that her motivation was to make life better for Dad and Cassie, but that was only an excuse. Deep in the corners of her heart lurked the truth. She'd really wanted to prove her way was the best.

Now she would have done anything to be able to take back her self-centered actions, but she couldn't. She could only apologize and then put the kitchen back as it had been.

He needed some time alone to compose himself, but she couldn't stay inside any longer and do nothing. She had to set everything right—to heal the anguish she'd caused. Quietly she opened the patio door and tiptoed across the deck to the steps. His back was to her as he sat alone on the bench where he and Mom had snuggled so many evenings, facing the western horizon, waiting for the sun to dip low and cover the evening sky with fire.

She inched across the yard until she stood behind him and gently placed her hand on his shoulder. She could only whisper. "Daddy, I..." But no more words would come as hot tears stole her voice.

The hand she'd held so many times reached up and covered hers, and she heard the nickname she'd had all her life. "Hey, Baby Girl, it's OK. Come sit with me."

Slowly she walked around the bench and eased down into her mother's seat. This time her words mingled with tears and gushed forth like a rain-swollen waterfall. "Daddy, I'm so sorry. I never intended to hurt you. I'll put it back tomorrow."

Her father's arm encircled her and pulled her close until her head rested upon his shoulder. "No, leave it as it is. You did a fine job."

"But Daddy..."

"It's OK, Katherine." He kissed the top of her head. "Life's marching on, and I can't continue to live in the past. That's not what your mother would have wanted, and it's sure not being a good steward of the years I have left. However many they are, I need to make the best of them. Thanks for helping me take the first step." As he rested his cheek on her head, his voice was soft, warm. "Besides, we both know organization was never one of your mother's strengths. In fact, her disorganization and spontaneity were two of her most charming qualities."

With her head still on her father's shoulder, she closed her eyes as the warmth of the sinking sun blanketed her heart with peace.

"Baby Girl, open your eyes, or you'll miss it."

The western sky was ablaze with color. A celestial paint canister had spilled a puddle of bright gold on the horizon, it's spreading fingers gradually darkening to orange and then crimson as they reached upward into the royal blue sky overhead. Her breathing caught, and she could only whisper at the magnificence before her. "Oh, Daddy, it's beautiful."

They sat in comfortable silence as the yellows and oranges turned to deep burgundy and then on to dark gray blending into the now navy sky above. The evening breeze brushed the wind chimes hanging above the deck, and they tinkled a sweet accompaniment to the rhythmic percussion of the cicadas. She could have stayed here where peace reigned forever.

"I hear Clark stopped by yesterday. How's he doing?"

Cassie was at it again. "Good, I guess." Better than she was anyway. He still had a job and a paycheck. "Looks like business has picked up, and I'll be able to have my job back in a few weeks—if I want it, that is."

"If you want it? I thought this was your dream job."

She'd been sure of that, too. "I love the work. It's not that. But the idea of having Clark as my boss again is uncomfortable, to say the least. He's different.

Everything changed after his proposal."

As she sat up and faced him, Dad drew away and turned toward her. "Of course it did, sweetie. You can't expect it not to. It's hard for a man to be rejected by a woman he loves. Clark's hurt, but he'll come around in time. I'm sure he loves you as much as ever."

"That's one of the problems, Daddy. Sometimes I wonder if Clark really does loves me. Maybe he never did. If he does, would he have let these weeks go by without calling me? It's more as if I'm the next step in one of his action plans. College, career, marriage, family."

"Maybe he just needed some time to sort things out. He knows your hopes, and I'm sure he was hurt and surprised when you turned him down. I think the fact that he showed up here is a sign he's working through everything and still cares for you. So, maybe the real question is not about his love for you."

They'd never dated for fun. From the very beginning, Clark had let her know he was dating her with the intention of marriage at some point in the future. And now that the time had come, she was afraid. Engagement was the next logical step in their relationship, but the thought of marrying him smothered her, just as his embrace had yesterday.

So maybe Dad was right. Maybe the true problem had nothing to do with Clark but with her. An idea that had been slowly germinating in her heart over the past few weeks suddenly mushroomed. Clark was a wonderful man, perhaps she couldn't marry him because she'd been wrong all along, and she wasn't designed to get married—to anyone. Perhaps she simply needed to surrender and accept that her

Father's answer might possibly be "No."

Yet she couldn't erase years of her life as if they'd never happened. Not continuing to hope after she'd invested all these years waiting seemed wrong. Her heart's desire was still to be married, and she wasn't ready to ask God to remove that longing from her spirit. More than anything, she wanted to be a wife...just not Clark's. "When did you know Mom was The One?"

"Oh, you mean she was The One for me, and I was The One for her?" He smiled.

She nodded. "Yes. Could you imagine your life with anyone else?" The idea of the two of them not being married was inconceivable.

"Not now. I loved her more than I ever thought possible." His smile warmed as he slowly shook his head. "I proposed to your mother three times. She turned me down twice because she thought we were too different and it would never work. And turns out she was right. The first couple of years were rocky. She even went home to Grandma one time."

Shock gripped her stomach like a vise. Neither of her parents had ever shared this with her. Their relationship had always seemed ideal, as if they'd never doubted they were anything but the perfect match. Their warm smiles, their tender glances, a gentle hug or squeeze of the hands when they passed one another. She'd grown up in a home where the love between a father and a mother was never a question, and that's exactly what she wanted. "I...I had no idea, Daddy. You two always seemed like soulmates."

"We learned to be because we loved each other." As he looked toward the ground, his smile disappeared. When he turned back toward her, he rested his hand on hers. "Sweetie, I've never really bought into the idea that God has one perfect person picked out for each of us. Maybe He does. Maybe He doesn't. I don't know. But the world is a mighty big place, full of billions of people. And thinking, that in all that mass of humanity, God has chosen only one person for each of us has always seemed to me as if we're trying to place limits on a limitless God. But I do know this. When you find the person you want to promise your love and faithfulness to in marriage, then he or she becomes The One. Your One and Your Only."

This idea was contrary to anything she'd ever been taught in youth group growing up or in all the women's Bible studies in college. There had always been this belief that if she prayed hard enough and looked thoroughly enough, God would reveal The One, His One, for her. But what happened if she missed him? "Daddy, you remember that notebook from that Passion and Purity Conference in middle school?"

"You don't still have that thing, do you?"

She nodded. "Clark has every quality on that list—everything I've looked for in a husband all these years. But what if I make a mistake and marry him and then find out there's someone else who would have been a better match?"

He patted her arm. "You know, you and I are a lot alike—wanting to follow the rules, to do the right thing, wanting everything to run according to plan."

She hadn't thought about that before. No wonder Dad had always understood her in a way Mom never had.

His voice dropped to a whisper, and his eyes glistened as he turned away from her. "I needed some of your mother's free-spiritedness as balance in my life. I'm convinced that one of the strengths of our relationship was the way our differences complemented one another, and I'm beyond glad I found her, and that we had these years together. She was My One."

Perhaps that was the problem between Clark and her. They were too much alike. "Maybe I should be looking for someone like that. Someone different from me."

As he turned back toward her, his gaze held the gentle warmth she'd seen all her life. "If I could fix it for you, I would, Baby Girl. But only you can decide that. Seems to me you're pretty comfortable in the security of that little boat, though."

Boat?

"You've been sittin' there rowin' for quite a while. When a storm comes, you just pull your oars in and hunker down until it passes. You might feel the boat rock and hear and see the waves lap against the outside, but they don't touch you. You never feel them. You're nice and dry."

"Daddy, I'm not sure—"

"Honey, maybe it's time to give yourself permission to do something different and trust in something other than the boat. Why don't you consider stepping out onto those crashing waves and see what happens?"

The screen door on the deck creaked open and then slammed shut. "I'm home."

Her father squeezed her hand and grinned. "Speaking of crashing waves...I think I'd better go visit with your sister while I can still string a few words together. My body's several time zones away.

Coming?"

"In a minute."

He stood and then pecked her on the forehead. "Just remember, for people like you and me, the hardest part of life is not necessarily the doing and working but more often the waiting."

As he walked across the yard to the deck, she glanced upward. Clouds partially obscured the first few stars of the evening. Their lives had been covered with clouds these last few months. Before her mother died, she would have described her life in Dallas as fulfilling. But she had been fooling herself. Her life had been simply full—full of activities and deadlines, of doing and working, just as Dad had said. Every moment of every day was busy, regimented. The checkmarks in her notebooks were visual evidence of all she'd accomplished. Yet, like the hours she'd spent at the gym on the treadmill, she'd been clocking hundreds of miles but never making any progress toward a final destination.

So, maybe Dad was right. Maybe it was time to throw away the book and try another approach. Essentially every night for almost fifteen years she'd prayed for God to bring the man on the list into her life. But now she realized that had been the wrong prayer.

At some point, she'd begun to place her faith and trust in the list she'd made. She'd clung to the sides of the boat to ride out the storms instead of trusting in the one who could conquer them. How had she gotten so off course? *Forgive me, Father.*

The metal chimes clanged incessantly as the mild breeze transformed into blustery winds, rustling the trees and bushes. Someplace close by, a storm was brewing. The winds had shoved the previous clouds over the horizon revealing thousands of stars—some mere pinpricks overhead. The sky was filled with more sparkling jewels than she could possibly count, more than human eyes could even see, and her Father knew each one by name. He was a God of plenty, of vast creativity beyond what she could ever understand or even imagine. He'd created her and knew her heart, her desires, her needs.

And He knew her by name, too.

~*~

Clouds had rushed back across the navy canopy above, obscuring the stars and sprinkling rain down upon her as she walked down the driveway to the curb. Tomorrow was garbage day. If she didn't do it now, she might lose her nerve.

Slowly she opened the garbage bin. Daddy was right. Waves or no waves, storm or no storm, it was time to step out onto the water and head toward a destination she could have never reached by staying within the security of the boat. Heart pounding, she laid the old notebook from middle school on the top of the black plastic bag and lowered the lid.

She raised her face upward. The gentle drops were refreshing, cleansing, melting away the invisible chains that had held her captive all these years. Her heart was renewed, and she was free.

Maybe in the storm, she'd find her peace.

13

Sam navigated around the trash container on the edge of the curb, pulled up the driveway, and parked about half way between the street and the house. The garage door was up, and her father's car was gone. Good. One less excuse for her not to go with him on this well-planned, "impromptu" outing. He shifted the car into neutral and cut the engine. As he opened the driver's side door, he grabbed Cassie's water bottle from the passenger seat. That girl was his accomplice unaware. One of these days, if everything went as planned, he'd have to thank her.

After pressing the doorbell, he jumped to the side of the porch, out of sight of the peephole in the door and flattened himself against the brick wall adjacent to the doorframe. The deadbolt shot back, and then the inner wooden door whooshed open followed by the creaking of the outer storm door. Katherine's voice squeezed through the open sliver. "Good morning, Sam."

Oh, man. She wasn't surprised at all. He stepped over in front of the door and spoke with mock anger. "What are you doing opening that door? It could have been some weirdo." She looked amazing. Fresh-scrubbed face again. T-shirt and shorts. So pure and natural.

She opened the door wider and focused her gaze over his shoulder. "You'll have to be sneakier if you want to conceal your identity. Since James Bond doesn't visit Crescent Bluff very often, there was only one other choice. The weirdo." Her eyes sparkled as a smile lit her face.

The car. He'd forgotten it was visible from the doorway. "Oh, yeah. What can I say? Weirdos are us."

"I like your water bottle. Pink's a good color for you." The corners of her mouth twitched slightly as her pursed lips hid a smile. Something about her was different. She seemed more relaxed than usual.

"Funny." Looping his finger through the strap, he held the bottle up. "I thought Cassie might need it before practice tomorrow."

"Thanks, Sam. But you really didn't have to come over here just to return the bottle. We have plenty of others. Mom must have bought Cassie one a month. She could have waited a couple of days."

Game time. "Well, actually, I have a bit of an ulterior motive. I'm headed to Bluebonnet Park to do some jogging, and I thought it would be nice to have some company. What do you say? I'll even buy you lunch after."

"Well, Sam, I was going to..."

"Going to what? Reorganize the linen closet?"

Her faced reddened. "No. I wasn't...I mean not exactly. Not that closet, anyway." She paused.

He'd caught her.

Shaking her head, she smiled. "The game closet in the family room."

"Oh, I see. Do you think those games'll self-destruct if you wait twenty-four more hours?"

"No, of course not. But..."

"But what?"

"Look at the sky. It's cloudy and the weatherman said there's a sixty percent chance of rain today."

"That also means there's a forty percent chance of no rain. I've lived in the UK for the last seven years. Believe me. I'm not afraid of a little precip. Besides, running in the rain can be quite refreshing."

Her eyes softened.

He had her.

"I'm not much of a jogger. Actually, I'm not a jogger at all."

"Well, we could skip around the trail if you'd prefer."

She crossed her arms. "You can be so infuriating sometimes, Sam Tucker." Her eyes said yes. "OK, but only if I can walk."

"Deal. Grab your sneakers. I'll wait out here."

~*~

No wonder Katherine hadn't recognized Sam before the mission meeting. Now, with his hair grown back enough, she could see little Sammy Tucker in the man. It was still as blond as ever. Women she knew at her church in Dallas paid good money, and lots of it, for hair that color.

So what exactly was she doing? She'd had her whole day planned, and now she wouldn't get any of it accomplished. She should have turned him down, but he was right. Nothing on her list would mysteriously disappear if she didn't get it done today. Besides she'd made a decision last night, and now it was time to see if she intended to follow it through. So, she was taking the first step out of that boat. That's what she was doing.

"You're quiet." His words pushed their way into her world. "Everything OK?"

"Sorry. Everything's fine. I was just rearranging my schedule in my head." Not exactly the truth. She was doing some rearranging but not of her schedule. Her goals, her dreams. She was, as Dad suggested last night, giving herself permission to try something new.

"I'll take you back home if you really want. We can do this another time." As his gaze briefly left the road and glanced her way, the warmth embraced her.

"You know, I worked really hard to get everything done before my dad got home from his trip. I think I've earned a little time off." She pushed herself back into the seat and closed her eyes. "I could definitely use a break."

Throwing the old notebook away last night had taken every ounce of courage she'd been able to muster. To get rid of something that had been a part of her and her dreams for so many years had made her almost physically ill. But once she'd closed the lid on the trash can, a sense of excitement—of freedom—had coursed through every inch of her body. She was no longer confined by those glass walls Mom always mentioned, where she could see what was going on outside but was restrained from participating by the invisible barrier. She was free. Today began a new adventure—one driven by relationship and trust rather than rules and lists.

But even that excitement couldn't completely displace the old fear planted deep within her heart that she was making a mistake. Old habits died hard. Mom's words resounded in her mind. The journey ahead would most likely be bumpy. Change was never easy, but in the discomfort of change came growth. Peace flowed over her, ebbed away, and then flowed back again like a gentle wave tickling her feet at South Padre Island. She would do this.

Sam's hand squeezed her knee. "You've definitely earned some downtime."

"What...? Oh, yes, some time off."

His tone was gentle. "Lean back and close your eyes, if you want. I'll wake you when we get there."

~*~

The park was deserted. Apparently, most of the town agreed with Katherine's weather forecast rather than his. Even though the temperature had dropped some, the air hung on her shoulders like a soaking beach towel as they slowly jogged around the track. So far, she'd been able to keep up with him, but that wouldn't last much longer. Besides, he was definitely holding back.

"You're doing great." His voice was as steady as if he'd been sitting in a recliner watching television.

"I think it's more like 'I've done great.' I've about had it, Sam. Plus, I know I'm slowing you down. You can't possibly be getting much out of this workout." She slowed to a brisk walk.

"Today is about quality time more than quality workout." He matched his pace to hers.

"Really, I'm sure you want this to be of some benefit to you. I'm fine walking by myself if you want to run on. We can meet up at the beginning of the trail when we're finished." She slowed even more.

"I have an idea." Suddenly he sprinted ahead about ten yards and then ran backward until he met her again. "Good skill practice." He ran forward again, but this time for a longer distance.

This past fall she and Clark had gone to the park three times a week after work. He knew she didn't like to jog, so he'd run on and leave her to walk alone. Some days that was OK because she needed the space, but other times, she wanted companionship and had asked him if he'd walk with her. He'd just complained, saying he really needed a good workout and walking with her didn't provide that. If she wanted to exercise together, then she needed to start jogging. So she'd smiled and told him to go on...just as a good girlfriend should.

Sam was back. He'd done several mini trips forward and backward before he came all the way back to her. Tiny beads of perspiration covered his forehead as he matched his pace to hers again. "You doing OK?" His breathing had quickened.

"I'm doing great." And she was. Last night's time in the garden had left her with a refreshed sense of optimism.

"Time for some laterals." He turned sideways and kind of galloped-shuffled up the path and then back a couple of times. He changed sides and made several more roundtrips until he took his place beside her.

They walked on in comfortable silence until he jumped in front of her and held up his hands in two-step position. "Time for you to practice your footwork."

He had to be crazy. Outside, in broad daylight. "Sam! Not now. Not here. What will people think?"

He looked over his left shoulder and then his

right. "What people? The place is deserted. I can't believe the hint of a little rain would scare everyone away."

Over the past several weeks she'd learned enough about him to know once he got an idea in his mind, dissuading him was next to impossible.

Pressing his hands toward her, he reinforced his invitation. "Just cashing in on that rehab you promised." As his eyes sparkled, the Caribbean called to her. The sooner she agreed, the sooner they could do something else.

She stepped forward and grasped his left hand, and the electricity from his touch flowed from her fingertips up her arms until it filled her entire body. When he placed his right hand against the middle of her back and drew her closer, the path beneath her feet disappeared.

He smiled and bent forward slightly. "Ready?"

As she nodded, he began counting the cadence of the steps. At first, they moved slowly and deliberately. But soon he increased the tempo and they began gliding and turning down the path. Counting was no longer necessary as she'd followed him enough by now that she could feel any slight change or correction he made, just as Juanita had said when she'd tied the bandana over Katherine's eyes.

As his hands directed her to a side by side position, he gently draped an arm across her shoulders and then began leading her into a series of quick turns and twirls. Laughing, she floated down the path like the ballerina she'd dreamed she'd become when she was five years old.

But Sam was silent. Usually when they danced, he'd make little amusing comments, and since she was no longer facing him, she couldn't see his expression. When she came out of the next turn she glanced up at his face. He was smiling. All was well.

As he led her into the next turn, her foot became entangled with a small root that had overgrown the outer edge of the trail, and she lost her balance. As she fell backward, grass, trees, and gray sky swirled around her in slow motion like in a movie. She tried to let go of his hand to catch herself, but he held tight and then placed his free hand behind her back and pulled her upward against his body to hold her close until she could get both feet planted securely back down on the path.

"I'm so sorry. Are you OK? I should have remembered that spot. I almost tripped myself when I was doing the laterals earlier."

"I'm fine."

Neither of them moved as the whole world faded into the background. No birds sang, no leaves rustled in the wind, no clouds passed overhead, the earthy aroma of impending rain disappeared. Only one thing filled her senses.

The soft bass of his voice drew her back to reality. "I think that's enough for today."

14

Katherine sat on one of the large flat stones next to the ancient riverbed. Since the beginning of time, this small tributary of the Brazos had diligently and painstakingly etched its path through the limestone until it was now flanked by two walls of small cliffs full of nooks and crannies.

Sam set a small cooler down next to her and then dropped onto the rock himself. "How in the world did you ever find this place?"

"When I was a kid, my parents and I would come here on one of my mother's expeditions. After church some Sundays, we'd stop by the Dairy Delite, pick up some sandwiches, and come here to eat them. Then we'd hunt for fossils or dinosaur footprints."

The memories filled her soul with a strange mixture of joy and sorrow. Mom always had a childlike sense of awe and fascination with the world—something she'd passed on to Katherine when she was young, but something Katherine had rejected as she'd grown and matured. Things like pretending to be paleontologists became inappropriate behaviors for a preteen-practically-adult-serious-person. She'd give anything to have some of those times back—to have Mom back. If she could rewind the hands of the clock, she'd do a better job of enjoying the moments instead of wishing her life away.

"Fossils?" Sam handed her a sub sandwich.

"Thanks. Yes, this is the same river that runs through Glen Rose, through Dinosaur Valley State Park. My mother had me convinced that if we looked hard enough, we'd find some undiscovered fossils or footprints. We never did, of course, but I used to get so excited at the prospect—" Her throat choked closed. One more word and the tears might escape.

In the silence, Sam reached over and gently brushed her arm with his hand.

She pushed her words out in a whisper. "I wish I'd told her how much I enjoyed those times instead of pretending to be too cool after a while."

"I'm sure she knew." The warmth of his voice surprised her. "Parents are smart like that."

She could only nod.

"Hey, if the weather continues to hold out, we could do our own expedition this afternoon—in honor of the past."

"I think I'd like that."

As they ate their sandwiches, the only sounds were the wind rustling through the trees above and the water gently trickling over the stones below.

You lead me beside still waters. You restore my soul. Yes, yes.

Here—away from jobs and jumbled closets, away from lists and responsibilities, away from broken dreams—here in creation was peace and restoration. She was not some inconsequential, disconnected island. She was a vital part of this complicated system of checks and balances that a perfectly organized and loving Creator had set in place eons ago and continued to hold in His hands.

So this was why Mom had loved the outdoors so much. After all these years, Katherine finally got it. Creation gave a glimpse into the vastness and beauty of the heart of God. *Thank You, Father.*

Sam's voice jolted her back to the present. "Hey, are you up for a random question?"

"Depends upon what it is. Go for it."

"OK. When did you become Katherine? You were always Beth in school."

"No laughing. Promise?"

He nodded.

"I had always been Katherine until third grade when I read the Little House series of books. I started watching reruns of the old TV show and fell madly in love with Almanzo Wilder." It all seemed so ridiculous now. "I loved that he and Laura had special nicknames for each other. She called him Manly, and he called her Beth. And since my middle name is Elizabeth, I adopted that nickname, too. Some days, I'd go out to the garden, move my mother's patio furniture over under the arbor, and pretend it was my 'Little House' and that I was waiting for Almanzo to return from a hard day's work in the fields." She couldn't believe she'd shared this with him. "Silly, I know."

"Nothing's silly about having hopes and dreams. Life would be pretty boring without them." He winked. "Besides, there's not much difference between that and some young boy with orange plastic cones set up in his backyard, pretending he just scored in a shootout to win the World Cup."

She should have known he'd understand. "Anyway, when I left for college, I decided I needed a serious name for a serious time of life, so Katherine it was, and Katherine it is."

"Katherine Elizabeth Herrington. I'd say that's a pretty serious name."

A cool gust of wind raced down into the small canyon and rippled the water as it skimmed across the stream.

Sam stood and offered her his hand. "Well, Miss Katy Beth, if we're to get that expedition in, we'd better start now so we can be back before any rain comes—that is, on the microscopic chance that your forecast is right."

Katy Beth...she liked that.

He led her across the rocks and down a slight rise to the river bed and then turned to face her. "So—just out of curiosity—did Almanzo ever show up?"

If she'd only heard his words and not been looking at him when he'd said them, she might have thought he was making fun of her. But he wasn't. His eyes were warm and gentle. "Not yet. He must have gotten lost somewhere out there on the prairie."

"Poor guy. He's gotta be exhausted and starving by now. You sure that wasn't him that came the other day after we finished working in your mom's garden?"

"One hundred percent positive."

They'd been hiking for about fifteen minutes when several enormous raindrops splatted like miniature water balloons against the rocks. At first, she thought they were a few random drops and nothing more. But the temperature had dropped at least ten degrees since they'd begun their "expedition." And now the wind whipped down the gully between the two cliffs, bringing with it the earthy scent of the approaching storm.

Sam's voice sounded above its roar. "OK, I surrender. Looks as if your sixty percent positive beat my forty percent negative. There'll be no fossils today. Guess we better turn back if we have any chance to make it to the car before the storm breaks loose."

"Good idea." Back to the car, back to life. She needed to figure out a way to carry home the earlier sense of peace she'd discovered here. As the storm approached from someplace upstream, the previously clear, calm waters were now as murky as a latte from The Perks.

He reached over and took her hand. "Come on. We'd better move to outrun this thing."

They began a careful jog over the slippery rocks back downstream toward their picnic spot, but the storm was faster.

The thundering of raindrops pelting against the riverbed and the adjacent stones was as loud as if an entire herd of wild horses was chasing them.

Katherine looked over her shoulder to see a wall of rain about twenty feet away. She squeezed Sam's hand as she yelled above the clatter, "We'll never make it."

They quickened their pace in vain, as icy needles stung her shoulders and the backs of her legs.

"Hurry, in here." Sam pushed her into a small crevice in the stone cliff.

She hadn't noticed it when they'd walked by earlier. It was about five or six feet wide at the opening and several feet deep, tapering closed in the back. They planted themselves toward the rear, out of reach of the biting rain.

While the raindrops could no longer touch her and her arms and legs weren't being prickled by hundreds of needles anymore, the combination of her wet skin, the cold stone walls of the small cave—if one could even call it that—and the plummeting temperatures made her shiver.

"Cold?"

"F-freezing."

He reached down and grabbed the hem of his T-shirt. "Here. It's wet, but you can have this."

As he began to raise his hands, she replied quickly, "No, that's OK. I refuse to take your shirt." The last thing she wanted was a replay of the soccer field. She didn't have a seatbelt to restrain her today.

Eyes twinkling, he grinned. "OK. But I can't watch you shiver like that. Come here." He grasped her hand and gently pulled her close, completely wrapping his arms around her so that he could rub his hands up and down her arms.

She should pull away, but the heat from his body had already began to counteract the shivers. Besides, his hold wasn't much different from the times they'd slow-danced together—except there was no music and they were completely alone.

As the warmth of his body began to relax her, she rested her head on his shoulder, and he tightened his embrace. His heart pounded against her.

He barely drew away and then, with his fingertips, softly brushed the wet tendrils of hair off her cheeks. "Better?"

She nodded and placed her head back against his shoulder. She raised up to look into his eyes. They were dreamy and filled with desire she'd never seen before from him, from Clark, from any man she'd ever dated.

He wanted to kiss her, and she wanted nothing more, but something was stopping him. Maybe he thought she was still involved with Clark. That part of her life was over, and she'd tell Clark as soon as she got the chance. But still, Cassie had mentioned the proposal at the soccer field the other evening. So Sam knew they were serious—or had been—and maybe he thought they still were.

"I'm breaking up with Clark for good." The words rushed out before she could put on the brakes.

"I'm sorry."

"Do you really mean that?"

"Well, yeah, of course. It's gotta be tough if you guys were at the point where he would propose. You two obviously have some history together. Feelings like that don't usually happen overnight."

Sam was right. Saying no had been hard. All of their friends, Dad, Clark's family, and especially Clark had just assumed she'd say yes. Living up to what everyone thought would happen and accepting his proposal would have been, in some ways, the easier choice. But she hadn't been able to do it. And whether or not, as Cassie thought, the two were connected, the layoff after the rejected proposal had ended up being a blessing. It had given her time away to really think and reevaluate. And after last night, especially to pray. Not that God would bring her The One, but that He would bring her a man who would become Her One.

"Clark's a wonderful man, and he'll make someone an incredible husband someday. Just not me. Turning him down was hard, but I'm not sorry I did it. Even though he has every quality I want in a husband, marrying him would have been a mistake. I understand that now."

As a gust of wind blew rain into the small cave, she shivered again, and Sam turned his back to the doorway in the rock to shelter her from the cold. He held her close, and while habit told her to pull away, she refused to obey as the old Katherine would have done. Instead, she placed her head back on his shoulder, and he began slowly swaying back and forth as if they were dancing. Stepping out of the boat meant taking risks she'd never taken before. And yet something about him felt safe.

"Hey." Barely audible above the splatting of the rain against the river rocks, his whisper warmed her hair.

In response, she turned her face up toward his. They were eyelashes apart.

"Whatcha thinking?"

How close you are. "Nothing."

"Nothing?" His eyes probed hers until he had to be able to read her thoughts. "I'm pretty sure that's impossible."

How close you are. And how much I like it. "Nothing...really."

"Sorry, but I'm not buying." He gently rested his forehead against hers. "Let me see if I can pick up some telepathic communications here. Look into my eyes."

She was floating in the ocean, the sunlight sparkling on the gentle, cerulean waves. *Kiss me.* "Sam, I—"

"Quiet, please. I need total silence to ensure accurate results." As she continued to stare into the blue pools, tiny lines crinkled at the outer edges, and he drew his head away. "I got it."

"You have, have you?" For some ridiculous reason her voice quivered.

"Yes. You have a question you want to ask me."

"Oh, I do? And what would that be?"

"You're wondering why I haven't tried to kiss

you."

Her face was on fire as she moved away. There's no way he could have possibly known her thoughts.

"And you think it might be because I'm not attracted to you." He entwined his fingers with hers and then raised their clasped hands to draw her back to him. "But you're wrong."

The rain had slowed to a gentle sprinkle as the storm marched on downstream. In minutes, the two of them would exit the cave, and these moments of forced intimacy would be gone as quickly as they had come. She needed to take advantage of the little time they had left. "Why haven't you then? Every other man I've ever dated would have at least tried by now."

"I'm not every other man."

He was right about that.

"Besides, I'm waiting for an invitation."

So that was what had been going on. It wasn't that he didn't want to kiss her. He just needed to know she wanted him to.

"Yeah, I screwed it up the first time, and I won't the second time."

The first time? Snipe hunting. "Oh, is that what that was supposed to be? A kiss? Thanks for the clarification. I thought it was a sneak attack of some sort." She couldn't help but grin at the memory, but the man before her was not the boy who had ambushed her years earlier.

"Let's just say, I've had plenty of opportunities to practice since then, and I'm confident I can do a better job."

"And upon what do you base that conclusion? As an auditor—even one who's currently unemployed—I can't simply accept some blanket statement without analyzing the supporting facts."

"I see. And how would you do that?" His voice was soft.

"I could interview some of the other participants. But that doesn't seem feasible." Hundreds of tiny butterflies swarmed in her stomach. "I guess the only way to determine the validity of your conclusion is by personal investigation."

He removed his hands from hers, gently cupped her face with them, and gazed into her soul. "I'll take that as an invitation."

Very slowly he leaned forward and, as her eyes fluttered closed, he kissed her softly on her forehead, then her right cheek, her left cheek, and finally the tip of her nose. She could hardly breathe.

Her heart raced as he pulled her close and his lips finally met hers. His first kiss was gentle, sweet, searching. The second, though, was more deliberate, as passion she'd never felt before burned through her body like fire consuming dry kindling in the fireplace before the logs burst into flames. She drew away while she still had the will to do so and leaned her head on his shoulder.

As he rested his head on hers, he whispered. "Well, Miss Auditor?"

"Upon first analysis, I would say that the facts seem to support your stated conclusion. But I will need to do some further investigation at another time to confirm."

As she pushed away from him, he laughed. "Whatever I can do to assist your evaluation."

"Oh, look, Sam. The rain's stopped. Guess we better get going." She pushed him aside and bolted out of the cave before he could argue.

"Wait, Katy Beth!"

As she turned back, he stooped down at the mouth of the cave. He picked up a rock, studied it, and then tossed it into the stream. "Nah, not a fossil. Oh, well, I thought maybe today would be your lucky day, and you'd find something."

If only he knew.

~*~

The notebook must have been under the trash can. Sam hadn't noticed it until he was on his way back down the driveway from returning the can to the side of the house for Mr. Herrington. He'd figured it belonged to Cassie. It would be just like her to lose it.

But then he'd opened the cover. In the upper right corner of the first page in fat, round, schoolgirl cursive was the owner's name: Beth Herrington. The following words jumped out from the center of the same page: Passion and Purity followed by the year of the conference. The same one he'd attended.

He should return it to her, but if she'd wanted it back, she wouldn't have thrown it away in the first place. So, he'd brought it home and, after arguing with himself about respecting her privacy, his curiosity had won out, and he'd begun flipping through the pages.

Reading it had been a mistake. He closed the spiral notebook covered with fluorescent butterflies and dropped it on the floor beside his bed. He'd been on such an emotional high after this afternoon. Everything was moving along better than he'd hoped. Even the weather had cooperated.

But, he'd just had to read the notebook.

The first part was filled with notes from the conference, and about half-way through he found a page entitled, The List. He'd read over the numbered attributes. She was obviously stating the qualities she wanted in a husband. At the bottom of the page was some Bible verse about God granting the desires of one's heart.

He'd told himself he shouldn't open the book, and now he really wished he hadn't. As he'd flipped from page to page, her hopes and dreams were expressed. Some pages contained a male name, often embellished with hearts and flowers. She was obviously comparing the real to her ideal.

The List was restated multiple times. Some items were eliminated as new ones were added. Others were rearranged. But the top three entries never changed.

He was working on the first one. After being so far away from God over the last several years, his heart had begun to hunger for something more than the world could give him. His morning Bible studies with Brad had only increased that longing.

The second one he possessed and had for years. He loved her unconditionally. As ridiculous as it seemed, she'd been the standard he'd measured the other women by, and they'd all been nothing more than caricatures of the real thing. The fear that his teenage memories had, over time, airbrushed her into some fake representation of reality was obliterated the night of their date at the Cattlemen's Hotel. She was so much more than he remembered.

But number three...he'd had one chance at that one, and he'd blown it. How realistic was it anyway in this day and time? He'd been tested, and he was clean. Plus, he'd been celibate for about a year now—since he'd decided to come back and look for her.

God couldn't rewrite the pages of his past, but He could, Brad had assured him, direct his future. All Sam could hope was that Katherine would come to love him enough that number three wouldn't matter.

15

Katherine drove with her window down, but even the breeze on her face didn't help calm her rolling stomach.

I'll call you tomorrow. Those had been Sam's last words to her as he'd hugged her good-bye last night. And as each minute of the day had crept by at a snail's pace, and the phone call hadn't come, the nausea had only gotten worse.

Yesterday in the little canyon had been amazing. The kiss that she had agonized over these past few weeks had been more wonderful than she could have ever imagined. And the longing in Sam's eyes had told her he'd felt the same.

The first thought she'd had this morning was of Sam. She'd wanted to see him, to smell the clean fragrance of his cologne, to feel his heart beating life into hers. She'd grabbed her phone from the nightstand, and then she'd glanced at the clock and discovered it was way too early to call him. Besides, even though it seemed kind of old-fashioned, she wanted him to call her—to want to call her. And he had promised he would.

When she hadn't heard from him by late morning, she'd told herself he'd just slept late. But then noon had come and gone and still not even a text from him.

Several times, she'd picked her phone up to call him but then put it right back down again. She'd even called her cell from the house phone just to make sure it was working. It was.

The whole day was gone, and he hadn't called.

There had to be some reason. Maybe she was nothing more than an answer to boredom. After all, he was stuck here in Crescent Bluff with lots of time on his hands and nothing to do. Perhaps she wasn't cosmopolitan enough for him. Or maybe she'd misread him, and he didn't enjoy the kiss as much as she'd thought. After all this time of waiting, maybe he'd been disappointed.

Whatever the reason, he hadn't called, and now as she turned onto the street that dead-ended into the soccer complex, a part of her prayed he wouldn't be there this evening. But as she rounded the corner, the red car, backed into a corner space, came into sight. Her prayer wasn't answered.

She pulled into a parking place at the other end of the lot, cut the engine, and rested her forehead on the steering wheel. Maybe she was unfinished business from his past, and now he'd checked her off his list just as she'd checked the game closet off hers this afternoon. One more conquest completed so he could move on to the next.

But if all this was really true, he should have made a move long before yesterday. She was so confused. And nervous.

So much for stepping out of the boat and taking a chance. She was sinking in fear and disappointment and taking the peace she'd felt the other night in the garden down with her. She wanted the old notebook back, but it was too late.

Somewhere deep inside a quiet, gentle Voice asked for her trust. She should give Sam the benefit of the doubt and at least wait until they could talk. Yes. She would try to do that.

Taking a deep breath, she stepped out of the car and closed the door. As she made her way across the complex to the far field, the earthy scent of the ground, still damp from yesterday's rains, enveloped her, and she was again in his arms in the cave. If only she could be there now.

The team was gathered on the sidelines, Brad and Sam giving instructions to the players and their parents. As she approached the group, Sam's gaze found hers, and heat from yesterday's memory crept up her neck to her face. She tried to smile as if everything was normal, but her lips quivered and gave her away. She couldn't let him see her cry.

~*~

Something was definitely wrong. She had the same look on her face as she'd had that day at the church when she figured out who he really was—embarrassment, betrayal. After yesterday, he'd been sure their relationship was well on its way, but apparently there'd been some sort of setback that only she knew about.

"Think you and Katherine could handle that, Sam?"

He'd missed what Brad had said. "Sorry, man. What was that?"

"Would you and Katherine mind taking care of the planning for the tournament next month?"

Sam glanced at Katherine. She opened her mouth to reply, but he jumped in first. "Sure, we can do that."

"Great," Brad continued. "OK everybody, Sam and Katherine will try to have some packets ready to hand out at the game Saturday."

By the time Sam picked up his bag, Katherine was halfway across the field, marching full speed toward the parking lot. Good thing Cassie was still on the bench changing into her slides because Katherine couldn't leave without her sister. He jogged on ahead so they'd have a few seconds alone before Cassie showed up. "Wait up, Katy Beth."

She paused slightly. She'd heard him even though she didn't turn and acknowledge his words. She returned to making a beeline across the complex, obviously pretending she hadn't.

When he caught up with her, he matched his pace to hers. "Hey, you OK?"

"Fine." Her gaze was trained straight ahead.

"Fine? You sure?"

She stopped and turned toward him. Her eyes were red. She wasn't angry. She was upset about something.

"Baby, what's wrong?" He reached out to take her hand, but she pulled it away.

"Please don't, Sam."

"Sorry. I didn't mean to upset you." When he'd kissed her yesterday afternoon in that primeval setting, they'd been alone in a world of two. Even the rain had been an accomplice by forcing them into the cave. Nothing could have been better.

But then last night he'd read the notebook, and in a matter of minutes, that world had disappeared. He wanted her, but he didn't deserve her. She must have come to realize that, because, despite what she'd said, something between them was definitely wrong.

"Really, I'm OK." Her face still said otherwise as she broke eye contact and shifted her gaze, focusing on some point to his right. "How was your day?"

He didn't want to talk about his day, but she obviously didn't want to discuss what was on her mind, and some conversation was better than none. "A mess. I had the final doctor's appointment for my knee in Dallas, but the doctor was tied up in surgery. So, I decided to wait rather than reschedule. I read every magazine in the waiting room, including some three-year-old ladies' magazines. You'll be glad to know I should be able to make a pretty mean apple pie while teaching a child how to tie his shoes using the bunny ears method."

She nodded as she shifted her weight back and forth but no smile, and she still wasn't saying anything, so he'd better keep going. "And to top it all off, my phone died. You know all that rain yesterday? It must have fried my phone. I didn't realize it until I tried to call you on the way to Dallas this morning—and nothing."

As her gaze found his, her face lit up. "You tried to call me, but your phone was dead?"

"Yeah, it was in my pocket yesterday, and it must have happened when I had my back to the opening of the cave. I was, shall I say, a bit distracted at the time. I guess it got wetter than I realized. It's home in a bowl of rice, but I don't have much hope for a recovery."

As a smile covered her face, she grasped his hands. "Oh, Sam, I'm so sorry."

He'd never seen anyone so happy about being sorry. "You don't seem that sorry."

Her laughter was musical. "Oh, trust me. I am. I really am."

Whatever. At least she was smiling and talking to him now. "I need to go to the phone store tonight. Want to come along? We could go to The Perks after and work on the agenda for the tournament."

"I'd love to."

~*~

Katherine had no idea where they were headed. Sam sped down the highway toward some secret destination that he assured her would be fun. Going on yesterday's date had been a surprise, too, and it had turned out better than if he, or even she, had planned it for days. Neither one of them could have created the rainstorm that forced them into the cave and brought them together. The growth their relationship had experienced in just a few minutes might have otherwise taken days or weeks to come to pass. If at all. So, maybe she needed to rethink her stance on spontaneity. Impulsiveness wasn't such a bad thing after all.

As Sam shifted the car into fourth, Katherine softly blew across the top of her cup. They had finished the information packets for the tournament so quickly that her latte was still hot.

"That was a bit too easy, if you ask me." Sam glanced her way and smiled.

A bit. Over the past few weeks, his accent had morphed into something more Texan than British, but every now and then isolated words or little phrases sneaked back in. Something about the change was really cute.

"What's so funny?"

"Nothing. I was just wondering why Brad assigned the two of us to do a job that would have been a snap for one person. That's all."

"I think he was trying to help me out."

"You mean he didn't think you could do it by yourself? That's ridiculous." Sam was no dummy. Besides, even Cassie could have compiled the information with no trouble.

"Not that. I think he wanted us to have an excuse for a date." He reached over and rested his hand on her knee.

"Oh, I see. Well, I don't think you need his help. Anyway, that's a good sign. You didn't kiss and tell." As she entwined her fingers with his, a sense of belonging suddenly filled her. It was as if she'd stepped through the front door after a long trip. She was home where she was meant to be. Their hands had been created to complete one another. She'd always imagined feeling like this in her relationships. She'd wanted to, but never had. And now, she never wanted to let go.

"No, ma'am." As he squeezed her hand, he winked. "What happens in the cave, stays in the cave."

"Groan..." She'd never noticed how long his eyelashes were until now when the streetlights shining through the windshield made them glisten bronze.

As he slowed the car, they pulled off the highway and turned into a newly developed neighborhood about halfway between Crescent Bluff and Dallas. "We're here."

"Where?"

"Our date location." He continued through the

subdivision to the back where the roads had been laid out but no streetlights or houses had yet been built. The crescent moon glowed softly, so most of the light came from the car headlights and the stars overhead.

He pulled the car over to the curb, turned off the lights, and cut the engine.

Suddenly her heart began to race as fear prickled from her stomach throughout the trunk of her body into her arms and legs. No one knew where they were. They'd been alone together on several dates, and she'd never been afraid or uneasy—until now. How well did she really know him, anyway? She remembered the young boy he'd been and knew about the man he now presented himself to be, but she didn't really know him. What if he was some psychopath? He didn't seem to be, but that's how they reeled in their prey.

"Ready?"

Blood surged through her ears. "For what?"

He opened his door. "Your driving lesson."

"My what?"

"You heard me. Come on. We need to switch places." He stepped out of the car and walked around to her side.

The relief lasted only a couple of seconds until he opened her door. When she'd tried this a few years ago, she'd done nothing but make a fool of herself. "Sam, I really don't want to. What if I ruin the transmission?"

"You won't. I promise. But if by some weird chance you do, it can always be replaced. Come on." He grasped her hand and gently helped her out of the car. As she stepped onto the street, he drew her close, his words tickling her ear, "Who knows? Your future husband might have a car like this, and you'll want to be able to drive it. But even if not, everybody should know how to drive a stick."

~*~

Sam had laughed so hard over the past hour or so that his sides were sore. A couple of times he'd been sure she would take off her shoes and throw them at him. But she'd finally gotten it. She'd figured out the tension between the clutch and the accelerator, and she was doing great. "Brilliantly done, Katy Beth. I think I'll let you drive us home tonight."

Her eyes never left the road, and her left hand was welded to the steering wheel, her right to the gear shift knob. "If I'm doing well, it's no thanks to you. I pretty much had to figure this thing out on my own because my teacher was laughing too hard to speak."

"It's kinda the Socratic method of driving lessons. You know, figure it out on your own. I was here in case you couldn't."

She pulled the car over to the curb and stopped. "A poor excuse for rotten teaching, Sam Tucker. You'd better stick with soccer and forget any aspirations you might have ever had to teach."

"Don't worry. Never had any. Never will." He placed his hand on top of hers. "You did outstandingly."

A grin spread across her face. "I did, didn't I? Thanks, Sam."

"You betcha. It's almost time to go, but I want you to try one more thing. See that hill ahead? Drive up to the intersection at the top and stop at the stop sign. Then I'll tell you what you need to do."

As smooth as silk she pulled away from the curb, drove to the intersection, and stopped. She did a great job. If everything went as he hoped, this car would be hers one of these days, and now she'd be able to drive it.

"Ready."

"OK, when you take off, the car will want to roll back down the hill, so you'll need to ease your right foot over so you can kind of hit both the brake and the gas at the same time. When you get ready to go, you'll need to slide your foot over to the accelerator, give it some gas, and pull the clutch out just enough to act as the brake, but not enough to kill the engine. Don't be afraid if the engine races until you get the feel of it. Ready?"

"Not really, but here goes."

The first three times the car rolled back and the engine died.

She pursed her lips in frustration. Her voice was higher pitched than normal. "I can't do this, Sam. Let's switch places and just go back home. I'll try it again later."

"No, you can do it. You just need a little more practice. Come on, three more tries and then we'll call it a night. Go ahead and restart the car."

Right after the engine turned over, headlights shone through the back window of the car. She looked over at him with eyes the size of quarters. "Sam, there's a car behind us. Where did that come from?"

This would be interesting. But the hardest part for him would be not to laugh. She was way out of her comfort zone. He could change places with her right now and save her, but not everything in life was under her control, and it would do her good to work through this. Not that he wanted to control her life, either. She needed spontaneity.

Besides, this would be hysterical. He cleared his throat. "It's OK. Just take a deep breath and remember everything we talked about."

"Sam, I can't do it." Her eyes had grown to the size of those silver dollars his father had always kept in his sock drawer. "Please?"

"Just try."

On the first attempt, she let the clutch out too fast, the car died, and began rolling backward. "Hit the brake, Katy Beth." The car stopped.

"Sam, please..." She pleaded with him.

"One more try." He covered his mouth with his hand so she wouldn't see him grinning.

The second attempt was a rerun of the first.

"I can't do this. The car's right on my bumper now. If I try it again, I'll roll back into it." She put the window down and waved the car around. "They're not moving!" She stuck her hand back out and exaggerated her motions. "Why aren't they moving, Sam?"

Suddenly blue lights flashed through the back window. He rested his head back, and the laughter he could no longer stifle exploded. "That's why."

"This is not funny, Sam Tucker."

"Yes, it is, Katherine Herrington."

Her eyes were now the size of hockey pucks, and policeman or no policeman, he wanted to pull her close and hug away all that fear and tension, but that would have to wait.

An amplified voice broke into their conversation. "Stay in the car. I repeat. Do not get out of the car."

"Sam..."

"It'll be OK, just sit still, place your hands on the

steering wheel, and let me do the talking."

~*~

The policeman was at her window. One hand rested on the grip of his pistol as he shone a flashlight into the car with the other. "Evening, folks. Having a little problem here?"

Sam leaned forward and smiled. His hands were on the dashboard. "Good evening, Officer. Just teaching my girlfriend how to drive a standard."

"License, please, sir."

Sam slowly pulled his wallet out of his pocket, extracted his driver's license, and handed it across her to the policeman. He studied the license, looked at Sam's face, and then back at the picture on the license. "Don't see one of these every day."

"No sir, it's a British license. I live outside of London."

Maybe it was illegal to drive here without a Texas license. She wouldn't remain silent while they got arrested. "I have a valid Texas license in my purse in the backseat. I'll be happy to get it."

"That won't be necessary, ma'am. I believe y'all. I just thought somebody had stolen the car and didn't know how to drive it."

Relief flooded over her as he removed his hand from his gun and smiled.

"Samuel Tucker." The officer handed the license back to Sam. "I know you."

The officer couldn't possibly know Sam. He may be a professional soccer player, but he was not as famous as some.

"My brother played on your club team in middle school—Kent Strickland," the officer continued.

"Kent. He was a great striker." Sam leaned across her and offered his hand. "Good to see you..."

"Daniel."

"Daniel. How's Kent doing?"

"Married with four kids. Coaches high school soccer in Waco. He's doing good, but by the looks of things, not as good as you."

"I'm not so sure. Sounds as if he has a really great life."

"He's happy."

"Tell him hi for me next time you see him."

"Will do." Daniel leaned down and pointed toward Sam, "Oh, and for the record...the guy who tripped you and tore your knee up should've gotten a red card. That was a lousy call."

Sam laughed. "I won't disagree with that."

16

Katherine nestled back into the passenger seat as Sam closed her door. Thank goodness he'd agreed to drive. Despite how much she'd pretended to be perturbed with him for laughing at her earlier attempts to drive his car, the first part of tonight's driving lesson had been much more fun than she could have ever imagined. No matter how frustrating he could be, she always ended up enjoying their times together.

And tonight had been no different. Because he'd told her she could do something she knew she'd fail at, she'd proven herself wrong and him right. Since their first date, he'd nudged her, sometimes not so gently, to move beyond the comfortable and safe into the unknown and...fun.

Sam was changing her old attitude of control. She was being shown a different personality within herself, and she liked who she was becoming. For most people, these changes would have been nothing more than baby steps, but for her they were huge strides. They were growth. Something as silly as dancing blindfolded with him was growth in learning to trust another person.

Throwing the old notebook away had also been evidence of growth. Somewhere over the years, she'd begun to place her trust in the wrong person—herself.

She'd designed a comfortable, tidy little world in which she was queen, and she'd forgotten who the ruler of her heart was supposed to be. She hadn't really wanted the notebook back today. She'd just wanted the feeling of security it provided. So, this afternoon she'd listened to the wrong voice, and she'd failed to trust.

Please forgive me.

The residue of the doubts and fears from earlier today coupled with the episode with the policeman had left her emotionally drained, and all she wanted to do was put her head back and let Sam chauffeur her home.

One of these days, they'd look back on today and laugh. Her breathing caught. For the first time in her life, her heart suggested a forever-ness with a man. This man...Sam. Something inside her burst open like Mom's morning glories as they'd awaken to the newness of the day. Although the emotion was foreign, her heart recognized it. As improbable as it seemed, she loved him.

She hardly knew him, yet she loved him, and she wanted to know him better so she could love him more. But that desire was all wrong. While the notebook was in a landfill somewhere, The List was still written on her heart and might be forever. It couldn't simply be erased like a misspelled word on a homework paper, and he didn't possess the number one quality she wanted in a husband.

She'd taken a step out of the boat as Dad had suggested, but that didn't mean she should disregard every quality on the list and not use the common sense she'd been given. God couldn't really want her to pursue a relationship with a man who didn't share her faith. A few—a very few—items on the list were completely non-negotiable. And that was one of them.

A quiet Voice deep inside encouraged her to trust and take another step away from the boat. She needed to tell Sam how she felt. If she scared him off, she scared him off. But better to end their relationship now before it became even more complicated. She leaned her head back against the seat and took a deep breath to steady her stomach.

As he opened the driver's door, his new phone began to ring from the cup holder in the console.

Reflexively, she glanced at it. The display read "Lizzie" and showed the picture of an attractive blonde. When Sam slid into the seat, Katherine quickly redirected her gaze so he wouldn't realize she'd seen the image. He grabbed the phone and glanced at the screen. "Sorry, Katy Beth, but I really have to take this. I'll only be a second."

Sam stepped back out of the car, walked to the curb on the other side of the street, and turned his back. Quiet, comfortable laughter floated across the asphalt and in through the open window. His words were unintelligible, but the tone of his voice was warm. "Lizzie" was neither a casual acquaintance nor an unwelcome caller.

Her relationships had consistently followed the same pattern. She'd always been in control, dating her current "one" until she'd determined whether or not he had enough of the qualities on the list to possibly become The One. If he did, they'd continue their relationship.

But they had all ended the same: he would declare his love for her, and she'd realize he wasn't The One and break it off. Even with Clark she'd eventually said no.

How could she have been so cruel? She'd placed more importance on ink blotches on a piece of paper than a person's feelings. Her priorities had been so misplaced. These were people, not business proposals that were open to scrutiny and revision. But now she understood, because she was no longer the person in control.

Sam was.

Today's fears returned, darkening every inch of her heart.

As he dropped the phone in his pocket and turned toward the car, she pushed her head back against the seat. She needed to deal with this but not now when her emotions were all over the place. A few seconds ago she'd been ready to set caution aside and tell him her feelings. But the phone call had changed everything. Before she said anything she'd regret, she needed time to compose herself, to go home and think...and pray.

He dropped into the driver's seat, reached over, and squeezed her hand. "Sorry about that, Katy Beth."

"Please don't, Sam. Not right now."

As he drew his hand back and shut the door, his words were short. "Sorry. I apologize for overstepping the boundaries. I guess I didn't see them." He pushed back against the driver's door. "Sometimes you're a little hard to read, Katherine."

A heavy silence hung in the car like an invisible curtain separating them until he turned his keys and the engine rumbled to life to began the trip back to her house.

She couldn't wait any longer. "Who's Lizzie?"

"What?"

The light from the dashboard was just bright

enough for her to see the surprise on his face. Yeah, he didn't know she'd seen his phone. "Lizzie. Who's Lizzie?"

The surprise melted away, and a grin took its place. "Lizzie? Now I get it. A bit jealous, are we?" His eyes sparkled. "Well, she's sure not one of my sisters."

"Cut it out, Sam. Can't you just give me a straight answer for once?" Her earlier hurt was quickly morphing into anger.

"Well, of course I can. The question is, 'Will I?'"

He was playing with her again, and she'd had enough of his smugness. She'd get out and call Dad to come get her. "Enough." As she reached over to open the door, he hit the "lock" button.

"And the answer is, 'Of course, I will.' Lizzie is my coach's daughter, and she's also his administrative assistant. And she's married—with two kids. She was calling me because the team has a job for me to do tomorrow."

"Really? A business call, at this hour?" Surely, he didn't think she was gullible enough to believe that. "Must be pretty early over there—like six o'clock in the morning."

"Actually, it's four. She'd tried to get me earlier, but my phone wasn't working...as you may remember...so when her baby woke her up, she thought she'd give it one more try. They want me to go to Austin tomorrow to scout out a possible recruit." A self-satisfied grin covered his face as he sat in silence, obviously waiting.

Relief mixed with embarrassment flooded over her. "Sorry, Sam. I don't know what's going on with me."

"Whatever it is, it's quite flattering."

As he reached over, grasped her hand, and lifted it to his lips, every bit of insecurity from today melted away. She'd never acted this way about a man before. Because she'd never really loved a man before. The urgency to tell him was gone, though. The place and time needed to be special, and her words needed to be well-planned and not some sort of disorganized ramblings.

"Hey, Katy Beth, I want to ask you something, and I want you to know up front either way you answer is OK with me. It's kind of short notice, so I know you'll want to think it over. Plus, I don't want you to do anything you'd be uncomfortable with." His free hand gently brushed against her cheek. "Come with me to Austin tomorrow. It'll be fun. We'd have to leave early in the morning, and we'd need to stay the night in a hotel—separate rooms, of course. Then we could come back the next day." He gently placed his forefinger against her lips. "No need to answer right now. Just think about it, and you can let me know when we get to your house. Or any time before six tomorrow morning."

More than anything she wanted to go, but she wasn't sure she could trust him. But even worse than that, she wasn't sure she could trust herself. When she and Clark had taken a few similar trips, trust had never been an issue because desire had never been an issue. But in the cave yesterday, Sam's kiss had stirred a longing in her that could only be satisfied one way, and that scared her—not the longing, but her desire to surrender to it.

As he turned back toward the front of the car, his knee brushed against his keys and, in the dim light of the dashboard, a metallic glint flashed from a silver ring she had never noticed before—a band with a cross engraved in it. He had a purity ring very similar to the one at home in the box on her closet shelf.

She loved him even more, because she could trust him. "Yes."

He turned toward her. "Yes? That was quick."

She leaned over and kissed him on the cheek. "I'd love to go."

17

Like a satin ribbon, the Colorado River unfurled itself golden, as it meandered through the Balcones Canyonlands below. Painting long cooling shadows over the sultry Texas hill country, the setting sun slipped behind rolling hills covered with live oaks and cedars.

Sam wound his car along the two-lane road northwest of Austin.

Mom had insisted the scraggly trees were some sort of juniper, but everyone Katherine knew called them cedars.

"Sure you don't want to drive? This would be a great road for you to practice your skills on."

"You're kidding, right?"

"Maybe there's another policeman around here. You could try again for a ticket."

"Hey, you're the one who insisted I drive last night. If I'd have gotten a ticket, it would have been your fault."

He chuckled, and a warm smile covered his face. He reached over and squeezed her hand. "I'm glad you came."

"Me, too." She squeezed back. "So, how many autographs do you think you signed?" After today, she knew how girlfriends of celebrities felt. All the players and coaches from both teams had presented whatever they could find for him to sign. When paper wasn't available, T-shirts, sports bags, balls—anything large enough to write on—was substituted.

"Oh, I don't know. I didn't exactly count. Just smiled and signed."

Yes, and he'd looked so cute doing it. "Guess."

"Forty-two?"

"Wrong. Seventy-eight."

"Really? You counted?" His eyes never left the road as he nodded his head. "Not too long ago, I would have thought that was totally awesome. But lately..." His words ended in a sigh. "You know, it's not all it's cracked up to be."

The playful, smug part of him that she had a love-hate relationship with had faded to reveal the sincerity she'd rarely seen. "What isn't?"

"Fame. I'm pretty well-known—in small, specific circles. But very few people really know me. They think they do. But all they know is the me my football club wants them to know. And that's it. I've spent my life working hard to be who I thought I should be and who other people wanted and expected me to be, but now I'm realizing I'm not who I want to be and maybe not even who I was meant to be." The car slowed as he glanced her direction. "I'm rambling. I just want people to know me and like me for who I really am rather than who they think I am." He paused for a few seconds. "Sorry. Didn't mean for the conversation to turn so heavy. I'm just tired of pretending."

As his words died away, the only sound in the car was a country song on the radio accompanied by the revving of the engine as he downshifted into a hairpin turn. The first star of the evening sparkled in the gray-blue dusk.

None of the other men she'd dated had ever been this vulnerable and honest with her. They'd always seemed to need to have everything under control. He was right. He wasn't like them. "Sam, I don't know who you were meant to be, but I like the you I've come to know. A lot."

"Thanks, Katy Beth. I don't think I can fully express how much that means to me. But one of these days, I'll try."

When he said no more, she pushed her head back against the seat and closed her eyes. This morning had begun well before sunrise, and the motion of the car along with the encroaching darkness was lulling her to sleep.

~*~

Katherine took one final look in the full-length mirror tucked in the corner of the dressing area off her bathroom. Not knowing exactly where they'd be staying or what they'd be doing, she'd packed a sleeveless black dress with a variety of accessories so she'd be prepared for anything.

The hotel was really more of a spa-like resort. The contemporary elegance of the fresh white linens and leather upholstery combined with the massive oak furniture and stucco walls produced a sophisticated Texas ranch look. Her room had a corner balcony that jutted out over the tree-covered hills surrounding the resort—the perfect setting for tomorrow morning's quiet time.

She smiled at the image in the mirror. The dress

hung perfectly, accentuating all her assets and diminishing the areas that needed work due to a lack of time spent at the gym. The silver and turquoise necklace, bracelet, and earrings, in combination with her cowboy boots, were the perfect look for tonight. "Texas chic" Mom would have called it. She especially wanted to look good for Sam. And she did. She looked really good.

The clock read eight fifty-eight as she took one last look around the room. Everything was in place. Her current notebook was on the nightstand by her bed, ready for her to check off today's list and plan for tomorrow before she went to sleep tonight—although, for the first time in years, the list was almost nonexistent. She had nothing planned, no agenda other than to be with Sam tonight and tomorrow. Thus far, this letting-someone-else-do-the-planning thing was working out better than she would have ever imagined possible.

She closed the door and walked down the hall toward the elevator to meet Sam in the lobby. Their rooms were on different floors as Sam had requested, a small gesture for some people, perhaps, but one that, for her, was huge—a sign of his respect for her. Of course, it could have been a way to ensure they both exercised self-control and remained true to their promises.

Their arrival had been a replay of the Cattlemen's Hotel. The valet called Sam by name, liked his car, welcomed him back. The desk clerk was friendly and welcoming, without the blatantly suggestive invitation. Their dinner in the private dining room Sam had reserved would be ready at nine.

The dropping of the elevator only intensified the

excited fluttering in her stomach. She must have been living in some sort of vacuum these last few years. Everyone seemed to know who he was—except her. And if Dad and Sam's aunt hadn't set up the blind date, their paths might never have crossed.

As the elevator doors slowly drew apart, everything in the scene before her faded into the background except this incredibly handsome man. Dressed in gray pants, a white button-down shirt, and cowboy boots, Sam stood leaning against a wooden column—a single yellow rose in his hand. His short, blond hair was neatly combed, and his eyes sparkled the same color as the stones on her bracelet.

Breathe, Katherine, breathe.

Grinning as he stepped forward, he offered her the flower and then his arm. "They didn't have any tulips." As he leaned close, the spicy fragrance of his cologne enticed her while his words tickled her ear. "You look amazingly lovely tonight."

Her heart raced as warmth washed over her. "Thank you, Sam. So do you."

"Well, I can't say that lovely was the exact look I was going for, but it'll do."

"You know what I mean."

He laughed. "Yeah, I think maybe I do. Thanks."

They turned left and walked in silence toward the room at the end of the hallway. The plaque beside the double doors read "Canyon Overlook." As Sam held open one of the doors for her, she stepped into the huge, dimly lit room. Taking her hand, he led her toward the far wall of windows and out onto a balcony which overlooked the canyon below. Above them the onyx sky was covered from horizon to horizon with more twinkling stars than she could possibly have ever counted, the absence of any city lights enhancing their visibility.

The night earlier this week when she and Dad sat together under the same heavenly canopy replayed in her mind. *And He knows their names...*

~*~

Sam peered out at the night sky and the stars above.

Katherine actually gasped. "Oh, Sam, it's so beautiful."

"Yes, but not as beautiful as you."

She leaned into him.

He placed his arm around her and drew her closer. Everything in him yearned to kiss her. But not now. Instead, he slowly turned her toward a table covered with a white cloth at the far end of the balcony. In the center a single candle flickered, shielded from the evening wind by a cylinder of glass in a wrought-iron stand. He had something similar on the mantel in his flat in London—a hurricane, the decorator had said. Why something that protected a candle from the wind was called a hurricane was beyond him. Anyway, the one on the table was doing its job, and that was all that mattered. "I ordered us some dinner. It should be here in a few minutes."

"Thank you."

Her arms encircled his waist as she leaned even deeper into him. Something was different tonight. The always-present tension was gone. As difficult as it was not to, he still wouldn't kiss her now. The servers should be here with the food any minute, and he wouldn't risk putting her in a potentially embarrassing situation.

She gently swayed to the soft ballad sounding in the background. "My mom loved this song. One night when I was about six, I had a bad dream and went out to the den looking for my mother. This song was playing, and she and Daddy were slow dancing. I still remember how I could feel their love for each other and the sense of peace that brought me. I just turned around and went back to bed. They never even knew."

"Yeah, my folks liked this, too. It's a old song." Turning to face her, he held out his hands in invitation. "Shall we continue the tradition?"

Her voice was barely more than a whisper. "I'd love to, Sam."

She smelled great—sugar cookies and lemonade again. As she leaned her head on his shoulder they began to move in time with the music. "As I said earlier, I'm so glad you came."

Her eyes found his. "And as I said earlier, I am too. Very glad."

"You know, when I asked you I was surprised you agreed. It's great that you did—don't get me wrong—but I totally expected you to turn me down."

"Really? Why?"

Choosing his words carefully, he waited for a few seconds before he replied. "Well, let's just say you're different from most of the girls I've dated in the past. I wasn't sure you'd be willing to go away—just the two of us—if you know what I mean."

She nodded slightly. "I know exactly what you mean. In today's world, there aren't many of us out there. Especially at our age."

In his world, attractive, single women were

everywhere, regardless of their ages. But she had always been the yardstick against which none of them had ever measured up.

As she stopped dancing, she drew away and smiled up at him. "When I saw it, I knew I could trust you, so that made agreeing to come easy."

What? "I don't know...Saw what?"

"The ring...on your keychain. I've still got mine, too. But it's at home in a box." Her eyes sparkled in the candlelight as she placed her head back on his shoulder and began moving to the music.

Way too soon. He wasn't ready to have this conversation. Especially not here, not now. He would have it at the proper time and place, but before then he needed more time for their commitment to each other to deepen.

If he told her now, he stood the chance of destroying everything he'd been working on the last year or so. But then...if he didn't tell her, she might feel as if he'd been lying to her when he finally did, and he'd destroy it anyway. Neither option was a good choice at this time, but he had to decide.

As the pounding of his heart rocked his entire body, she peacefully hummed along to the song. That was it. That's what was different. She believed she could trust him, so she did. And that trust had erased the tension between them.

But by not telling her the truth and letting her believe a lie, he would betray her newly-placed trust. He would be lying to her. He turned them so he was facing the canyon. The river below was white, purified by the reflection of the sliver-moon and glistening stars above. Not too long ago, the choice would have been easy. He would have done what was best for him, but the morning studies with Brad were changing him. Life wasn't all about him and fulfilling his desires.

He had no other choice. He'd do it. "Katy Beth, I need to tell you something. I..."

A gentle but insistent tapping interrupted his words, and then the door from the hallway slowly opened. "Room Service, Mr. Tucker. Your dinner is ready."

~*~

The part of the dinner Katherine had eaten was delicious, but she hadn't been hungry enough to eat much. Love had stolen her appetite.

Sam signed the check and then closed the leather case. He'd been quieter than usual during the meal, but maybe that was a good sign. He was comfortable enough with their relationship that he didn't feel the need to be "on" all the time and could relax. Today had begun early, and he had to be tired. She'd been able to sleep some in the car, but he'd been up since before dawn this morning.

Katherine reached across the table and grasped his hand. "Tired?"

He raised her hand to his lips and then winked. "Maybe a little."

She stood and gently tugged on his hand. "Let's go. We don't have any deadlines for tomorrow, so we can sleep late in the morning."

As he stood, a soft smile covered his face. "Sounds good, but what about one last dance?"

As he drew her into his arms, everything was right. She leaned against him and remembered.

"Weren't you about to tell me something when our dinner arrived?"

He tightened his embrace. "Yes." He leaned his head on top of hers as the music continued.

"Well?"

"Katherine, there's something I've got to tell you. I want to wait, but I can't." Drawing away he grasped both her hands in his and looked deeply into her eyes.

The vulnerability from earlier today had returned. Whatever he was about to say was difficult for him. She squeezed his hands and smiled. "It's OK."

He took a deep breath and then began. "Katherine, I know I'm not the man of your dreams. I'm sure I don't have all the qualities you would want in a husband. But I'm working on it."

Her heart pounded throughout her entire body. "Sam, I..."

"Please, let me finish." He leaned forward and placed his forehead against hers. "You know Brad and I have been doing some studying together, and I'm beginning to realize just how off track my life has been. All these years, I focused on the wrong things. But now, life is finally beginning to make sense. And, Katherine, I'm telling you this now, so you can be ready. When I get it all figured out, I'm going to ask you to marry me. I love you more than you will ever know, Katy Beth."

She'd heard similar words from men before, but she had never wanted to hear them as badly as she'd wanted to hear them from him. She melted against him and said the words she'd spoken to only one other man. But this time she said them because she wanted to and not because she was expected to. "I love you, too."

~*~

Sam dropped onto his bed. He hadn't been man enough to do it. And then after he'd told her how he felt, she'd told him she loved him, too. Shocker. He sure hadn't expected that—not this soon, anyway. She definitely cared for him. Her kiss had told him that.

He'd always gotten what he really wanted out of life, so he'd known he'd get her, too, eventually. He just hadn't expected it this early in the game.

All his life he'd been driven. He'd told himself over and over again if he'd reach the next milestone, he'd be satisfied. But with each conquest came an emptiness followed by another goal to be attained. Today he was at the top of the list. He'd thought if he could find Beth again and win her love, the deep yearnings he'd felt would be quenched. There was nothing else he wanted more in life.

Over these last few weeks he'd been happier than he'd been in years. And tonight should be the happiest moment of his life. Yet, still something was missing. An empty corner in his heart, unreached by the love and joy he felt at this moment, still quietly begged to be filled. Surely as her love for him grew, the emptiness would disappear.

And if not, maybe he'd have to accept that the peace and wholeness he craved were unattainable. No. He'd never compromised his goals, and he never would.

So maybe this is what Brad had meant when he'd said there was a void in his heart only God could fill.

18

Closing her Bible and her notebook, Katherine snuggled back against the canvas cushion of the redwood lounge chair on her balcony and gazed at the understated beauty before her. A soft, gray mist blanketed the river below and spilled over into the adjacent canyon, obscuring the surrounding landscape and transforming the tree-covered mounds into mere suggestions of their physical realities. A pink glow barely tinged the eastern horizon, heralding the coming of a new day.

She took a sip of the pomegranate tea she'd made a few minutes earlier when she'd decided to have her devotion on the balcony. Joy, not sleep, had been her companion last night. A few weeks ago, after their blind date, she could have never guessed the abrupt turn into uncharted territory her life would take.

But deep inside, woven together with the joy, laid a single thread of fear. If Sam had asked her to marry him last night, she wasn't sure she could have said anything other than yes. The possibility that her feelings for him would cause her to make such a life-altering decision in a seemingly careless manner scared her. This was not the Katherine who'd stayed in the security of the boat for so many years.

Yet entwining itself with the thread of fear was

another tiny thread—one of peace. The focal passage of this morning's devotion had been those verses about trusting God rather than trying to do the impossible—understanding His thoughts and His ways. She had stepped out onto the waves, and she was definitely trusting. And Sam...as he'd said last night, he was working on changing.

Every book about marriage she'd ever read and every singles conference she'd ever attended always stressed one thing—don't marry someone with the idea he will change or you can change him. But the more she was with Sam, the more she loved the person he was, and the less she wanted him to change. Except in one area—his faith.

Considering a possible future with a man who would be her lifelong partner and the father of her children, a man who should know her more intimately than any other person on earth, but who could never understand her deepest love or share what was most important to her, was an impossibility. A definite deal-breaker.

Time. Father, we just need some time.

An entire chorus of birds welcomed the coming of the day as the pink band on the horizon deepened. She walked to the edge of the balcony and rested her arms on the dew-covered railing. Her soul sang a song of gratitude as she waited for the eminent gift from her Father. Morning, when new life—fresh and full of promise—pushed away the darkness of night and restored her soul. Seeing the glorious creation before her as a new day emerged was worth any loss of sleep early rising caused. *Thank You, Father.*

Sudden movement at the far end of the balcony grabbed her attention, and Katherine sprang away from the railing back toward the door to her room. A snake of some sort was slowly creeping, no, descending from the balcony above hers. She placed one hand over her mouth to keep from screaming and madly groped for the door handle with the other—but then stopped.

Something about that snake wasn't right. She turned back toward the railing to take a closer look. The snake was about eight to ten feet long and made of black terrycloth with a knot tied in the middle of its body. A small, white piece of paper was safety-pinned to its most southern end. Whoever was in the room above her had tied together the belts from the hotel bathrobes, pinned a note to them, and was using them as some sort of primitive mode of communication.

Only one person she knew would do something like this.

She walked over to the snake and unpinned the note.

Good morning, Katy Beth. I'm in the mood for a walk and hope you'll go with me. Call me when you get this.

Sam

She stuck her head out over the railing and turned her face upward.

Sam was tying the northern end of the "snake" to his balcony railing.

"You almost scared me to death, you know."

As he leaned forward, his gaze found hers, and he smiled. "Well, good morning, early bird."

His mouth continued to move, but none of the words reached her ears. The sight of him overcame all her other senses. He was dressed in soccer shorts. Soccer shorts...that was it. No shirt. He might have had on some sort of shoes, but his feet were hidden from view. His face was covered with a day's beard growth, and he looked amazingly handsome.

"...but I didn't want to call or text in case you were still asleep. So, what do you say?"

She cleared her throat. "Say? Say about what?" Lots of things to say were whirling around in her mind—none of them at all appropriate at this point in their relationship.

He shook his head. "Do you want to go on a walk before breakfast or not?"

"I'd love to."

"Last one in the lobby has to buy root beer floats at Dairy Delite."

"Sam..." He was gone.

She ran into her room, pulled on some shorts, a T-shirt, and hiking sandals. Then she jumped into the bathroom to brush her teeth and her hair and was done. Three minutes. That had to be a record.

After grabbing her phone and key-card, she quietly closed the door, ran on tiptoe down the hall toward the elevator, and pushed the "down" button. The red light above the door showed that the elevator was on the sixth floor, she was on the third, and Sam was on the fourth in the room right above hers, she now knew. The light above the five blinked on for a second and then above the four. As long as it didn't stop she'd be OK. The light above the three blinked on as the bell dinged and the door opened. Empty.

She bolted between the doors and pushed the "down" button and then the "close-door" button in rapid succession. She'd done it. She'd finally beat him.

~*~

Sam leaned against the same column as he had last night and smiled as the doors drew apart. The elevator bell dinged in the lobby. The look on her face in a few seconds would be priceless.

Her face was alive with excitement...until she saw his and shock set in. "Looks as if you'll be buying the floats, Katy Beth."

"Sam, this is impossible."

He loved getting the best of her. She needed a dose of that every now and then.

"How did you...?"

"Seems there're these old-fashioned things called stairs." He threw a backpack over his left shoulder and held out his right hand. "Ready?"

As her fingers grasped his, she shook her head. "I don't know if I'll ever be ready for you, Sam Tucker."

"Sure you will." He squeezed her hand and led her down the hall and out the back door. "Come on, or we'll miss it."

Sometime in the sleepless dark of last night, he had decided exactly where they needed to go this morning and exactly what needed to happen when they got there. They passed the swimming pool area, empty at this early hour, walked around the fire pit, and stepped through a narrow break in the privet hedge. As the pink strip on the eastern horizon slowly widened, he turned west. If they hurried, they should make it in time.

The path snaked between trees and over rocky rises until the hotel was no longer visible behind them. She was uncharacteristically quiet—no questions or seeming concerns about where they were going or why. His diligence was apparently paying off. He'd earned a measure of her trust, but exactly how much remained to be determined. In a few minutes, he should know.

Making a sharp turn to the right, the path abruptly ended, a fence serving as the only barrier between them and the canyon below.

"Whoa!" She dug in her heels and pulled back on his hand as she read the sign nailed to one of the fence posts, "'Public access beyond this point strictly prohibited.'"

He looked straight in her eyes. "Trust me?"

The immediate yes he'd hoped for, but absolutely not planned on, didn't come.

"I don't know. Maybe..."

"Trust me. You've only got a few seconds to decide before it'll be too late, but I promise it'll be worth it."

"It better be."

He carefully climbed over the fence and then turned and offered his hand.

"Sam, I'm really uncomfortable doing this. Didn't you read the sign? 'Public access prohibited.'"

"No, I didn't read the sign. You did. Besides, this isn't public. It's private—just you and me. And no one's here monitoring us, anyway."

She gripped his hand, as he helped her over the fence.

"I must be crazy. I can't believe we're breaking the law," she muttered.

"I wouldn't exactly call it a law, KB, more of a suggestion for our safety. We'll be careful."

Sam led her toward the edge of the cliff to where a rock platform jutted out over the canyon below them. He eased down onto the small promontory and then helped her as she followed him. Facing west, he inched to the edge, placed his arm around her, and pulled her close. The fragrance of last night's cologne had softened and become a part of her. "You're awfully quiet," he whispered.

"I'm awfully scared," she whispered back. "It's too high. I want to go back."

As he kissed the top of her head, he tightened his embrace. "I won't let anything happen. Just watch."

The sun had risen enough for its rays to barely clear the horizon behind them and paint the tops of the hills across the canyon in copper. As the sun continued its ascent, the copper turned golden and washed down deeper into the canyon until the predawn mist disappeared and the river below caught fire. The light had chased away the darkness.

The sight was even more beautiful than he'd remembered—maybe because he was sharing it with her.

She leaned into him. "Oh, Sam. It's breathtaking. Thank you for making me break the rules."

Expectant, she turned her face up to him, and he placed his lips on hers. As he drew away, she leaned more deeply into him and every inch of his body ached for more, but no. Time to chase away some more darkness. Her face was rosy in the morning light.

Leading her away from the edge, they sat, resting their backs against the cliff. He opened the backpack. "Hey, love, I need to share something with you." She was not the first woman he'd called that, but this was the first time he'd really meant it. He reached into the backpack and pulled out the notebook. "This."

Her expression deepened as she sat up and crossed her legs. She was obviously embarrassed.

"How did you get this?"

"I found it in your driveway one day when I brought you home. I thought Cassie had lost it so I picked it up to give it back to her. But then I opened the cover and saw your name. Here." He held it out, but she didn't take it.

"Did you read it?" The tone of her voiced pleaded with him to say no.

When he had read through it, he hadn't planned to return it to her. He'd thought she'd never know. "I, uh, not exactly. Well, not all of it...Yes, most of it."

She took it from him with one hand and then gently ran the fingertips of the other across the cover as if the notebook was some fragile treasure that needed to be handled with extreme care. To her it was obviously more than only ink and paper. It was a part of her and her history.

"And did you laugh?"

"Laugh? Of course not." He brushed the back of his hand against her cheek. "I thought it was kind of...cute. And very insightful. Both thought-provoking and encouraging at the same time."

"Encouraging?"

He held out his hand for the notebook. "May I?"

When she handed it back to him, he slowly paged through the seminar notes until he came to the first "List." He scooted closer to her so they could look at the page together and pointed to the last attribute on the bottom. "Nice car...check." Then he moved up the list. "Captain of the football team...check. Tall. How tall is 'Tall?'"

"Taller than me. Check." She grinned and patted his leg. "Remember what Juanita said. No Great Danes and Chihuahuas here."

"Blue eyes. Check."

She linked her arm through his and leaned her head against his shoulder. "I've never heard these read out loud before, but now that I do, it's kind of embarrassing. They all sound so shallow. And there was a time in my life when these qualities were what I prayed for in a husband because I thought they were important. How silly."

"Don't be embarrassed, Katy Beth. Growth is part of life. Priorities change over the years—hopefully, anyway—and we often find what we thought we wanted out of life may not be the right or best thing for us. Besides, those were some of the parts I thought were cute."

He leaned his head on hers and took a deep breath. Time had come. He'd actually prayed about this last night when he couldn't sleep. Or in reality, he hadn't been able to sleep because he had been praying about it. At first, he'd wondered if God would even listen after all these years, but then, about sunrise, an illogical sense of peace had gently calmed his heart. He needed to do what he knew was right, and God would take care of everything else.

He flipped over to another list closer to the back and held the notebook so that both of them could see. "Here's some more stuff. Sense of humor? A good provider?"

"Check on the first. Don't really know about the second one."

"Let's just say I've gotten some wise advice over the years and made some good investments." He could never touch a soccer ball again and be financially secure. "My job comes with a lot of perks, and my lifestyle is pretty simple."

Carol James

She sat up, took the notebook from him, and turned over a few more pages. Her fingers followed the list and stopped part way down the page. "Wants children." As her gaze left the page and found his, her face flushed red. "You've never said whether or not you want a family."

"Check, check, and double-check."

"Kindhearted and compassionate." Her eyes sparkled with laughter. "Yes, except for the times you're mean to me."

"Mean to you? I would never be mean to you. Give me one example."

"Just one? How about when you almost got us killed when you forced me to learn to shift your car? Or worse than that, you made me beg for a kiss?"

"You can't imagine how hard it was to wait that long for a kiss." He gently eased her back until she was lying flat, and then he pulled up on one elbow above her. Here in this private spot, it would be so easy to relax and let things go farther than they should. But he couldn't. He had to stick with the game plan. "Love, there's something I want to tell you." As he quickly kissed her on the forehead, his shorts pocket vibrated. He should have left his phone in the room. He'd ignore it.

"You want to get that?"

"What?"

"Your phone. I felt it vibrate."

"Not really. I'm busy."

"You'd better check it just in case there's an emergency. It's awful early for a social call."

She was right. He rolled over onto his back and pulled his phone out. Lizzie. "It's work."

She smiled. "Go ahead."

~*~

As he stood and walked a few feet away, her heart fluttered as if one of the hummingbirds at Mom's feeders had taken residence in her chest. The phone call had been a blessing. This was the first time she'd ever been with a man and not cared about her commitment to purity. Giving in would have been easy if he'd asked. But he wouldn't. And in that knowledge was security and trust. And joy.

His conversation with Lizzie had moved from friendly give and take into a more serious tone. He was reporting on the player he'd scouted yesterday.

She opened the notebook and flipped back through several of the lists. Suddenly a lightning bolt pierced her heart. He had every quality they'd discussed—even the silly ones—on the lists, except one. And for that one, she'd take another step farther into the ocean and trust God.

She stood and carefully inched closer to the edge of the cliff. Suddenly the rock below her seemed to bend downward into the valley. She grasped on tightly to a tree to steady herself. The hummingbird inside her chest beat its wings wildly, trying to escape to freedom. Looking down at the notebook in her hand, she tossed it out. She didn't need it anymore. The pages fluttered open like a hatchling's first awkward attempts at testing its wings, and then, catching an updraft, it floated back and forth as it spiraled downward into the canyon below.

Throwing it away this time was easier than the first time. As the notebook disappeared under the leafy canopy, the chains that had bound her for so many years fell away, and she was finally free. All these years of searching and waiting had come to an end, and God had brought her The One.

She turned back.

Sam stood, phone by his side, his face stony. "I have to go back to London."

Her prayer for more time wasn't to be granted.

19

Katherine sat in an isolated booth in the back corner of The Perks. The soft jazz playing over the audio system was the perfect accompaniment to the laid-back atmosphere of the coffee shop. This was as ideal a setting as possible for this afternoon's encounter. She'd deliberately chosen not to sit in an overstuffed chair in one of the casual groupings meant to promote conversation among the patrons. Today's agenda deserved more privacy.

She and Sam had spoken very little on the way home from Austin the other day. Lizzie's phone call had changed everything. Of course, she'd known his stay in Crescent Bluff was temporary and every moment together meant his time to leave was one step closer. But those fewer than five minutes on the phone had stolen away the time their relationship needed, the time she'd asked from her Heavenly Father.

Sam was sure he could get management to give him a few more weeks here, but whatever the decision, today's conversation needed to happen. As her stomach churned, a part of her was ready to turn around and swim back to the safety of the boat. But she couldn't, even if the waves were crashing up over her shoulders.

She glanced at her phone. Clark was

uncharacteristically late. Only by a few minutes, but ten minutes by Clark Standard Time was more like an hour for anyone else. She'd wait at least five more minutes before she called to check on him.

She took a bite of the croissant she'd bought not because she was hungry, but because the bland pastry might help calm her stomach. As she sipped her iced coffee, the bell on the door chimed, and in he walked. Dressed in khakis and a buttery yellow polo shirt, he was a walking ad for an upscale men's store. He certainly was handsome enough to have been a model.

The perfect hair he had never liked for her to touch was so meticulously combed into place, it looked like a wig. No, not a wig exactly. If he'd had lighter hair he would have looked just like a male fashion doll. "Mr. Plastic" Cassie had called him, and she was right. Despite the seriousness of the next few minutes, the perfect nickname made Katherine grin as he turned her direction and waved. Hopefully, he'd think she was smiling because she was glad to see him, not because she was laughing at him—well, not really at him, but at Cassie's comment. How had she never noticed that before?

He ordered his coffee—black with two sugars— and made his way to her table. Her heartbeat intensified with each step he took, closing the distance between them. By the time he slipped into the seat across from her, the pounding was so intense she could hardly breathe.

"Hi. Sorry I'm late."

She willed the shakiness out of her voice. "No problem. Thanks for agreeing to stop by on your way back from Austin."

He reached over and patted her hand. "Sure. I

really wanted to see you, too."

She'd broken up with several guys before, after she'd compared them with The List, but this time was different. She loved Clark, but more like a brother, not enough to marry him. Not like Sam. "Another conference?"

"No. Katherine, we need to talk." He looked down into his mug and then back up. As he took a sip, his hand shook. He was more nervous than she was.

She reached over and rested her hand on his forearm to try and calm him. "Clark, are you OK?"

"No...yes. Yes. Katherine, I..."

Since she'd first met him, he'd always known what to say. He was never at a loss for words.

As he broke eye contact, he blew out softly. "This is so hard." His gaze found hers again. "Katherine I met someone. Well, not exactly met. Re-met. An old college sweetheart of mine was at the conference the other day. We were both alone, so we decided to have dinner together that Friday night, just to catch up, you know, and well, we, uh, we discovered that, I mean it wasn't my intention, but we...she...I..." His words trailed off.

She'd never seen him like this—little-boy vulnerable.

She gently squeezed his arm and smiled. "Sounds like she was, and is, a very special person in your life."

"In my lifetime, I've proposed to two women, and you were the second. I'm sorry I never told you about her. After college, when she refused to leave her career so I could pursue mine, we broke off the engagement. I thought I was over her and she was over me. I mean, it had been so many years." He smiled and rested his hand on top of hers. "Katherine, I never would have proposed to you if I'd had any idea this would happen. I..."

"What's her name?"

"Lauren."

"Lauren is a very blessed woman."

Relief softened his face. "Thanks. I want you to know my feelings for you were real."

"I know that. Mine for you were, too."

His smile was warm, sincere.

Her heart had slowed, and the churning in her stomach had disappeared. "I'm really happy for you. You'll make Lauren a wonderful husband. Have you set a date yet?"

His face reddened, and he grinned sheepishly like a grade school boy who'd gotten caught passing notes. "No. Not specifically. We're talking about the fall. October."

No sorrow, no regret. She really was happy for him. He deserved much more than she could have ever given him.

"I want you to know that the job offer still stands if you're interested. Just call me when you get back from your mission trip."

Dream job or not, when she'd left Dallas, her heart had known she'd not be going back. It had just taken several weeks for her mind to catch up. And now, with Sam in her life... "I appreciate the offer, but I think I'm ready to try something new."

"Maybe with someone new?"

Her face and neck were on fire. Her lips curved into a smile she couldn't contain. "Maybe."

As he reached across the table and squeezed her hand, he winked. "With the water hose man?"

~*~

Sam's car was parked at the top of the circular driveway. He wasn't supposed to be here for another hour, but that was OK. No, it was great. They'd have some time together before they had to be at Brad's to finalize the plans for the soccer tournament next week.

Katherine could tell him she was free to go with him to London—whenever management wanted him back. He hadn't asked her, but he would. A few months ago, she would have never made a decision as serious as this without weighing, reweighing, and re-reweighing her options. But only one option mattered. Being with Sam.

Lizzie's phone call would not be the end of their relationship, just like that fence blocking the path to the canyon hadn't ended their walk. It had only caused them to pause before stepping into something glorious. They'd get past this minor hiccup in their relationship just as they'd carefully climbed over the fence. Great reward never came without great risk.

She stepped through the kitchen door and looked into the empty family room. The lights were off, the TV dark. No soccer game as she'd imagined. She placed her purse on the kitchen island and made her way toward the back doors.

The two men stood on the lower patio beside the rocking chairs where she'd first apologized to Sam for her behavior at the soccer fields and where he'd first demanded her penance. That seemed like years, not simply weeks, ago.

She grasped the door knob as the men shook hands. But then she froze as Dad placed his hands on Sam's shoulders and both men bowed their heads. Her heart quickened. They were praying. Praying. Or at least Dad was praying. Sam's head was bowed and occasionally nodded in what must be agreement with Dad's words. Dad had never prayed with any of the other men she'd dated—not even Clark. Or, at least, if they had she'd never seen them.

Their heads raised, Dad pulled Sam into a brief fatherly hug, and then they turned toward the deck.

As a wave of guilt seeped into her heart, she drew back into the darkness of the den so they couldn't see her. She'd been intruding on what was obviously a private moment. Quickly, she stepped into the kitchen to get a bottle of water. As she opened the refrigerator, deep, musical, laughter tumbled into the room, and the two men she loved most in the world walked through the back door.

"Hey, look who's back. Hi, sweetie."

"Hi, Daddy." Heat filled her cheeks. "Hi, Sam. You're early." If Dad hadn't been there she would have pulled Sam into her arms.

"Didn't have much going on today, so your dad and I went to lunch. You know, some of that famous male bonding time over barbecue."

Another first. None of the other guys she'd dated had ever gone out with Dad—just the two of them. "That's nice."

"Actually, Sam treated me to lunch." Dad stepped forward and kissed her on the cheek. "How was your meeting?"

"Good. No, great." An awkward silence replaced the polite conversation as she turned from Dad and plunged into Sam's Caribbean eyes.

Clearing his throat, Dad broke the silence. "Well, if you two young people will excuse me, I'll head upstairs to the office and finish my sales report." He offered his hand to Sam. "Thanks again, son."

"My pleasure, sir."

The stairs creaked as Dad padded up them.

Sam closed the space between them and drew her into an embrace. "Come here, you."

Her body melted into him as his arms encircled her and his lips briefly, but firmly, met hers. As he rested his forehead on hers, little smile lines crinkled the corners of his eyes.

Tears of relief welled up in hers.

His eyebrows raised, and he drew away. "What is it, love? What's wrong?"

"Nothing. Nothing, really. I'm just a bit emotional."

"Want to talk about it? Anything I can do to help?"

A warm droplet trickled down her cheek. "I just met Clark at The Perks and officially broke up with him. Or he broke up with me. Actually, I guess we each broke up with the other."

He grasped both of her hands. "Rough?"

"No. That's just it. It turned out better than I could have ever anticipated. He was relieved. He's begun dating an old girlfriend again and seems happier than I've ever seen him."

He cradled her face in his hands and kissed away the droplet that had escaped. "And you? What about you?"

Yes, what about her? "I'm in love with a soccer player."

~*~

Katherine was grateful for the breeze provided by the overhead fan as she sat on Megan and Brad Thompson's patio.

Megan stepped through the sliding glass doors, a pitcher of iced tea in her hand. Tall and with a flowing mane of blond curls, she barely looked six months pregnant, much less nine.

Katherine had seen her before at some of Cassie's games and had spoken briefly with her, but they'd never really talked much before tonight. Katherine really liked her, and had she planned to stay in Crescent Bluff, the two would assuredly become close friends. It was a shame that wouldn't happen, though, because Katherine wasn't staying here. She was moving to London. The decision was made. Sam just didn't know it yet.

Megan filled Katherine's glass and then nodded her head toward the backyard where Brad and Sam stood hunched over the grill, keeping their eyes on dinner. "It's good to see those two together again. It makes me think of our early college days when they were inseparable. But then their lives went opposite directions. Sam followed his soccer dream, and Brad did an about-face and began studying for the ministry."

"Yes, I have to say, in high school I would never have predicted Brad's life would follow the course it has." The transformation was almost unbelievable.

"When I met him our freshman year, he was in a bad place. On the verge of flunking out and close to losing his soccer scholarship because he was too busy partying to study. His coach hired me as his tutor, and as illogical as it sounds, after the first session I knew

Brad was the one. Oh, he was definitely a work in progress. He was dissatisfied and searching, but I could see his tender heart."

Dissatisfied. Searching. Tenderhearted. Those words pretty much summed up Sam's current state.

Megan had been willing to take a chance on her work in progress, and now she was married to a wonderful, godly man.

"Were you ever worried? At first, I mean."

"Worried's not the best word. Wary, perhaps. Certainly cautious until I got to know him well."

Cautious. Maybe Katherine needed to be more cautious. Lately, when it came to Sam, she had almost forgotten such a state could exist. But she had spent her life being cautious, and now, for once, she was following her heart.

"We sat down at one of the tables in the library that first night, and by the end of the session an illogical peace filled me. It was as if I could see the direction his life would take, and I wanted to go with him."

Brad and Sam stepped onto the patio, and Brad set a plate of grilled burgers on the table. "Thanks, again for agreeing to take over the team mother duties, Katherine. You've really helped take some pressure off Megan."

"Yes," Megan said. "When none of the other moms volunteered, Brad asked me to step in and help. But there's no way I could have done it as well as you have." She gently rubbed the top of her belly. "Especially now. I just can't tolerate the heat. And if I'm on my feet too much, I develop elephant ankles. But not for much longer."

"Yeah, that little girl has to stay in there for two

more weeks—just until the Monday after the tournament." Brad bent down and spoke directly to Megan's tummy. "Hear that, sweet Olivia? Be a good girl, and obey your daddy."

Sam slipped into the chair beside Katherine.

Megan laughed. "I hope she listens to Daddy."

Sam reached over under the table, grasped Katherine's hand, and entwined his fingers with hers. As he smiled and winked, her mind read his. Maybe one day this would be them.

Katherine looked back toward the table.

Brad grinned at her.

She had become the center of attention. As embarrassment burned her cheeks, Megan's eyes twinkled. "So, Katherine, how did you do it? How did you tame the wild beast?"

"Yeah, a lot of women have tried, and all have failed," Brad chuckled.

"All right, guys. Cut it out. We've been out of college for a long time." Sam squeezed her hand. "Besides, priorities change."

Brad smiled at Sam. "Yeah, they do. And I'm glad you've finally realized that."

20

Sam's arm was warm on Katherine's shoulder as they walked away from the flower kiosk toward the mall food court to get something to drink. They had an hour to kill until the girls' bouquets would be ready.

Katherine placed her arm around his waist, closed the space between them, and leaned her head on his shoulder. "Great job, Coach Sam."

"Great job yourself, Team Mom Katherine. I think the girls will like the flowers you picked out. A splendid idea, Katy Beth."

"I can't take the credit. My mom used to do that at the end of every season. I think she always wanted a ballerina daughter, and when Cassie took up soccer, Mom knew giving her a bouquet after the final game of the season was as close as she'd get to a ballet recital. Then it grew into a team tradition..." Emptiness choked off her final words. She missed her Mom much.

His lips brushed the top of her head. "It's OK, love."

She turned her face upward to place a quick kiss on his cheek. Lines creased his forehead as his eyebrows knit together. "Is everything OK?"

Even his smile didn't completely erase the furrows in his forehead. "I've got a bit of a headache from being out in the sun today. That's all. I forgot my sunglasses at Ginny's."

"C'mon." She grasped his hand and led him toward the grouping of loveseats that faced the fountain in the center of the food court. She particularly chose the one that was set back in an alcove flanked on three sides by banks of foliage— mostly palms and those other variegated spiky plants. What was it her mother called them? Oh, yes, Chinese evergreens.

"Would you like something to drink?"

"Maybe in a minute, but not right now."

Katherine knelt on the loveseat, scooted next to him, and carefully began to rub the back of his neck. No wonder he had a headache. He was unbelievably tense. As he leaned forward, she continued to knead the knotted muscles. After a couple of minutes when the tension had disappeared, she slowly walked her fingertips up to the top of his head, rubbed his scalp, massaged his temples, and then ran her fingers through the short, blond silk.

"That's nice. Thanks." Sam smiled as he sat back up.

Yes, it was. "I'm glad you liked it. My dad used to rub my head like that when I'd had a rough day at school." She sat down, leaned back into the loveseat, and soaked in the sight of the man she loved. Her mind shifted into "then and now" mode. The bald, short stranger who had taken her out for Mexican food weeks ago had transformed into a just-the-perfect-height man with a head of golden hair. And, unlike Mr. Plastic, he didn't care if she touched it. "Better?"

"Yeah. The headache's almost gone. Standing on the sidelines watching, knowing you can't get out there and do anything, is much more stressful than being on the field. Who knew?" He shrugged his shoulders and grinned at her.

"Are you surprised Cassie's team made it this far?" She would have never predicted they'd win all their games in the tournament and be slated to play in the finals against last year's champions. Sam's advice had transformed the team.

"I knew they had the potential if everything fell into place. They're playing really well today, but at lunch I could tell they were nervous about the final game. I'm glad Brad took them to a movie. It'll distract them and give them a chance to get out of the heat and relax before the final game."

As long as each girl played her personal best, the outcome of the championship was unimportant, at least to Katherine and the coaches, if Brad's postgame talk was evidence. The girls, however, felt differently. They were on fire.

And the tight muscles in Sam's neck had been confirmation the tournament was more important to him than his words let on.

A pure, clear male voice broke through the soft roar of the cascading water from the fountain and the bustle of the Saturday shoppers. A young man holding a rose stood on the edge of the fountain wall. He was singing that country song about being amazed by a woman. Leaning over the balcony above the fountain, a young woman, also holding a rose, added harmonies and transformed the solo into a duet.

Sam grinned and grasped her hand. "Lovely."

"What do you think it is? An ad for an upcoming musical?"

"Whatever, it's really cool."

A mall security guard materialized at the end of

their loveseat. He should know what was going on. "Excuse me sir, do you know what this is about?"

He smiled and shrugged his shoulders. Then he held up a rose, stepped forward, and made the duet a trio. Suddenly people all around them began to join in.

"Sam, it's a flash mob! Let's go watch."

Katherine stood and pulled Sam to his feet. The noise of uninterested, disconnected shoppers dissolved as they too paused and became one in the moment.

Joining the chorus, people holding roses popped up all around the food court and overhead on the second floor. They began to move toward a young brunette eating pizza with a girlfriend at one of the tables nearby. She looked as confused as Katherine had felt a few seconds ago as participants danced up to her, handed her their flowers, and then danced away.

As the singers began the final chorus, the glass doors from outside into the food court drew apart, and a young man on a Segway zipped through the opening. He wore a white cape and a plastic crown and held a plastic sword above his head—today's version of a knight in shining armor. "Oh, Sam. It's a proposal." Butterflies filled her stomach.

Sam raised her hand to his lips, kissed it, and then encircled her with his arms. Memories of her parents' reactions when they'd snuggled together watching a romantic movie or attended a wedding filled her mind.

Mankind possessed the universal desire to love and be loved by another. And in watching others walk along the path to love, a small portion of that craving was satisfied.

If a person had found The One, as her parents had, their love for each another was rekindled. If someone was still waiting, the hope in the heart was affirmed.

She melted into the man she loved, The One she wanted to become Her One.

Cheers and applause rose from the crowd as the knight stopped by the table, now piled high with roses, and dismounted from his two-wheeled stallion. As he reached into his pocket, produced what could only be a ring box, and dropped down onto one knee, Katherine's heart pounded wildly in her chest.

The knight spoke words they could not hear and held out the box. Silence filled the food court and surrounding area of the mall as the crowd held its breath in anticipation.

The young woman sat in stony silence.

Katherine's heart pounded even harder. She recognized the look on the woman's face because she'd felt the emotions before. Fear. Embarrassment. A desire to be anywhere except here.

The crowd erupted into shouts of "Yes, yes, yes," and as the knight offered the box again, cheering and whistling accompanied the manic chanting.

The trapped young woman stood, looked right and left for some path of escape, and then raced away toward the restrooms, to a place where the knight could not follow her.

A deathly silence blanketed the food court.

Katherine wanted to race after her, to pull her into a comforting embrace, and tell her everything would be OK. But she couldn't. They were strangers. And then what about the shattered hopes of the young man?

Recorded instrumental music combined with the white noise of shoppers suddenly filled the empty silence of the mall as life returned to normal. But not for the young couple. The lady was sequestered in a fortress of cinderblock and granite, and the kneeling knight had been defeated in his quest. He wouldn't ride away with his lady today. If ever.

~*~

"Losing in a shootout. You can't get much closer than that." Katherine reached over and patted Sam's knee as he pulled out onto the highway to begin the long drive back home.

"A shootout's a lousy way to lose—or win, for that matter. They played spectacularly for ninety minutes but just couldn't get the ball into the goal. Some days are like that. You're doing everything right, but it's just not working. To lose one to zip in a shootout is painful and in no way reflects what actually went on in the game. I really feel for the girls. They were great. Especially Cassie. We'll get 'em next season." He grinned and squeezed her hand.

Next season...if only that were true. By next season he'd be back in London—actually, long before then. She didn't know exactly when, but it had to be in a very few weeks. She couldn't think about that now, though. She had absolutely no control over this situation. No notebook, no list, no amount of planning would have any effect on the wishes and demands of his employer. He was under contract, so right now his life, his future, was not really his.

"Whoa!"

Her attention jerked back to the road in front of them. "What? What is it?"

"See that old highway over there paralleling the interstate? I remember that from when I was a kid playing in soccer tournaments and going back and forth between Amarillo and Crescent Bluff."

"I see." It was just an old highway.

"No, I don't think you really do." He downshifted as they approached an exit ramp and he steered the car off the interstate over to the old highway. "This is the first place my Dad ever let me drive. The road is straight, you can see forever, and it's completely deserted. Perfect."

"Perfect for what? You're not making me drive again, are you?" She'd only had that one lesson and wasn't really in the mood to have an encounter with a policeman tonight.

"Only if you want. But I had something else in mind." As he stopped the car and looked over at her, his eyes sparkled like a little boy's on Christmas morning. "Ever since I got this car, I've wanted to see what she could do, and this is the perfect place."

"You mean how fast the car can go?" He must be kidding. She could see the numbers on the speedometer. "I don't think so."

"Come on, Katy Beth. It'll be fun. Besides, look at how straight the road is. You can see for miles." His eyes pleaded with her to agree. "I'm a good driver."

"I'm not doubting your driving skills, but accidents happen—even to the best drivers. And all it takes is one little jerk or a millisecond of distraction for things to go bad."

He stared straight out the windshield toward the pinprick on the horizon where the old highway disappeared into nothingness.

Her stomach rolled. She knew him. He'd come back alone. "Please Sam, I don't want you to come back out here." Her voice shook. "I've lost one person I loved in a car accident, and I can't lose another. Promise me you won't come back. Please."

When he turned toward her, she expected to see frustration or impatience, but his eyes were gentle. He reached over and brushed the back of his hand against her cheek. His words were soft. "I promise."

He leaned over, gently kissed her on the cheek, and then drove the car back toward the interstate. "But love, I've never been afraid of death. There's worse things than dying. Having this one life and not living it fully—reaching the end and looking back in regret wishing I'd accomplished more or done things differently—that's what scares me. A life wasted, spent on the wrong things, would be so much worse than death."

21

Katherine slipped into the sandals she'd worn on their first date. Sam had mentioned how much he liked the dress she'd worn then and asked if she'd wear it again tonight. Most guys didn't even seem to notice stuff like that. She could have probably worn the same dress on every date with her exes, and they wouldn't have noticed.

Except for Clark. He was the exception. When it came to clothes, he was more like a woman than a man. He even noticed something as simple as her earrings. How she looked was important to him because the wardrobe of the woman he dated was as much a reflection of his image as the clothes he wore.

Sam had never made her feel like an accessory or as if she'd been inappropriately dressed. But for some reason, he remembered this dress and that was cause enough for her to happily agree to wear it.

The rumbling of a car engine vibrated through the windows into her bedroom. Slipping out of sight behind the curtains, Katherine peaked through the sheers to get a candid view of the man she loved. The car door opened and out stepped The One she hoped to spend the rest of her life with.

He wore jeans and the same shirt he'd worn the night of their blind date. Any disappointment she'd felt those weeks ago had long since been erased. He was the most attractive man she'd ever known. She'd never thanked Dad for setting them up on that first date, but that was something she'd remedy tonight.

Tonight, Sam looked much taller than he had then. After he reached up and patted down the blond hair that had been ruffled by the ever-blowing Texas wind, he dropped his arms to his side, shook them, and then blew out. She'd seen him do that before on the sidelines at Cassie's games and then right before Juanita had asked them to demonstrate their fledgling dance skills that night at the Cattlemen's Hotel. Come to think of it, he'd made the very same gesture after he'd first stepped out of his car the night of their blind date.

She now knew what it meant. She smiled so widely her cheeks hurt. He was nervous, and he was unbelievably cute being such.

Tonight, there would be no stalling by counting to twenty while someone else answered the door. She grabbed her purse and ran down the hall toward the family room.

Dad muted the TV and smiled. "From the sounds of it, I believe James Bond has arrived."

Her face warmed as butterflies swarmed inside her. She was nervous, too. "Yes, he has." She leaned over and kissed his cheek. "Thank you, Daddy. Thanks so much."

He smiled as he grasped her hand. "He's a fine young man, Baby Girl. I'm happy for you."

~*~

An unfamiliar feeling hammered in Sam's chest. Sure, there were times he was nervous, but not much, if anything, really scared him. Yet fear was the only name he could give the emotion that was shaking his whole body. As he reached to press the doorbell, he took a deep breath. He was entering new territory—completely uncharted, completely unknown. In a few hours, his life would change forever.

The door swept open, and there she stood—the woman he'd loved for as long as he could remember. Her face was rosy, her eyes sparkling with anticipation, though she could have no idea what lay ahead tonight. Her voice was hushed. "Hi, Sam." Her smile only intensified the pounding in his chest.

He fought to find enough breath to answer. "Hi, love. You look utterly gorgeous."

Her smile radiated joy. "Thanks. So do you."

Her words made him laugh, and the laughter dispelled his fear. He needed to relax. After all, she did love him. She had told him that. "You're the only woman who's ever called me beautiful and now gorgeous."

"Good. I want to be special."

He placed his arm around her and drew her close. She smelled pure, like sweet spring rain. As his lips touched her ear, his whisper raised goosebumps on her arm, and she giggled. "Mission accomplished, Katy Beth."

~*~

The ride in the car went by more quickly than Sam anticipated. Thank goodness, she was chatty tonight.

He was in no mood to make small talk, and if they'd ridden in silence she would have known something was up. She seemed content with his few words of agreement or his quick answers to her questions designed to keep her talking.

He turned off the road and drove his car toward the edge of the small cliff overlooking the riverbed and cave where they'd shared their first kiss.

Her narrative stopped mid-sentence as she looked around. "Oh, Sam, I'm so glad this is where we're having our date. When you asked me to wear this dress and then you showed up in the same shirt you wore on our first date, I just assumed we were going to The Cantina. And as much as I love their food, I really wanted to be alone tonight—just the two of us."

He'd wondered if she'd remember the shirt, but he should have known she would. "I'm glad." He cut the engine and then walked around the car to help her out, a gesture that would have made Mom and Dad proud.

Hand in hand, they made their way down the path to the river. The sun would set and twilight would fall in about thirty minutes, providing him with plenty of time for what he had planned. The riverbed was already in shadows.

Farther ahead, a warm glow radiated from their cave.

She stopped when she noticed it. "Sam!" A smile covered her face as she dropped his hand and hurried toward the golden pool.

He stepped into the cave right behind her.

"Oh, Sam. It's beautiful."

He had to admit, it did look pretty darn good. The battery-operated candles scattered around the cave softened the deep colors of the Mexican blankets and pillows he had borrowed from Ginny and warmed the cool gray of the stone floors. The vase filled with pink tulips he'd had flown in from Michigan sat atop the cooler that contained the fajitas from The Cantina.

His love turned toward him and pulled him close. She placed her hands around his neck and drew his face to hers. As their foreheads touched, she whispered, "It's perfect. I love you, Sam Tucker."

His body welcomed hers as if they'd been created for one another. No other woman had ever felt this right. "I'm so glad." They stood in silence for a while, enjoying a measure of oneness that could go no further. He barely relaxed his arms and whispered against her ear. "Hungry?"

She drew away and looked dreamily into his eyes. "Starving."

A year ago, he would have taken that comment as an invitation to something other than dinner and happily obliged. But not anymore—not since he'd vowed to find her and win her heart. And certainly not from her.

He led her to one of the pillows, set the tulips aside, and then removed the two plates from the cooler. "Tonight's menu includes a choice of fajitas or fajitas. Which would be your preference?"

"Hmmm. It's hard to decide. They're both so good, but I believe I'll have the fajitas. No, wait, I've changed my mind. I'll take the other fajitas instead." She giggled and reached for the plate in his left hand.

"Fajitas, it is."

He placed his plate on the cave floor, pulled his phone out of his pocket, and set it on a country station. "A little mood music."

They ate in comfortable silence for the next few

seconds. He forced down a few bites until his rolling stomach rebelled. His nerves and the Mexican food were not a good combination at the moment. Maybe he'd feel like eating more later.

"I've made a decision." She set her plate aside. "I'm going with you."

What? "Pardon?"

"To London. I'm going with you when you go back."

"Katy Beth..."

Her words tumbled out. "Now, don't try to talk me out of it. I have it all worked out. One of my roommates from college works at the US Embassy in London, and she's invited me to come visit her numerous times. I always wanted to go but couldn't get the time off. So now I have the time off, and she said I could come and stay as long as I want. I've got a little money saved up, so I think it would be a wonderful time for me to explore the British Isles. Oh, and by the way, she's a big fan of yours."

Her gaze dared him to try to change her mind, but he wouldn't think of doing so. He'd hoped she'd agree to come with him. He'd just had a different idea about who she'd be living with, but they could discuss that later. He leaned forward and kissed her on the cheek. "Thank you. You've just made me a very happy man."

A smile warmed her face. "Good. So, when do we leave?"

"One month. I spoke with Lizzie earlier today and management agreed that I could stay for the mission trip. They thought it would be good PR. You know, 'Pro Athlete Donates Time to Help Underprivileged.'" He hated that the team would try to capitalize on the misfortune of others, but that was all part of the game of promotion. Plus, it allowed him a few more weeks here. "We'll need to leave the Wednesday after we return, and I'll have to report for pre-season training the following Monday."

A song they'd danced to with Juanita began. Katherine jumped up and held out her hand. "Come on. Let's see if we still remember the steps."

They stepped out onto the path in front of the cave so they'd have enough room to move. He opened his arms, and she eased into his embrace. After she counted the cadence one time under her breath, they began. Juanita would have given them at least a B+. As the song ended, he dipped her, and her laughter echoed softly through the small canyon. He'd never been happier, and yet he'd never been more afraid that he would lose the source of that happiness.

As twilight blanketed the riverbed, an evening breeze skipped across the surface of the water, bringing a welcome cool to the end of the day. The song that the flash mob had danced to and sang began. He drew her closer. "Shall we?"

She rested her head on his shoulder. "This song makes me sad."

"Sad? It's a beautiful love song."

"Yes, but I'll never hear it that I won't remember the face of that broken-hearted young man at the mall." She snuggled her head even closer. "I'm glad I'm not a man."

"Not nearly as glad as I am. Trust me." He chuckled, but she was silent.

She stopped dancing and drew away. "No, really. There's so much pressure on guys today. When did a personal time like a proposal become such an impersonal event? Some contest that focuses on who can come up with the biggest, most involved spectacle and then post it all over social media? It should be an intimate time shared by two people who love each other, not an opportunity to outdo all your buddies. I don't blame that young woman for running away. Being put on the spot in front of a mob of strangers cheapens what should be one of the most precious moments in a relationship."

This wasn't going according to his plan, but she'd cracked open the door, so the time had come for him to ease his way in. He'd wanted to tell her about the other women first, but suddenly he couldn't. The risk of losing her was too great. Even though he'd prayed about this moment off and on all day, he wasn't sure it would do any good—that God would even listen to a person who'd been running away from Him all these years. Much less answer his prayer.

He held open his left hand in front of him like a piece of paper, gripped an imaginary pen in his right hand, and began making invisible notes.

"What in the world are you doing?" She tilted her head to the side.

His heart began to pound in his chest. After these next words were out of his mouth, there'd be no turning back. This was a once-in-a-lifetime moment. He'd never done it before, and he'd never do it again. He took a deep breath and then answered her question. "Canceling the flyover by the fighter planes. And the fireworks display. Oh, yes, and I'd better not forget the marching band."

The corners of her eyes crinkled with amusement as laughter flowed forth like the little stream beside them. Then the unspoken meaning of his words sank in, and the laughter stopped abruptly as her eyes opened wide.

He slowly eased down onto one knee and grasped her hands in his. "Katy Beth, I love you. I've always loved you. I loved the girl you were when we were in school together. I loved the memory that was you. I loved the young lady I dreamed you were when we were apart. And I love the woman you've become. I will always love you. Nothing you could ever do will change my feelings. That's why I came back to Crescent Bluff. To find you and ask you to marry me."

He reached into his pocket and pulled out the tattered and faded red velvet box. She recognized it before he even lifted the lid.

As her bottom lip began to quiver, tears glistened in her eyes. Her words were whispered. "How did you...? Where did you...?"

"Your dad. Our time together the other day was more than a casual lunch. I told him my intentions and asked for his blessing. Even though you've been on your own for years, it just seemed like the respectful thing to do. Anyway, he insisted I take this. He said your mom would have wanted you to have it. So, Katy Beth, my only true love, join me in this adventure called life. Please say you'll be my bride."

She knelt down so they were face to face. The candlelight escaping from the cave transformed the tracks of her tears into sparkling golden strands on her cheeks. "Samuel Houston Tucker, I've been waiting for you all my life—I just didn't know it would be you. You, Sam, are The One—My One."

As she offered her left hand, fingers slightly spread in invitation, he started to remove the thirty-year-old diamond engagement ring from the box, but then he stopped. Her face. Amidst the tears she was smiling. Her eyes were full of joy, innocence, trust. Trust. Some unseen vise squeezed his chest so hard he struggled to breathe. They weren't even engaged, and he was already being unfaithful to her by letting her believe something that wasn't true. In his lack of honesty, he was being dishonest. He was planting seeds of deceit that would one day bloom into complete distrust.

Slowly he stood up and helped her to her feet. He pulled her into a tight embrace. "I love you so much."

"Well, I certainly hope so since you just asked me to marry you. But you know what? I don't think I gave you my official answer." She chuckled and squeezed him tightly.

"Then don't. Not yet. I want you to say yes more than anything I've ever wanted in my life, but not like this. Not under false pretenses." The sound of blood coursing through his body roared in his ears so loudly he could no longer hear the trickle of the stream

She drew back and looked up at his face, her brow wrinkled. "What is it, Sam?"

Trust or no trust, God or no God, he loved her too much to let their married life begin under these circumstances. "You know that purity ring you saw on my keychain?"

She smiled and nodded.

"It's only been there about a year."

22

The ride home had been silent. Too much had been said earlier beside the river. Even now, while she gripped the doorknob to the kitchen door and Sam leaned against his car, neither one of them wished the other "Good night." The pain and disappointment were too fresh to be brushed aside by polite pleasantries.

Her heart lifted a brief prayer. *Please, Father, let Daddy be asleep.*

She noiselessly turned the knob and pushed gently to open the door. The aroma of chocolate chip cookies drifted toward her from the plate on the kitchen island. Very quietly she tiptoed into the kitchen and closed the door.

"Anybody we know?" Dad's voice greeted her from the family room.

Of course. The rumble from Sam's car would have alerted him she was home no matter how quiet she had been.

Dad strode into the kitchen with Cassie on his heels. The huge grin on his face disappeared the moment he saw her. "Baby Girl, what's wrong? Where's Sam?"

She shook her head and forced her words past the huge lump in her throat. "I said no. He's not The One,

Daddy." Tears now washed her cheeks as he pulled her close.

"You turned him down, Beth? Are you kidding me? He's a great guy." Cassie looked at their father and shook her head. "She's crazy, Dad. I'd marry him if I was older."

"Cassie, you think you could give us some privacy, honey?" Dad asked.

"Whatever." She grabbed some cookies and left, muttering, "What's wrong with her, anyway? No wonder she'd not married."

"Want to talk about it, Katherine?"

How much should she tell him? "I don't know, Daddy. I think I just want to go to bed." She wiped away the stinging tears. Sam had hurt and betrayed her, but most of all, he'd let her believe a lie. He'd listened to her talk about them both being pure, and in not correcting her, he'd deliberately lied to her. And where there was one secret, there were bound to be more. She'd probably never know what other deceptions were hidden in his past. "Let's just say Sam's been lying to me. He's not the man I thought he was."

"Baby Girl, we all make mistakes in life. We all do things we wish we hadn't. And even though we might like to erase them, once they're done, they can't be undone. All we can do is ask forgiveness and turn our lives in another direction."

Sam must have told him. "When did you know?"

"The day he took me out to lunch. The day I gave him my blessing along with your mother's ring." He reached over and patted her hand. "I was impressed that he had the guts to own up to his mistakes. He didn't have to share that with me, but he wanted to start with a clean slate. To let me know he was a changed man."

"Lies are not isolated things. If a person lies about one thing, he's bound to have lied about others." She reached into her pocket and pulled out the ring box. "Here, I won't be needing this. Save it for Cassie."

Dad's voice followed her as she turned to walk out of the kitchen. "Sometimes the best gift we can give someone is forgiveness, but forgiving another is always the best gift you can give yourself."

She bolted down the hall, into her bedroom, and slammed the door. The open notebook called to her from her nightstand. She picked it up along with her pen and began x-ing through today's final entry, Date With Sam. Then she scribbled circles and lines through it until the original words were no longer discernible. A big black box stared back up at her from the page, reminding her of his betrayal. Grabbing the sheet, she ripped it from the notebook, wadded it into the tightest ball she could, and then dropped it into the wastebasket. Good. The page was gone.

While no reminder of this evening remained in her notebook, nothing she could do would ever erase it from her heart.

~*~

Sam carefully made his way down the rocky path to the riverbed. The words of forgiveness he'd prayed he'd hear from her hadn't come. But her reaction hadn't surprised him. In fact, it was exactly what he'd expected—and feared. If he'd told her earlier, long before they'd gotten so serious, she might not have felt so betrayed. The only words she'd spoken were, "I want to go home."

He stepped into the cave, where one surviving candle still flickered, to pack up the stuff and take it back to Ginny's. But instead he dropped down onto the stone floor. He couldn't go home yet. It was too early. There'd be questions, and he wasn't ready to answer them. The pain was too fresh, too raw. He'd return when there was absolutely no chance that anyone would be awake. Laying back against one of the pillows, he waited.

A burden sat heavily on his chest. While unfamiliar, the weight wasn't unknown. He'd borne it before, but not very often and not for very long. He'd always been able to shake it off or overcome it, though now it looked as though the two of them would become inseparable friends. Its name was Failure.

~*~

Katherine awoke, soaked in perspiration. The clock on her nightstand read three thirty. She waited quietly for the relief that she would surely feel as she became more awake and realized the memory of Sam's confession was merely a bad dream. But the peace she'd sought never came. The hours of sleep had only briefly deadened the painful reality. The man she'd fallen in love with was a liar and a fake—simply posing as someone he wasn't to get something he wanted.

He'd taken advantage of her trust. Instead of telling her the truth from the beginning, he'd wooed her and strung her along until she believed he was Her

One. If he'd truly loved her, he should have told her about his past earlier in their relationship, and he certainly should have corrected her when she'd made that comment about the ring. He should have been honest and allowed her to decide before she fell in love with a person who didn't exist.

Her life before Sam had been meaningful. Everything had been orderly and under control until Dad suggested she step out of the boat. She'd taken that chance, and she was worse off now than ever. She was drowning.

Guilt swept over her, mixing with the anger and pain. She should pray, but she couldn't. Not yet. Not in anger.

Hot tears dampened her cheeks as a patient Voice spoke deep in her heart. Her Father loved her. He understood her pain and her anger. And she could lay it all on Him. He could handle it.

~*~

Sam's back ached, and he was so stiff he could hardly move. Sometime during the last few hours, the battery in the last candle must have lost power. The cave was perfectly dark except for the gray predawn glow that filled the entrance. He stood, stretched, and then pulled his phone out of his pocket. Five o'clock. Somehow, he'd managed to sleep all night. Carefully he gathered the candles and wrapped them up in one of the blankets. He folded the other blanket, stacked it and the pillows together on top, and then headed out to pack them in the car.

Maybe he shouldn't have told her about all the

other women. If he hadn't she would have said yes, they'd be engaged now, and she'd be coming with him to London in a few weeks. Everything in his life would be just as he'd planned it.

No, he'd made the right choice. For once in a long time—maybe even the first time ever—he'd made a decision based not on his desires but based upon what was best for someone else. And while the pain of her rejection pierced deep in his heart, knowing he'd acted out of love for her brought him a sense of peace.

He placed the pillows and blankets in the trunk and walked back to the cave to get the cooler and the tulips. The tulips—throwing them in the stream shouldn't be considered littering. They weren't trash. They were organic, after all, and he didn't want to walk back into Ginny's house with them in hand.

The predawn sky had brightened, making it easier to see inside their cave. Their cave. The place where they'd first kissed in the spring rain. The kiss that had spoken more of her love for him than any words ever could. The place he'd known her heart was his.

The place she'd taken it back.

He picked up the cooler and the vase and stepped out onto the rock path that edged the riverbed. Then he leaned out over the stream and turned the vase upside down. Pink blossoms cascaded into the river and slowly floated downstream.

As he turned to watch them drift away, he jumped in surprise. Less than twenty feet from him stood a doe. She hadn't been there when he'd come back from the car a few minutes ago. She was drinking, and then she suddenly lifted her head to sniff the air. Her nostrils flared and she turned to look right at him, obviously trying to figure out whether he was a threat.

He froze. Not only was she beautiful, but she could be dangerous.

As her velvet eyes locked onto his, she leaned her head to the side, never breaking eye-contact. She could run. She could charge him. But she was thirsty, so she set aside her fears and gracefully lowered her head toward the stream. Why she would decide to drink with him, a likely danger, so near was incomprehensible. Not wanting to scare her, he stood motionless, watching as she quenched her thirst in the pink, predawn glow.

When she was satisfied, she raised her head, briefly looked his direction again, and then turned and slowly sauntered on downstream.

A mysterious longing stirred within his soul. Maybe this was what some people called a "God moment." Or maybe it was one of those once-in-a-lifetime coincidences that happened, because for some unexplainable reason he'd woke at the perfect time. Five minutes earlier or later and he would have missed the whole thing.

Whatever the reason or the cause, he would never forget it.

23

Sam pulled his car into a visitor parking space right in front of the church. After all, that's what he was. He wasn't a church member. Crescent Bluff hadn't been his home for years. He was a visitor. And one that wouldn't be around here much longer.

He stepped out of the car and walked up the concrete path toward the double glass doors at the front of the building. Maybe she wouldn't be at church today.

For about half a second, he'd thought about backing out of the mission trip and returning to London early. But he couldn't cancel on Brad right now. One of the other male chaperones, a carpenter by trade, had fallen at a job site and broken his leg. That left Sam as the only one with any true construction experience.

Besides he'd never been the type of guy to renege on commitments he'd made, and he wouldn't start now. He'd always been a man of his word—except in that one area that had cost him his relationship with Katy Beth.

His life would be so different right now if he'd only kept that promise, too.

Avoiding the smiling greeters, he walked straight through the foyer and then slipped through the wooden doors and headed for one of the chairs hidden in the blackness of the back corner of the auditorium. He was hiding—hiding from her, hiding from God. The only reason he came today was because they had that final meeting for the mission trip right after the service.

When he and his family had moved to North Carolina years ago, he hadn't left only his friends behind in Texas but also the God he was just getting to know. Soccer became his new god, and up until recently, he would have said it was a pretty good one. It had given him everything he thought he wanted out of life. But it was an idol—a false god that could never give him the one thing he wanted more than anything. Katy Beth.

So, he'd decided to turn back to God. Over the past several weeks he'd started reading his Bible again and praying—something he hadn't done since he and his family left Crescent Bluff. He'd thought he was on the right track, but she'd turned him down. The other night had been the test. If God had really wanted him back, He would have answered Sam's prayers, and Sam and Katy Beth would now be engaged.

As the worship band took their places, he saw the outline of her head on the third row. Her dad was on one side and Cassie on the other. She was here, and he wished he wasn't. No, that wasn't true. He wished he was sitting up there beside her.

~*~

Katherine's eyes filled. The next few hours would be difficult. Of course, there was always the possibility

Sam wouldn't come.

Never. He would be at the meeting after church. That was Sam. He wasn't one to shirk his responsibilities. When he was in, he was all in.

She leaned against the comfort of Dad's shoulder as he rested his arm on the back of her chair. She was safe.

Dad had been so understanding and supportive these last several days. Although he didn't completely understand or agree with her refusal of Sam's proposal, he supported her decision. Or at least he said he did. But then he also kept saying how everyone makes mistakes, everyone needs forgiveness, and everyone deserves a second chance.

She couldn't disagree with any of that. Sam had made a mistake, or apparently many of the same mistakes. No doubt he was sorry, especially because she'd turned down his proposal. And he certainly could have a second chance—just not with her. Forgiving him didn't mean she had to take him back and act as if the offense had never happened. Forgiveness meant only that she wouldn't hold it against him. And she could make herself do that— eventually.

These past few weeks had been surreal, like a slice-of-life episode from some TV show. But they weren't real life.

Clark had called yesterday. Since there was no longer any reason for her to stay in Crescent Bluff, she'd be moving back to Dallas and returning to her old job right after the mission trip. And Sam? He was under contract to his football club, so he'd be headed home to London in just a couple of weeks. Surely, as they both went back to their real lives and time passed, the pain would lessen, and she'd be able to forgive him and look back on this for what it was—a lesson in recklessness and what happens when people cast aside wisdom to follow their hearts rather than use common sense.

She just needed to get through today...and then tomorrow...and then the mission trip. When that was over, her life would return to normal.

~*~

Sam bowed his head for the prayer before the final song. He hadn't been able to concentrate on the sermon because she was sitting in the sightline between him and the pastor. Every time he looked toward Dr. Lewis, all he saw was the back of her head. And the memory of the fragrance of sugar cookies and lemonade from the first time they'd slow-danced together in the Longhorn Suite at Cattlemen's squeezed his chest until he could hardly breathe.

Up until a few days ago, he would have summed up his life in two words—no regrets. Not anymore. This last year of his life had been focused on one thing—finding her. He'd been willing to do whatever was necessary to win her heart, only to discover that nothing he could do would ever achieve that goal.

The worship pastor sat alone on a stool and gently coaxed notes from his guitar. The melody was straightforward and simple, and the words were poetic. Something about a deer drinking from a spring of water.

The image of the soft eyes of the doe staring at him by the river's edge the other morning filled his memory.

The screens hanging behind the worship pastor displayed a scripture reference—Psalm 42. He grabbed the Bible in the back pocket of the seat in front of him and opened it to the table of contents. He turned to the page number listed for Psalms and then kept turning until he came to Psalm 42.

As the deer pants for streams of water,
so my soul pants for you, my God.

He read on.

My tears have been my food day and night,
while people say to me all day long, "Where is your god?"

Yes. Where was his god? The god he'd trusted in all these years? He'd led a life many could only dream of. But it was all worthless, because all the stuff, all the prestige, and all the money couldn't get him the one thing he really wanted—the one who would bring him peace and fulfill his heart's longing. Katherine. He'd been trusting in the wrong god.

Again, the image of the deer flashed before him. She'd measured the cost and been willing to risk everything for the one thing that would give and sustain her life. That without which she would die. The risk would be worth the reward.

Sam's outcome had been different, though. He'd prayed and taken the risk. He'd lowered his head to drink, only to end up with a mouth full of life-choking dust. Katherine hadn't accepted his proposal. So much for trusting in something other than himself.

If God really loved him, wouldn't He have answered his prayers? Wouldn't Katherine have said yes?

~*~

Katherine stepped through the door into the fellowship hall. Chairs ringed a solitary table, but Megan was the only one there so far. Olivia was asleep in her stroller.

"Katherine, I'm so glad you could make it." Megan stood and gave her a warm hug. "Brad was hoping you'd still come with the group."

"Why would I not?"

Megan's face turned red. Megan knew. Sam must have told Brad. "We just...well, I mean, Brad would understand if you changed your mind. You know, with Sam still coming and all..."

"A promise is a promise, and I always keep my commitments." She sat in the chair nearest the stroller and looked at the precious treasure who slept there. "She's absolutely beautiful." Her next words surprised even herself. She'd never been much of a baby person. "Could I hold her?"

"Of course." Megan lifted the pink bundle and placed her in Katherine's waiting arms. She looked at the tiny features on Olivia's face. The silky eyelashes, the button nose, and the heart-shaped mouth. And then for some unexplainable reason, more instinctual than rational, Katherine leaned over and breathed in the pure fragrance of this sweet child.

Megan chuckled. "That was one of the first things I did after she was born and I had counted all her fingers and toes. My mom says it's a 'Mommy' thing."

Katherine had never thought of herself as a "Mommy" but had always assumed that she would be. One day. Yet now, maybe not. Life seemed to be leading her down a different path than she'd always imagined. Plenty of unmarried, childless people led fulfilling lives, and she would, too.

Other chaperones had filed in and taken seats around the table, but Katherine had been so completely engrossed in her thoughts, she hadn't noticed until this moment. At the far end of the table, only one chair remained open, and only one person was missing. Maybe he had changed his mind and wasn't coming.

"Thanks to all of you for being here," Brad spoke. "We'll be brief so you can get to the cafeteria before the congregation down the road does." A polite snicker at the old joke made its way around the table. "In case you haven't heard, Charlie fell and broke his leg. He's OK, but we'll be shorthanded, so if any of you know another man who could chaperone on such short notice, please let me know."

The door opened one last time, and in slipped Sam. "Sorry, I'm late." He made his way to the empty chair and sat down.

"No problem. We were just getting started." Brad passed out packets, and Megan set one on the table in front of Katherine. "You can go over it later," she whispered.

As foreign as the idea seemed in her spirit, holding this baby felt right in her heart. She studied each tiny pink fingernail, then the wrinkled brow, followed by a smile that science attributed to gas. The love shared by Brad and Megan had brought forth this sweet child, this beautiful gift. The miracle of new life sprang from an intimate love meant for one person to share with only one other.

Brad was praying for the mission trip.

At first Katherine bowed her head, but then she looked up toward Sam. His eyes were fixed on her. They were not filled with anger, but with what

Katherine could only believe was a warmth, a longing, a resignation that she, his love, would never hold their baby.

But it was all his fault. She did not look away but slowly shook her head. What they both yearned for in the core of their beings would never come to pass.

24

Ten more days. In ten more days, she'd be on her way back to Dallas, and Sam would be on the other side of the world, or at least making his way there. For the first time in her life, she'd had one of those famous summer romances people usually had as teenagers or college students. Passionate, unexpected, irresponsible. A relationship that exists only because it is short-lived, momentary. The only differences were theirs had been in the spring, and neither of them had wanted it to be temporary.

"He's not going." Cassie's pouting voice broke through the silence as Dad turned the car into the church parking lot.

"Who, sweetie?" Dad asked.

"Sam. He's not going. And it's all your fault, Beth."

This was the same verdict Cassie had been delivering for a couple of weeks now. But she had no idea where the fault lay, and Katherine was not about to discuss an adult issue with her barely teenaged baby sister. Besides, it was private, between two people. Well, not exactly two. Him, her, and apparently lots of other women.

"Now hold on there, young lady. Don't go blaming your sister for something that's not under her control. Sam's an adult, and he can make his own choice about what to do and what not to do. Besides, what would make you think he's not going, just because you haven't seen him in the first two seconds after we've arrived?"

"His car, Dad. His car's not here."

"Sam's not dumb. I doubt he'd leave a car like that in the church parking lot for a week." Dad chuckled. "I would have offered to car-sit it for him, if I weren't going out of town part of this week."

"There he is. I see him. It's a good thing for you, Beth."

Sam hopped out of the pick-up that had parked behind the bus. An ache began in the center of Katherine's chest and spread through her entire body. He looked wonderful. His blond hair was spiked on top as if he'd just rolled out of bed. His face was covered with chestnut stubble. Katherine had seen him unshaven only once before—that morning they'd trespassed out onto the rock ledge overlooking the Balcones Canyon—but that was with one night's growth, not a week or so. While the beard camouflaged his boyish cuteness, it only intensified the brilliant blue of his eyes.

As Cassie jumped out of the car and slammed the back door shut, Dad placed his hand on Katherine's shoulder. "Your mom would be proud of you for going. Thanks for taking her place."

Her eyes burned. Dad didn't mean it the way she heard it. Her mother truly would have been proud, but no matter how hard Katherine tried, she would never take Mom's place.

"Baby Girl, your mother was really good at living in the moment, at enjoying the journey. That woman packed so much into each hour of every day. She lived more life in the few years she was with us than I ever will, no matter how many years I have." He leaned over and pecked her on the cheek. "You and I are both destination people. I know this week will be challenging for you, but don't wish the time away. Live every minute of the journey because you'll never get any of them back."

She hugged him tightly. "I will, Daddy. I promise."

~*~

Sam was in the bed of the truck, loading the luggage, sleeping bags, and other cargo for the trip. When Brad had asked for a volunteer to drive the pick-up, Sam had jumped at the chance. He'd rather be alone in a truck where he didn't have to make small talk with anyone, instead of trapped on a bus where he'd have to be "on" for hours. Normally, the bus ride would have been fun—cutting up with the kids—but not today. This week needed to pass as quickly as possible. Then he could leave, and just like when a football match was over, he put that game behind him and move on to the next. As he turned around to get some more cargo, his heart skipped a beat.

"Morning, Sam." Mr. Harrington lifted up a purple flowered suitcase. Had to be Cassie's.

"Good morning, Mr—Jim. How are you, sir?"

"Sleepy. Five came awfully early this morning."

Yeah, it had. Especially when he hadn't been able to fall asleep until about three.

"Are you driving this all the way to Oklahoma?"

"Yes, sir."

Jim handed him up a black, nondescript suitcase. Katherine's. "You better take someone with you to help keep you awake."

"I'll be fine." He gently set the luggage down, and the fragrance of sugar cookies and lemonade invaded his senses and pierced his heart. "I've got an extra-tall, super-grande coffee from The Perks, and I'll crank the windows down and the music up."

"Just be careful, son."

Sam took Mr. Harrington's offered hand before he stepped aside. "I will."

"Good morning, Sam."

This was the first time he'd heard her voice since she'd asked him to take her home after the proposal. He recognized the look in her eyes. Their hearts shared the same feelings—regret and disappointment. Fortunately, they weren't alone, or he might have jumped out of the truck, taken her hand, and begged her to let him have one last chance to prove he was a changed man. Instead, he bent down to grasp the inflatable mattress she offered. "Hi, Katy B—uh, Katherine."

Jim had made his way over to Cassie, leaving just the two of them.

She reached to pick up the other mattress.

"Here, let me come down and help you with that."

"I don't need your help. It's not heavy." She lifted the rolled bundle up to him. "So what's with the whiskers?"

She was actually making conversation with him. "I'm going for an authentic construction worker look. What do you think?" She didn't return his smile or answer his question. "Actually, I thought it might make me look a bit older since I'll be bossing around high school students for the next week. I'll need all the maturity I can possibly fake."

"Oh." She glanced away. "I guess I'd better head over to the bus. Looks as if Brad's got everyone circled up for some sort of meeting before we leave."

"Wait, Katherine. Ride in the truck with me. Please. I'd really like the company." The only sound was the blood rushing through his ears as his heart pounded, waiting for her reply.

She shook her head. "I can't, Sam. I can't." Then she turned her back and strode over to mass of people beside the bus.

~*~

More than anything, she'd wanted to leave the gear for Dad to contend with, but Cassie had already deserted him. She couldn't do that, too. Plus running away never solved anything. If she and Sam were on this team together, she at least had to be able to carry on some semblance of a polite conversation with him. One down. She'd just done it, and she could do it for the rest of the week.

But to be trapped in a truck with him for six hours? Really? He had to be crazy if he'd thought the slightest possibility existed that she'd even consider agreeing to that. But then again, she didn't want anything to happen to him. After all, she loved him. What he'd done wouldn't change that. She just couldn't marry him. Exactly as she'd loved Clark but couldn't marry him.

No, this wasn't anything like her relationship and

breakup with Clark. She'd turned Clark down because she hadn't been able to see past a proposal. But she'd seen a life with Sam. Marriage, adventure, children, grandchildren. Not anymore, though. If she ever had those things in her life, it wouldn't be with Sam.

She slipped into the circle next to Dad and grasped his hand.

Brad was checking names off a list to make sure everyone was there before they prayed, boarded the bus, and headed north.

As Sam joined the group, Brad began, "Looks as if we're all here. As many of you know, Charlie Thompson broke his leg a couple of weeks ago and can't go with us, so Pastor Josh has offered to take his place."

As the kids broke into cheers, Dr. Lewis raised his hand and then said, "Let me pray for us, and we'll get this show on the road." His words asked for safety.

Katherine's heart asked for peace.

The prayer over, the young people began boarding the bus.

As Katherine gave Dad one last hug, Brad spoke, "Katherine, I've saved you the seat behind me. Your job is to keep me awake during the trip. And Josh, this is Sam Tucker. He'll be driving the truck with all the gear. I thought maybe you'd enjoy riding with him and keeping him company."

"Sam Tucker, the soccer player. I remember you. You'd just started going to our youth group activities when your family up and moved away to one of the Carolinas. Can't wait to hear all about your life since then." The two men shook hands.

Too bad the pickup was crammed with equipment. Katherine just might have changed her mind about riding in the truck and seeing exactly how much of his past life Sam would reveal to Dr. Lewis. Doubtfully very much, and certainly not all of it.

25

Her day began early—six—especially considering some of the girls hadn't settled down until after two. Katherine pulled on some clothes, grabbed her Bible and notebook, and carefully tiptoed through the patchwork of sleeping bags to the classroom door. Her introverted self needed some time alone before the day began.

Breakfast wasn't scheduled until seven-thirty, but maybe she could find a cup of coffee or something to hold her over 'til then. She headed toward the cafeteria, pretty sure she was going the right direction. A map would have been a good addition to the chaperone's packet.

This high school was huge, but it was the perfect place to house hundreds of teenagers with their raging adolescent hormones. All the guys were camped out in the classrooms on the north wing, the girls on the south. In the center were the common areas—the cafeteria, auditorium, gym and locker rooms, even an indoor pool—all serving as the great divide.

She walked into the cafeteria where several small clusters of other early-rising adults were huddled around tables, their conversations hushed, as if not wanting to wake a baby who'd been up all night and just fallen asleep.

Thankfully, chicken biscuits donated by a local fast food restaurant and coffee were set out for the "morning people." She placed the books on a tray, accessorized them with a cup of coffee and a foil-wrapped biscuit, and headed through the double glass doors at the back of the cinderblock room into a courtyard. She set her tray on a concrete table and eased down onto one of the benches facing the football field.

Painting the landscape before her in copper, the sun was rising over the building behind her. She opened her Bible to today's passage and began reading the words she'd read so many times. Yet today, one verse sprang off the page as never before. "Now to him who is able to do immeasurably more than all we ask or imagine, according to his power that is at work within us."

God was able to do far more than anyone could ever ask for or imagine. As the first bite of chicken biscuit hung in her throat, she struggled to swallow it down. Did she really believe that? She knew the verse. She'd probably read it hundreds of times over the years, even memorized it when she was in elementary school. But knowing and believing were two different things.

Did she believe this verse was true? And not just this verse but that other one about asking and receiving, seeking and finding.

She'd asked and sought—specifically—for her One over the years, and until very recently, she'd trusted he would come. So, if God was able, why hadn't He?

She crossed her arms over the open Bible and rested her head on them. As she tried to pray, exhaustion overtook her. This was only the first day of the trip, and already she was just plain worn out—physically, emotionally, and spiritually.

~*~

As Sam left the auditorium and headed toward the cafeteria, he shoved the roster for his team, the Black Crew, back into the manila envelope. What else could possibly happen to make this week any tougher?

Brad had told him the crew he'd supervise would be made up of students from all the youth groups attending, and he'd probably not have any kids from Crescent Bluff Church in his group. The idea was for everyone to start out on equal footing and make new relationships. No problem. Splendid concept.

And Brad had been right. Sam hadn't recognized any of the kids' names. But the female chaperone—that was a different story. It was as though God was playing some cruel trick. He and Katherine were working on the same crew. The Black Crew. How appropriate.

When he'd asked about making changes to the roster after the crew chiefs' meeting, they'd told him no. The assignments had already been handed out, and changing them would be too much of a hassle. Unless, of course, there was some overwhelmingly compelling reason—such as sickness or death. As far as he was concerned, his reason was every bit as valid as either of those, but he hadn't been about to share what it was.

For the sake of the success of the mission trip and the people they were helping, he'd make it work. Besides, it was only for a week. Not even that, really—just five days. But he ached for Katherine. His confession had wounded her deeply, and he didn't want her to be hurt anymore.

His stomach growled as the aroma of coffee and bacon grew stronger with each step. He was definitely headed in the right direction. As he stepped through the doorway into the cafeteria, his stomach groaned in disappointment. The line went all the way around the room.

Brad stood up at one of the tables and motioned him over. "I managed to get an extra tray for you. What took so long?"

"I had some questions, but they straightened everything out for me."

Several of the chaperones from their group, including Josh, were seated around the table. But no Katherine. Maybe she'd already eaten, maybe she'd be coming soon, or maybe she didn't normally eat breakfast, although she'd always seemed grateful when he'd brought bagels or something. But they'd never spent any nights together, so he had no way of knowing what her morning habits were.

"Questions?"

Sam took one more quick assessment of the group around the table. He barely knew all their names, so he certainly wasn't about to divulge his and Katherine's personal situation. "I'll explain later."

~*~

A warm hand gently squeezed her shoulder. "Katherine?"

She jerked up, shaking away the fog of sleep. "Jen." Childhood memories of Mom and Jen sharing cups of coffee around Mom's kitchen island warmed her heart.

Jen set a cup of coffee down on her table. "I thought it was you. Mind if I sit down for a sec?"

Katherine shook her head. "Please do." Pulling her phone out of her pocket, she squinted until the numbers came into focus. Seven fifty-two. She'd been asleep for over an hour.

"Rough night, huh?"

"Yeah." Katherine nodded in agreement.

"It was in my room, too. Don't worry, though. You'll be working so hard the rest of the week, even a bomb won't wake you once your head hits the pillow." As Jen's infectious laugh filled the courtyard, Katherine couldn't have kept from smiling even if she'd tried.

"Katherine, I'm really glad we're getting to work together on this trip. Your mother was so proud of you, and I know she'd be happy you're taking her place. She was a special woman."

Taking her place. Once again, the simple, stock phrase wrung her heart. She would never be the woman her mother had been. If only she could rewind life, if only she'd realized their time together would be so short, she would have been different. She would have made sure she'd argued less and cherished more.

Jen's words pushed into her consciousness. She'd been talking, but Katherine had missed everything she'd said. "Excuse me?"

"We probably ought to head on down to the gym." Standing, Jen took a sip of her coffee.

Katherine choked down one last bite of cold biscuit as she headed toward the trashcan.

After walking through the glass doors back into

the cafeteria, they set out down the hall to the gym.

"Katherine, have you ever been on a trip like this before?"

"I went on church choir trips when I was in high school. We'd stop at churches and sing along the way to a city where we'd lead a Bible school for disadvantaged children, but I've never been on a trip like this where we'll be doing construction."

"I promise you, this week will be a life-changer. There's nothing like helping people put their lives back together. I went for the first time three years ago, and now I'm hooked. I'm sure you will be, too."

From Jen's mouth to God's ears. Katherine's life could certainly stand a change. "Which crew are you on, Jen?"

"The Blue Crew. How about you?"

"The Black Crew."

Jen's laughter echoed down the hall. "Black and blue. Looks as if we're destined to become friends, too."

The roar of excited conversation confirmed they were headed in the right direction. Stopping in the gym doorway, they scanned the numerous huddles of people seated on the bleachers under various colored poster boards. A black rectangle had been taped to the bleachers in the back, left corner.

"There's my group. See you at dinner." Jen headed to the right side of the gym as Katherine began the diagonal trek across the wooden mirror beneath her feet. The floors were so heavily varnished, she could surely have counted her eyelashes in the reflection if she'd squatted down.

As she neared the Black team, all eyes turned in her direction, and the friendly banter dissolved into awkward silence at the arrival of an obvious outsider. "Good morning. I'm Katherine, the female chaperone."

A number of polite, but less than enthusiastic, hellos and good mornings briefly sounded before the silence set back in. Katherine, the female chaperone. Really? She couldn't have said something more interesting than that?

As she sat down onto the bottom row of the bleachers, a wave of applause and cheering flowed across the entire gym from the doorway to her corner. The crew chiefs were here, and the adventure was about to begin.

In the group of fifteen to twenty men, she saw only one. The chestnut stubble was doing its job. He looked older than his years. As the huddle advanced, men peeled off one or two at a time and headed toward the various colors of poster board. Surely the next group would be Sam's. But no. The closer he came, the more her heart pounded until he was the last man left, theirs was the only group without a chief, and her heart was about to leap out of her chest.

An excited voice sounded behind her. "We got the soccer player." Even here, in the middle of rural Oklahoma halfway around the world from England, Sam's celebrity had preceded him.

He was introducing himself, and he was definitely saying more than, "Hi, I'm Sam, the male crew chief." But his words were nonsensical. None of them broke through the wall of realization that the two of them would be working together this entire week.

Maybe she could get reassigned. Maybe there was another female chaperone who would be willing to change places with her. Jen. She could ask Jen. As soon as this little meeting was over, she'd find out who to talk to and get this straightened out.

But then, what reason would she give? *This man's a liar, I loved him, but he broke my heart.* Even though it was true, that sounded so adolescent. She was an adult. She could act like an adult. She'd make sure her personal feelings in no way impacted their mission work. One week. That's all it was. Five little days.

As the students climbed down the bleachers and exited toward the hall, Sam sat down beside her. "Morning."

"Hi." For the first time, she looked him straight in the eyes.

"I'm sorry about this. When I got the packet earlier, I tried to get one of us moved to a different crew, but when they asked why, what could I say? Personal reasons? That sounded lame, immature. I don't want to ruin this experience for you."

Just his acknowledgment, his concern for her feelings, brought peace. He was a compassionate man, and he loved her. Even though their relationship could no longer be anything outside of friendship, he truly cared for her. And she for him. "Thanks, Sam. I appreciate your saying that. We'll make it work."

His smile was soft, matching the tone of his voice. "My mom has always said things happen for a reason. Can't say I've agreed with her, but we'll have to see. Maybe she's right."

26

An awed silence crept through the bus until the only sound heard was the grinding of the engine.

The devastation surrounding them caused a quiet horror. Several of the kids were holding their breaths, eyes wide, no words spoken.

The landscape was unlike anything Katherine had ever seen—nothing but desolation from horizon to horizon. The handful of indigenous trees had been either uprooted or snapped off a few feet above the ground. The scene was the result of two tornadoes that had struck less than a month apart last year.

As the bus topped a small rise, the destruction continued, eerily dotted by havens where houses stood untouched. Some lived and some died. Some lost everything, and some lost nothing. The apparent randomness seemed so unfair.

The paths of the tornadoes must have changed as the road before them became some sort of asphalt dividing line. On the left the devastation continued. Occasional surviving concrete foundations were the only clues houses had ever existed on that side the road. The owners and tenants had moved on, either unable to afford to rebuild or unwilling to do so in this area.

The houses on the right side of the road were

untouched by the tornadoes but had been attacked by another destructive force. Poverty. Although millions of dollars of aid had poured into this region after the storms, these residents didn't qualify to receive any. This was the poorest section of town. In a larger city, this area would have been the slums. And while their group couldn't help those who had lost what little they had to the storms, they could minister to the remaining residents. They'd come to help poverty's forgotten victims.

Sam sat across the aisle from her, behind Pastor Josh, who'd volunteered to be their driver and assistant crew chief for their team. The conversation between the two men was now silenced by the scene surrounding them. She hadn't been able to hear their earlier words over the excited banter of the students, but the warmth between the two was evident in their smiles and relaxed manners. Obviously, Sam hadn't been transparent with Josh on the drive up here.

The brakes softly creaked as the bus inched to a stop before a small, one story, frame house that stood on the corner of the second block. Blue tarps, a flimsy but cost-effective barrier between the weather and the interior of the house, blanketed the roof. Stacks of plywood, shingles, and ladders hinted at the Black Crew's job.

Her stomach rose up into her throat as clamminess covered her body. She could never climb a ladder up onto the roof. Mom, however, would have been all over this. Probably one of the first up and the last down. But the thought of the height made her dizzy. Just one more way the two of them were completely unalike.

Without being directed, the group of eager

teenagers quietly exited the bus and formed a circle, waiting for instructions.

Sam began explaining their job for the week and covering safety rules, but the sound of fear coursing through her ears made it impossible to concentrate on his words.

The people on her right and left reached out and grasped her hands as Josh led them in a prayer. She'd look like such a wimp, but she couldn't do this. Maybe there was a job she could do from the ground. Maybe handing up supplies and tools. There had to be something.

The prayer over, the small circle dissolved as Josh and the young people headed back to the bus to retrieve their supplies and unload the coolers filled with water.

As a warm, familiar hand rested on her shoulder, she fought every impulse to lay her head against it.

"Katherine, I have a favor to ask of you."

When she turned to face Sam, he dropped his hand. Her shoulder ached with remembrance.

"I know this is probably not what you had envisioned, but the owner of the house is an elderly widow, and she's asked if someone in our group would be willing to help her with some chores inside the house. Not very glamorous, I know, but—"

"Yes." The breath she'd been holding suddenly rushed out of her lungs. "Yes, I'd be glad to help her."

The warmth of his eyes drew her in. "Thanks so much. I really appreciate your help. I doubt if any of the high school girls would go for it." A sad smile crossed his face. "But I had a feeling you just might."

He remembered her fear that morning at Balcones Canyon. "Thanks, Sam." She remembered their kiss, her unbounded love for him, the trust. Forever broken.

"Sure. So let's you and I meet..." He paused as he glanced down at the stack of papers on his clipboard. "Naomi Martin."

The small front porch was just large enough to hold two old, wooden ladder-back chairs, their white finishes dotted with gray blotches where the paint had flaked off over the years, now revealing the weathered wood underneath. The different intensities of color hinted at the varying lengths of time the individual spots had been exposed to the Oklahoma elements. The two had obviously been on the porch a long time.

Next to each chair was a terra cotta bowl, painted with brightly colored, glazed flowers. She'd seen similar examples in different sizes, shapes, and colors at the Mercado in San Antonio. Brittle brown sticks protruding from the dirt were the ghosts of the flowers that once bloomed there.

"Ready?"

She was positively ready. She could so do this. "Absolutely."

As Sam glanced her way and smiled, he rapped on the doorframe.

The inner door slowly creaked open, revealing an elderly woman who might be five feet tall on a good day. As she pushed her walker forward into the light, her white hair shone luminescent like new-fallen snow electrified by the morning sun. Her onyx eyes were filled with the sparkle of life. Although no words had yet been exchanged, Katherine liked her immediately.

"Mrs. Martin? Hi, I'm Sam Tucker, and this is Katherine Herrington. We're from Community Shalom."

"Land's sake, young man. I know who you are. I

been waitin' on y'all since they dropped off them shingles and stuff the other day." A bright smile covered her face. "And don't go startin' off on my bad side. Call me Naomi. None of this Mrs. Martin business."

"Yes, ma'am, Naomi." Grinning, Sam inserted a little Texas twang into his response.

Naomi turned her direction. "And you, Miss Katherine, are you gonna be my helper?"

She nodded. "I certainly am, Naomi."

"Well, come on in, sweetie. Let me get my list."

As Naomi turned her walker and stepped back into the house, Katherine glanced over at Sam before following and smiled her gratitude.

He nodded. "Her list. Well, you two will get along just fine."

~*~

How Naomi was sleeping through the incessant noise reverberating throughout the small frame structure was inconceivable. The roof overhead had been creaking with footfalls and vibrating with the syncopated pounding of hammers for the last three hours. Naomi had slipped into her recliner about nine thirty for her "mornin' program" and hadn't made a peep since then.

Katherine reviewed the list one last time. She'd completely straightened and cleaned every drawer and cabinet—inside and out—in the small kitchen. The cardboard box on the table was filled with the items Naomi had listed to be donated to charity—items she never used anymore, that her son and his wife did not want. Now, to clean the house.

Hopefully, Naomi had other lists for the rest of the week, or Katherine would need to downshift a gear or two. If she finished her job in here, she might have to work outside. The thought of having to go up onto the roof nauseated her. Anytime she'd glanced out of the windows this morning and Sam had been off the roof supervising or getting supplies, he'd never been unescorted. An entourage of teenage girls had been right by his side. Having to be in the middle of that might be worse than climbing a ladder up to the roof.

Although it hadn't visited her often, she recognized the little feeling tapping on her shoulder. Jealousy. She had no reason to feel the slightest twinge. She could have had him if she'd wanted. Probably still could. But the betrayal and breakup were too recent, too fresh. The day that her heart would catch up with her mind and she'd no longer love him couldn't come soon enough. Time. She needed more time.

A sudden silence thudded over the house, leaving her ears ringing and head pounding. The only sound in the small house was the theme song for the noon news coming from the television in the living room. She glanced at her phone. Lunchtime.

The clock on the mantel began to strike twelve, and the recliner creaked as Naomi sat up. "My lands, noon already. How's it goin' in there, sugar?" The wheels of the walker squeaked as Naomi shuffled into the kitchen.

"Everything's done in here except the floors." Katherine opened the cabinets one by one, showing their reorganized interiors.

"My lands, girl, you're fast! Everything looks great. Woulda taken me a whole week, and I still couldn't have reached them top cabinets. Don't be workin' yourself to death now."

"I enjoyed it. I'll work on the rest of the list after lunch, and then we'll see what I can do tomorrow."

"Lands, honey, I don't expect you to spend your whole week in here with me. You need to be outside with them other young people. I'm grateful for today."

She would find something to do inside. "We'll figure it out, but right now it's lunch time. Let's go outside and get a sandwich."

A wall of heat met her as they stepped out onto the front porch. The blowing Oklahoma wind burned against her bare arms and face. The temperature on the roof must be tens of degrees hotter than below.

Every inch of shade was covered with knots of teenagers as they sought relief from the blazing noon sun. The two pecan trees were completely ringed. Others huddled under the eaves of the small house, or against the side of the bus as a country song drifted from its radio through the open door and windows.

Katherine got Naomi settled into one of the ladder-back chairs and turned to go get their lunches. She almost fell against him.

"Mind if I join you?" Sam stood on the top step, three boxes stacked on one arm and three bottles of water in the crook of the other.

"Land's sake, Sam. You don't need no invitation. We'd be delighted to have your company."

"Thanks, Naomi." As Sam turned toward Katherine, his eyes spoke the pages his voice did not. "Would you give me a hand here, Katherine?"

The couple of feet between them may as well have been miles. Her heart missed him. Longed for his nearness, his touch. She'd have to wait for the yearning to fade. And it surely would...one day. "Certainly." Katherine took a box and a bottle of water and set them on the empty chair. Then she took another set and helped Naomi get settled.

Sam sat down on the top step.

"So, how're you and the kids doing up there?" Naomi asked.

"Great. Some of them have done this before, so there wasn't as much of a learning curve as I'd figured there'd be. We're right on schedule to be finished in a couple of days, and then that'll give us an extra day to thoroughly tidy up the yard."

Tidy up. He was sitting in front of her right now, but his mind had begun the return to his life in London.

Katherine didn't want to talk. As awkward as his presence was, it allowed her to sit in silence while he entertained Naomi.

As their conversation shifted to Sam's work, the twang of live guitar music accompanied another country song now playing on the radio. Josh and one of the teenage boys had dug their guitars out of the back of the bus and were strumming along. The few minutes of rest and some fuel had apparently revived the kids, and several of the girls had gotten up and were trying to Two Step to the music. Laughter rolled across the front yard at their failed attempts.

"Sam, Katherine, why don't you two show these young people how it's done?" Josh's voice boomed up the sidewalk to the front porch. His eyes sparkled with mischief.

A knot rose in Katherine's throat. She'd never told him, but he knew. And that knowledge confirmed one of the topics of conversation between Sam and Josh on the ride up here from Crescent Bluff. But Sam wouldn't have dared to tell him everything.

Sam made eye contact with her, read her thoughts, and then turned back to the group. "No. I don't think so."

A low chant crept through the group. "Sam, Sam, Sam..." With each syllable, the volume grew.

As his gaze asked again and hers answered, Sam turned back to to the group. "C'mon, guys. Cut it out. Not now." But his words did nothing to dissuade them.

The kids could tell Katherine, the female chaperone, not Sam, was the one who didn't want to dance. This was certainly not the way to change the original stick-in-the-mud impression she'd made.

One of the songs they'd danced to that night at Cattlemen's began to play, and as if she'd lost all control of her body, she stood and held out her hand. "They won't let it go."

"Thanks." As Sam stood in response, a cheer rose up from the kids. "One time, guys. That's all."

His hand was warm as he grasped hers and led her down the steps. When she turned to face him, and he placed his hand high on her back, the pressure of his touch sent electricity surging though her body. They'd danced together enough by now that she no longer had to concentrate on the steps, his hands told her everything she needed to know. She closed her eyes. As they moved and turned, everything disappeared except Sam. She missed his nearness, she missed his touch—she missed him so much.

When the song ended, Sam quickly dipped her and then drew her close. The feeling of home she'd felt the first time he'd held her hand swept over her entire body. She wanted to stay in his embrace forever. She belonged here. Looking deeply into his eyes, she saw regret and wanted to kiss it away and say the words he longed to hear. Cheers and applause rising up from the kids pulled her back to reality. She couldn't. Despite how much her heart told her she belonged here, this could never be her home.

A group of girls gathered around them. The short blonde, Hannah, if Katherine remembered correctly, spoke. "Katherine, you were great! Would you teach us some of the steps?"

Sam dropped her hand and grinned like a proud parent.

"If we have time at the end of the day today or tomorrow, I'd be happy to." She was no longer an outsider. She smiled her appreciation at Sam. "But the most important part is finding a good partner."

~*~

The afternoon sped by. The pounding on the roof had stopped. The group packed tools in the back of the bus and stacked large pieces of debris by the road for pick up later this week. Any Two Step lessons would have to wait until tomorrow.

The rest of Naomi's house had been cleaned from top to bottom, and although the list was completed, Katherine had an idea for tomorrow. "Naomi, unless you have something else you'd like me to do tomorrow, I thought I'd repaint the chairs on your front porch and plant some flowers in the pots."

Josh was already planning a trip to the local hardware store for some supplies. He wouldn't mind adding a few items to the list.

"As I said earlier, I don't want to take up all your time. Plus, I think them girls out there are expecting some dancing lessons." She smiled and winked. "But it would be nice to have that porch prettied up some."

"It shouldn't take me all day, so I'll have time to show them a few steps either at lunch or at the end of the day tomorrow."

"You and Sam, right?" Her onyx eyes sparkled. "I didn't know you two was an item."

"We're not an item, Naomi. Just friends." A more transparent reply would have substituted the words "no longer" in the place of "not."

"Uh-huh. Well, tell that to Mr. Sam. That boy's sweet on you. I seen it in his eyes. You can't tell me you don't see it, too."

She did more than see it. Just a glance from him filled her with a longing she'd never felt before him. "Sam's been visiting his aunt in Crescent Bluff over the last few months. We've dated a bit, but we're just friends. Really. He's flying home to London right after we return, and I'm headed back to Dallas."

The wheels on Naomi's walker squeaked as she shuffled over to the bookshelf beside the fireplace and picked up a black and white picture of a bride and a groom. Katherine had noticed it when she'd dusted the shelves earlier. Naomi's wedding picture.

She held it out to Katherine. "This was my Harold. Nary a more patient man walked this earth." As her fingers traced the faded image through the glass, she chuckled. "This man done asked me to marry him after our first date. I knew then he was crazy as a loon, and I turned him down straight away 'cause he wasn't the man o' my dreams. Turns out, he was so much more."

Naomi smiled as she gently placed the picture back on the shelf. "Now I can't imagine my life without him. That man loved me, and I loved him. Not with that fluffy love on them soap operas, but the kind of love that's weathered the storms and come out stronger." She grasped Katherine's hand. "Sometimes we can spend a heap of our years lookin' so hard for Mr. Perfect that we miss Mr. Right even though he's standing smack-dab in front of us. I almost missed my chance. Don't be mule-headed and miss yours."

27

Jen had been right. Katherine had fallen asleep seconds after her head hit the pillow last night, and she hadn't heard any sounds the girls had made after that. She silently pulled on some clothes, tiptoed through the maze of sleeping bags, and then walked down the hall to the cafeteria for some alone time before this second day started.

She filled the largest cup she could find with coffee and headed toward the courtyard. She'd always loved this time of day when the sun slowly revealed creation and everything was fresh and new. No amount of extra sleep was worth sacrificing the dawn of a new day. Holding the cup in one hand and her notebook and Bible in the other, she turned backward and managed to push open one of the glass doors onto the patio.

She placed her coffee and books onto the same table as yesterday and faced west, waiting for the sun to rise over her shoulder and awaken the landscape. An all too familiar bass voice sounded softly behind her. "Good morning."

Obviously, the solitude she sought wasn't on this morning's schedule. Going back inside now would be mean and hurtful, so she turned toward the table in the corner behind her and plastered on a polite, if not heartfelt, smile.

Sam sat at the table in the predawn gray morning. He'd watched her come out onto the patio and never made a sound. Maybe he'd hoped she'd go back in, or maybe he'd hoped she'd never notice him. No, that was ridiculous. He wouldn't have spoken if that were the case. "Good morning."

A book was spread open on the table in front of him. Not a book. Well yes, it was a book. The book. A Bible. She'd never seen him reading the Bible before. "What are you doing out here so early this morning?"

"Thinking. I couldn't sleep."

An uncharacteristic silence followed. She'd seen him at a loss for words only once—the long minutes between the time he'd proposed and told her the truth about his past and the time when she'd later closed the kitchen door, leaving him standing in silence on the driveway. "Thinking about what?"

Even though his voice was steady, his eyes glistened in the dim, predawn light. Tears. She'd never seen him cry. Hadn't even thought he was the type of guy who would. He was always so upbeat and playful. So in control.

"Nothing that would interest you." Quiet anger punctuated his words.

"Oh." She turned away.

"Wait, Katherine. I'm sorry. I didn't mean that the way it sounded. I'm just upset. I've been lied to."

She certainly knew all about that. And as momentarily satisfying as it might have been to point it out right now, she would have regretted it the second after the words were out of her mouth. She couldn't treat someone she loved like that. She turned back and waited.

"All these years, I've believed the lie that I could

run my life and have everything turn out just the way I wanted if I worked hard enough at it. But look where it's gotten me." He rested his head in his hands.

No matter how much he'd disappointed her, she still loved him. Nothing he could do would change that. Slowly, she stood and walked over to his table, and then sat down on the bench beside him. She placed one arm loosely around his waist and fought hard to keep from leaning her head on his shoulder.

"I've messed things up royally, and the one thing I wanted more than anything else in life, I can't have."

She could point out to him that the choices people made had consequences, but she wouldn't. He knew that. "I'm sorry, Sam. Sorry for both of us."

"I'm tired, and I'm done." He pulled away, picked up the Bible, and then stood. "I'm sure you wanted some time alone and didn't intend to begin your day like this. I'll see you on the bus."

Although her heart wanted to ask him to stay forever, the best thing to do was let him go. He'd be gone for good in a few days, and life would return to normal.

~*~

The bus ride had been different today. The shock from the first time seeing the desolation had been dulled, and excited chatter among the kids replaced yesterday's awed silence as they approached Naomi's house. Their work was making a difference.

Sam sat behind Josh as he drove the bus. Unlike yesterday, no friendly conversation passed between the two. Sam was not himself. Even if she hadn't seen him on the patio early this morning, his unusual quietness would have told her something was wrong.

As the bus pulled to a stop, Sam flipped some sort of an internal switch and was suddenly "on." He came to life, joking with the kids and barking out instructions about who should carry what and where the items should be put.

As Katherine picked up the shopping bags full of the sandpaper and white spray paint Josh had gotten last night, one of the boys carried a flat of portulaca from the back of the bus to the front porch. Painting and planting should keep her busy and off the roof for at least one more day. She'd worry about tomorrow later.

The kids set up ladders and got ready to climb up onto the roof.

Katherine knocked on the front door.

A quiet voice from inside answered, "Come on in."

The delicious aroma of fresh-baked chocolate chip cookies greeted Katherine as she stepped inside the small house. Suddenly she was sitting at the kitchen island at home and having a discussion with Dad about "James Bond" and his car. That night she could have never known the turns her life would take over the next few months. That in such a short time she would find—and then lose—Her One.

Blue and white striped linen dish towels spread across the table covered Naomi's handiwork.

"My goodness, Naomi, you've been busy."

"It ain't much, but I had to do something to thank them kids for all their hard work."

Katherine followed as Naomi pushed her walker over to the small desk in the corner of the living room.

"I was wonderin' if you'd bag 'em up for me so I could give 'em to the kids."

"I'd love to." She could work on the front porch later today. Every extra project Naomi gave her only ensured she'd have to spend less, if any, time on the roof.

Naomi opened the drawer and handed Katherine scissors, notecards, a marker set, and a hole punch. "The yarn and little sandwich bags is on the table. There should be enough for all the kids and adults to have three each."

"Naomi, you were so sweet to do this. I'm sure they'll all love them." Katherine sat down at the table.

"I'd have written the cards myself, you know, but my writin's gotten kinda shaky."

"I'm very happy to help."

"Would ya write this on one side of the card, and then sign my name on the other? 'God loves you with an everlasting love.'"

Katherine recognized the words. They were a paraphrase of a Bible verse she'd read hundreds of times in her life. "That's a really nice sentiment, Naomi."

"It ain't no sentiment, honey. It's truth." She scooted her walker toward the living room. "Well, I believe it's about time for my mornin' program."

From the living room drifted excited banter between the host and contestants on some TV game show.

Katherine couldn't help but grin. If yesterday was an example, Naomi would be asleep in minutes and probably have no idea what happened on her "mornin' program."

The pounding on the roof set in as Katherine

began to write the "truth" on one side of each card and Naomi's name on the other.

~*~

Katherine had remembered a basket in one of the upper cabinets and had arranged the bags of cookies in it for Naomi to present to the kids at lunch break. The remaining time this morning had been spent cleaning the refrigerator and oven. After lunch, she'd take on the porch chairs and plant the flowers Josh had bought.

A sudden silence fell over the house, the music for the noon news began, and Naomi's recliner creaked. "My lands, is it lunchtime already?"

A soft rap sounded on the door, and for some irrational reason Katherine's breathing caught at the anticipation of seeing Sam holding their boxed lunches. "Yes, it is."

As she picked up the basket full of cookies and opened the door, her heart fell.

Hannah and three other girls smiled up at her, lunches in hand. "Can we have our dance lesson after lunch? Please, Katherine?"

Looking over their heads, Katherine quickly surveyed the front yard. Sam was nowhere to be found. Not under the trees, not under the eaves of the house, and not sitting in the small strip of shade beside the bus. She covered her disappointment with a smile. "Sure. Where's Sam?"

"On the bus with Pastor Josh," a red-haired girl—Grace, Katherine was pretty sure—answered. "They're having some sort of a meeting. But he said they'd be done in time for the dance lessons if you wanted help."

Sure enough, Katherine could barely make out two silhouettes through the noon glare on the bus windows.

The bus started up, its radio once again providing both the dining and dancing music.

~*~

Josh stood and placed a hand on Sam's shoulder. "Let me know if you have any questions or want to talk about anything else."

"Thanks, Josh." As the pastor stepped off the bus, Sam finished the last bites of his sandwich. Josh had certainly given him a lot to think about. Maybe he was right. Maybe it was time to make some changes. Since he'd been a kid, his success had depended upon how hard he worked—his investment of time and effort. If he failed, he had no one else to blame. If he succeeded, he had no one else to thank. It was all about him.

And therein was the lie. Even though he'd believed the contrary, life wasn't all about him—his needs and his wants. The two had gotten so blurred over the past several years. So much of what he'd wanted had, in his mind, become needs, and he'd done everything he could to satisfy those desires...only now to come up lacking, empty. In the world of soccer, he was a success. In real life, a failure. And only one question remained. What would he do about it?

Four of the girls had lined up in the front yard, and Katherine was demonstrating the basic "quick, quick, slow...slow" sequence of steps. The girls all had their hands up encircling the empty air in front of them and moving backward around the yard. Despite their lack of partners, they'd all picked up the basic steps pretty quickly.

The dancing. That had been all about him, too. He'd learned in high school that girls liked guys who danced. They didn't even have to be good. They just needed to be willing to get out there and move to the music and keep them company. But, as usual, he'd wanted to be good—not necessarily the best, but good enough not to embarrass himself, and to stand out to the women. So, he'd taken ballroom dancing. Most of the steps weren't any more intricate than soccer drills. He just did them in street shoes instead of cleats.

No matter how he'd tried to present it, the real reason he'd spent all that time and money with Juanita hadn't been for Katherine, but for him. He'd never have done it if he hadn't thought he'd get something out of it. Winning her heart had been his ultimate goal. So just like everything else, that night had been all about him, too.

Yet, at some point in their relationship, something changed. He'd won her heart, and she would have accepted his proposal. He could have had what he came back to Crescent Bluff to get, but an unfamiliar Voice had urged him to say the words, to tell her the truth that might end their relationship. And he did. And it had.

If he'd only been honest with her the very first time she'd seen the ring on his keychain, she might not have felt deceived. She would have been upset, but she also might not have thought he'd lied to her and would have forgiven him. But he hadn't, and she hadn't.

And as much as it had hurt, still did hurt, and would always hurt, a sense of peace had begun to fill his heart. He'd loved her enough to set aside his own desires to do the right thing. That one act had been all about her. He would not have been worthy to receive the trust she would have placed in him had she accepted his proposal without knowing the truth.

Laughter floated into the bus through the open door and windows. The girls were giggling. Two of them had gotten tangled up and were now on the ground. The next steps were more difficult without a partner, and they were struggling. Katherine was trying, but some things were better taught by demonstration.

Sam stood and stepped off the bus. "All right, guys. I want to see some of you man up and help the ladies over here." As he made his way across the yard to the girls, four guys actually got up and followed. That was easier than he'd figured. "OK, Katherine, tell us what to do." This was another thing he'd do for her.

28

Like one of those songs that invades the mind so that one can't help but sing it all day long, the words she'd written on fifteen notecards this morning had haunted her all day.

God loves you with an everlasting love.

They'd been on her mind when she'd handed out Naomi's cookies, when she'd sanded and painted the chairs on the porch, and then when she'd planted the portulaca in the rainbow clay pots. Today certainly wasn't the first time she'd heard or read them. But today was the first time they'd ever filled her heart and soul so much she could think of nothing else.

As Jen dropped down onto Katherine's sleeping bag, the classroom suddenly came back into focus. The girls were scurrying around getting ready for the evening service. "You're quiet. You barely spoke at dinner."

"Sorry if I seemed distant. I've just got a lot on my mind."

"I told you this trip would change you." Jen smiled. "We've got a few minutes before we have to be in the auditorium. Why don't you find a quiet spot and just sit?"

Jen was the perfect chaperone. Katherine now understood why Mom had liked her so much. She was warm and compassionate. She had a great sense of humor and a quick, hearty laugh that filled the room and made people join right in—even if they had no idea what she was laughing about. But blink an eye, and she could be all business. The girls loved her and responded well to her fun-loving, yet straightforward, personality.

"I hate to not be available in case y'all need help with the girls."

"Don't you worry. We'll be fine. We can get them down to the auditorium."

The sun would be setting about now. "Thanks, Jen. I'll see you at the service." She headed toward her spot at this Oklahoma high school, slipped out of the cafeteria doors, and sat down at her table.

A storm was on its way, but it wasn't here quite yet. The skies that were blue only an hour ago were now filled with dark gray clouds, heavy with rain. Oklahoma weather was just like Texas weather. Wait five minutes, and it would change. Hopefully, the storm would move out as fast as it had moved in so they could get back to work tomorrow.

A heavy wind blew against her back.

I have loved you with an everlasting love.

The words resonated so loudly in her heart that she jumped. Everlasting love—having no ending. Lasting forever. As many times as she'd read this verse, her mind had comprehended the meaning, but her heart had never really grasped its truth.

Her Father loved her. He had loved her before she'd been born, even before the creation of the universe. His love kept no record of her wrongs. He loved her in spite of what she did or didn't do. She'd done nothing to earn His love, and she could do nothing to lose it.

Her Father was Love, and His love for her would never be withdrawn. It was everlasting, eternal. Unconditional, infinite.

And that's what He was asking her to do. Give the gift she'd been given but had never had to ask for, the gift she'd never had to earn. He was asking her to love with an everlasting love.

The wind gusted again, bringing with it the earthy smell of the impending thunderstorm. She lifted her face and let the sprinkle of raindrops wash away her tears. How could she so selfishly withhold the gift she'd been so generously given? *Forgive me, Father.*

She had to find Sam and ask his forgiveness. Now. Before the service began. She could not wait a minute longer.

Music from the band in the auditorium greeted her as she stepped back into the cafeteria. She jogged down the hall and stood in the doorway. Their group was about two thirds of the way back in the center section, just where they'd been the last two nights. The kids and the other female chaperones were all there, but none of the men. No Josh, no Brad, and no Sam. She'd wait in the hallway a few more minutes and then, if none of them showed up, she'd break the rules. She'd head over to the men's wing and find him.

The band began the second song. Maybe something was wrong. Sam had been really quiet today—certainly not himself. He'd been upset this morning, and then his dancing had been robotic, spiritless. The passion she loved so much had been nonexistent today. She'd waited long enough. They should have been here by now.

She walked toward the male wing of the school,

inched open one of the double doors, and slipped into forbidden territory. The hallway was dark, the only illumination being the red exit signs overhead and rectangles of light on the floor from some of the small windows in two of the classroom doors.

Pressing herself close to the wall, she crept down the hall, dodging in and out of recesses and doorways. The pounding of her heart shook her chest. Katherine, the rule-follower, the non-daredevil had abdicated her throne, and a complete stranger had taken over.

This maneuver wasn't well-planned. She didn't even know what room the guys were in, so how was she supposed to find them? And what if she got caught?

Around the corner a door slammed, followed by the low rumble of male voices. When she'd first stepped into the men's wing, she should have yelled, "Woman on the hall," but she hadn't, and now it was too late. Quickly she ducked into a doorway, pushed herself flat against the side wall, and held her breath. By now the entire school must be able to hear her heart pounding.

The silhouettes of two men heading in the direction of the auditorium passed by her. Neither of them was Josh, Brad, or Sam. Something was definitely wrong. Otherwise, Josh and Brad would never miss the worship service.

When the door into the main hallway closed, she peaked out from the alcove. Only one square of light shown on the hallway floor. It was from the window in the door three classrooms down on the right. That had to be their room. Crossing the hallway, she tiptoed toward the door and pressed herself against the wall beside it. On the count of three, she'd peek. One, two, three.

She slipped in front of the door, and as she glanced into the window, her feet froze to the floor. It was their room, all right, and all three of them were on their knees praying. Sam was in the middle between Josh and Brad, and each of them had a hand on his shoulder. Her hand involuntarily rose to cover her mouth.

The reverence of the picture before her brought back the evening's earlier tears. Had she stayed in the auditorium, had she not broken the rules, she would have missed this moment. Even now, one part of her felt like an intruder and respect encouraged her to turn away from this intimate scene, while another part was honored to be present to watch the man who had captured her heart make such a life-changing commitment.

She slipped back away from the door and tiptoed down the hall and back into the common area. She'd wait for him outside the auditorium doors.

The band transitioned to another song. Probably the last before the beginning of the sermon. She stood in the shadow across the hall from the auditorium doors. Josh was the first through the doors, then Brad, and finally Sam. Their conversation was punctuated with quiet laughter.

She stepped forward to reveal herself. "Hi, Sam."

The laughter died as the three stared at her.

Josh grinned and then spoke. "Brad and I'll save you a seat, Sam. Go on."

She and her love were left alone in the middle of the hall.

"Katherine, are you OK?" Sam's eyes were warm.

"Can we talk?" This wasn't the most private place.

Soft light shone through the glass doors of the library behind them. "In here." She led him to a reading nook filled with two chairs and a sofa, and then turned to face him.

He stood about ten feet away. "Shoot, Katherine."

She tried, but no words came. Only tears.

"Beth, what is it?"

"I need you over here beside me...please." As she held out her hand, he closed the gap between them. "Hold me, Sam." If her heart pounded any harder, it might burst.

He drew her close and encircled her with his arms. Then he rested his head on top of hers. She was back in their cave. He voiced no questions but stood silent, waiting.

Her voice cracked, transforming her words into a painful whisper. "Forgive me Sam, please forgive me."

"Beth, there's nothing—"

"Yes, there is. Please forgive me for being so self-righteous." She drew back and looked up into his eyes. "Please, Sam."

"Of course, I forgive you."

She placed her head against his chest as they stood still for a few quiet seconds. After all these years she'd found him, the man she wanted to be Her One. He was different than she had pictured, but he was so much more than she could have ever imagined. Slowly she drew away and dropped down onto one knee.

"Beth, please don't."

Her heart was racing. Butterflies filled her stomach. She loved him more than she could have ever thought possible to love another person, and she had to tell him. "Samuel Houston Tucker, you are The One I want to walk through the rest of my life with, and I pledge to love you with an everlasting love. Will you marry me?"

The ponderous silence only intensified the roaring of the blood rushing through her ears. Something was terribly wrong.

He took her hand, helped her up, and pulled her close. "Dance with me?" They began swaying to some imaginary melody only he could hear. "I can't put into words how much I love you, Beth. Don't ever doubt it. But I can't marry you."

Her feet were concrete, holding her rock still. He stopped swaying and tightened his embrace until she fought to breathe.

His breath was warm against her cheek. "Please listen carefully. I realize now that I thought marrying you would bring me happiness. And that would have been a terribly unfair burden to place on you. You would have failed. Not because you didn't try or we didn't love each other, but because my happiness is not your responsibility. True peace and joy come from only one place."

She struggled to push away, but he held her tight.

"Do you understand what I'm saying?"

She understood, all right. "You're saying no."

"No, Katherine. No, I'm not. I'm just not saying, yes."

"It's the same thing." As she wriggled free, he held her hand tightly.

"No, it's not. Katherine, I—"

His words were cut short as the lights flickered and an ominous thunderclap reverberated. The weather alert tone shrieked from his phone.

Josh burst through the doors. "Sam, come quick. There's a storm. We have to secure the roof of Naomi's house."

29

The quiet, but persistent, tapping on the classroom door didn't wake her because Katherine had yet to fall asleep. After Josh and Sam left, she had run to help the other chaperones move the students to sit in the hallways to wait out the storm. They'd had storm drills like this all through school, but this was the first time it hadn't been simply for practice. No tornado had materialized. Only lots of rain, lightning, and wind.

She jumped up quickly and tiptoed to the door before any of the girls awoke.

Josh stood alone in the hall. His hair and clothes were disheveled. Although his unreadable pastor face didn't give her a hint, something had to be wrong.

"I was hoping you'd be the one who answered the door."

Her heart rose into her throat. "What's wrong? Is it Sam?"

The door behind her opened again, and out stepped Cassie. They'd hardly seen each other the past few days. They were on different work crews, and during their downtime, Katherine had avoided hovering over her so Cassie could have the freedom to enjoy the trip without her big sister intruding—although Cassie didn't normally care about Katherine's opinion, so she probably wouldn't start now.

Cassie's voice was hoarse from sleep. "I heard you go out. What's up?"

"He's OK. He's in the hospital." Josh placed a hand on Katherine's arm. She could hardly breathe.

"Who?" Cassie was wide awake now.

"Can I go see him?" Tears burned Katherine's eyes.

"See who?"

Josh turned toward Cassie. "Sam."

"Sam?" Cassie pulled Katherine close. "What happened?"

Josh turned back to Katherine. "He's pretty banged up, but all in all, he's OK. Everything except his knee. We were on the roof of Naomi's house, checking to make sure the tarps were fastened securely, when the worst part of the storm hit. A huge gust of wind broke a branch off one of the trees in the front yard. It fell onto the roof and knocked Sam to the ground. His knee took the brunt of the landing. They did surgery, but I haven't heard the outcome. As soon as Sam was in recovery, I left to come get you."

~*~

The room was dimly lit and quiet except for the occasional droning and beeping of the blood pressure machine.

Brad stood and pulled her into a hug. "They moved him in here about ten minutes ago. The nurse said the doctor would be here soon to talk to us."

She nodded and made her way to his bedside. His face was peaceful as if he were simply sleeping. At least, that might be what he'd look like. She'd never seen him asleep. But the oxygen tubing beneath his nose was one clue it was more than a normal night's rest. The other was his leg. It was elevated, and his knee was bandaged in white gauze until it was at least twice its normal size.

The evening's earlier urgency to apologize rushed back into her heart. Tonight could have been a tragedy. She could have lost him. A tear dropped onto the metal side rail of the bed before she was able to wipe it from her cheek.

As the door to the room swished open, a tall man in blue surgical scrubs walked in. "Hello, I'm Dr. Andrews." He shook their hands and smiled. "There's a lucky guy laying in that bed. He took quite a fall, but he'll be just fine."

Luck had nothing to do with it. Sam was safe because of God and nothing else. Still, that he was OK was all she needed to know. He was OK. As the doctor answered Brad's questions and described the procedures, she turned back toward Sam. If only she could climb into the bed and snuggle beside him, kiss his cheek, and whisper that everything would be fine.

Reaching over the rail, she caressed the fingertips of his right hand and then traced the veins on the back of it. The hand she'd held so often. The one that had pulled her close when they were dancing, that had gripped hers when he'd made her shift his car after their first trip to the Dairy Delite.

She brushed the back of her hand against the chestnut stubble on his face—his camouflage to age him for this trip—and suddenly they were back on the outcropping over the Balcones Canyon watching the sunrise, his early morning whiskers prickling her face as he kissed her in the golden dawn.

Then as she ran her fingers through the blond silk covering his head, her mouth curved into an involuntary smile. He wasn't bald.

Suddenly the doctor's answer to Brad's question knifed its way into her thoughts. "Soccer? I can't imagine he'll ever play again. That knee's been through too much."

This loss would be devastating to him. Soccer was not only his profession, but it was so much of the person he was. It had been his world, his universe, for most of his life. As tears crept back into her eyes, she lifted his hand and kissed the back of it.

His eyes fluttered open and a soft smile warmed his face. "Hello."

She entwined her fingers with his as relief rushed through her entire body. "Hi, Sam."

He knit his eyebrows together. "Do I know you? 'Cause if I don't, I want to." His words were slow and childlike.

Dr. Andrews stepped over beside her. "That's the meds talking. He might be a little loopy for a while."

"Uh-oh. A doctor. This can't be good." Sam held on to her hand.

"I'm Dr. Andrews, Sam. Everything will be fine. I'll be back to check on you in a couple of hours."

"By-eee. See you later, alligator."

As the doctor left the room, Sam turned his attention back to her. "He didn't even say, 'After a while crocodile.' So what's your name?"

He was so cute when he was confused. "It's Katherine, Sam."

"Wait...Katherine...Are you sure I don't know you?"

Brad chuckled as he stepped up beside her. "Hey,

buddy."

"Brad. Great to see you, man. What are you doing here?"

Before Brad could answer, Sam had moved on. "She's not your girl, is she?" He was talking about her as if she wasn't even in the room.

"No, Sam. She's yours."

Sam's eyes flew open wide. "Mine? Are you joking?" Grinning, he turned his attention back to Katherine. "You're my girlfriend? Really? You wouldn't kid me, would you? Really? I'm the luckiest guy in the world."The smile vanished as quickly as it had appeared. "So, why aren't we married? If you're my girlfriend and I'm your boyfriend and we love each other, we should be married, right?"

If only things were that simple. She opened her mouth to answer, but his monologue trailed on.

"We do love each other, right?"

"Yes, we do."

"You're my girlfriend. I'm your boyfriend. We love each other. Then why aren't we married? Wait. Have I been an idiot? Is it because I haven't asked you? 'Cause if that's the reason, I can ask you right now."

Lying would be the easiest response. She could say they were engaged. After all, he had asked her. And if she hadn't been so self-righteous, they would be now. She'd tried to make things right and asked him, hoping he'd accept. But he hadn't. And no matter what she said in this moment, as the drugs wore off he'd remember the truth. "No. You've asked me."

His eyes blinked slowly, confusion clouding his face. "So, why aren't we married?"

"We love each other very much, but it's complicated." As she brushed his hair back from his brow, his eyes fluttered closed. Leaning over the rail, she kissed him on his forehead and then whispered the truth her heart must someday come to believe. "And no matter what we feel, no matter how long we've waited for each other, some things in life are simply not meant to be."

Carol James

30

The wooden runners creaked with the even cadence of a ticking clock as Katherine pushed the rocking chair back and forth on the sidewalk in front of Cattlemen's Hotel. These past weeks had gone by unbelievably fast. Summers had seemed so much longer when she was in school.

Dad dropped down into the chair beside hers and matched her rhythm. "Nice night, huh?"

Because Cassie and Sam still occasionally texted, he knew what tonight was just as well as she did.

He reached out and patted her hand. "Baby Girl, maybe in a few months you should go visit that college friend of yours over in London."

"I don't know. We'll see. Maybe it's time to move on and see what's around the bend."

Cassie burst through the hotel doors onto the sidewalk and struck a pose. "What do you guys think?"

She was total cowgirl—boots, tight denims, an old-fashioned, calico western shirt complete with fringe and pearl snap buttons, all topped off with a straw cowboy hat.

Dad grinned as he spoke. "I think you'll have to be careful, or they just might throw you onto a horse and ask you to run barrels."

"What do you think, Beth?"

"You look great, Cassie. Absolutely perfect."

Cassie smiled. "Thanks. You sure you won't come to the rodeo with us? I don't want you to be alone."

"I'll be fine, Cassie, really." Their relationship had come so far this summer. "I'll sit here and people-watch for a while, and then I'll probably go over to the restaurant across the street for dinner. The clerk at the front desk said they have western dancing on Saturday nights, and I think it'd be fun to watch."

Dad leaned over and kissed her on the forehead. "From one fellow introvert to another, enjoy the alone time." He smiled, and he and Cassie turned and walked down the sidewalk toward the rodeo complex.

The street was washed in peaceful gray as the sun slipped behind the buildings and evening approached. For the first time in her adult life, her heart was at peace. No agenda, no notebooks, no lists. For as long as she could remember, she'd been living in the future, always planning and dreaming about what would be instead of enjoying what was. For years, life in the present had passed her by.

She'd spent her days waiting, dreaming, making entries on lists, marking through entries on lists. And how people spent their days was how they spent their life. Once a moment was gone, it couldn't be gotten back.

Losing Mom and meeting Sam had taught her that.

The last weeks had been hard, but good. Cassie hadn't spoken to her for days after Sam left for rehab in Dallas. Yet sisterhood had eventually won out, and Cassie had forgiven her. Life was too short for agendas and grudges. For waiting and not doing.

Sam's words at that Oklahoma high school had run and rerun through her mind many times since they'd returned from the mission trip. Like his, her happiness would not be found in another person or in checking off entries on a list. What she had been seeking all these years through accomplishments, through jobs, and relationships had been right in front of her all the time, waiting for her to reach out and take it. But her "busyness" had obscured it.

Only in being still had she been able to see. True contentment and peace flowed from only one source. And no matter what direction her life was to take, she would learn to be content, because she finally understood the origin of true contentment. *Thank You, Father.*

And whatever the future held for Sam, her prayer was that he would find the same measure of contentment. And a still, small Voice deep inside suggested he would.

She loved him. She always would on some level. And while she would have been, and would still be, happy to be his wife, she was learning she could be content without him. But being the student was oftentimes difficult, and contentment didn't come by flipping a switch. Growing in contentment was a process, and many days she failed as often as she succeeded. Yet with the passing of each moment, feeling at peace with her situation became easier. Would she be happier being married? Maybe. But life wasn't all about her happiness.

Above all else, she knew one thing. Whatever road God placed before her would lead to one destination if she let it. True contentment and peace. He loved her with an everlasting, unconditional love.

As she lifted her eyes toward the sky, a small metallic glint flashed off a plane high above. Sam was flying back to London this evening. Maybe that flight was his. Maybe that plane was headed for Heathrow, and he was on it. *God bless, my love.*

The melancholy sound of a steel guitar floated across the road from the restaurant. She stood as its moaning melody beckoned to her. If she went on now, she'd have plenty of time to eat and then return to the hotel room and soak in the tub before Dad and Cassie returned.

The restaurant was packed with Saturday night patrons. Following the hostess to a tiny table in the corner, she wove her way between the couples on the dance floor. Some of them were good. But most of them were not any better than she and Sam had been. As Juanita has proclaimed, they were the perfect couple. She'd probably never find another partner like him. But then, she wasn't exactly looking anymore.

Watching the couples move and twirl around the floor birthed an empty sweetness within her. The sweetness of his playful spirit, his excitement with living, his tenderness toward her feelings. The emptiness that he was gone and no longer a part of her life. She would carry these emotions deep in her heart forever.

"Excuse me, ma'am." From out of nowhere a tall cowboy had materialized.

She shook off her memories and moved back into the present.

"I was wonderin' if you'd like to dance."

Her first impulse was to decline, just as she would have done before Sam. But a new woman was sitting in her chair. The one who was no longer a spectator to life—the one who was no longer simply waiting. "Thank you. I think I'd enjoy that."

She followed him to the dance floor, and then he turned and offered her his hand. "I'm Rusty."

"I'm Kath—Katy Beth, Rusty. Nice to meet you."

The band began the next song, the loudness of the music making any attempt at conversation fruitless. As her right hand grasped his left, and then she rested the fingertips of her left hand on his shoulder, he placed his free hand against her back, and they began.

At first, they simply scooted around the dance floor, and then his hands told her he was going to lead her into a turn. As she came out of the turn, she looked into his face and he smiled, but it wasn't right.

The fault, though, was not his. He was a good enough dancer, but dancing with him was just all wrong. She closed her eyes. He was too tall. Her arms were reaching uncomfortably upward. His hand was large and calloused, imprisoning hers. And he was wearing Clark's cologne.

As the music ended, they dropped hands and, following the lead of the other dancers, clapped for the band. "Thank you, Katy Beth. How about another?"

"Maybe later, Rusty." She didn't mean that. "You're a wonderful dancer, but I think I'll get something to eat. I'm starving." She didn't really mean that, either.

"Thank you, ma'am." He tipped his hat and sauntered back to join his friends at the bar.

She sat back down at her table and leafed through the menu. She wasn't hungry enough to order a big meal, and she sure wasn't in the mood to read all the pages of the gastronomic encyclopedia. Surely, they had some sort of grilled chicken salad and iced tea. She placed the menu into the chrome holder on the back of her table. Her gaze fell on the last page, and she changed her mind. Forget the tea.

"Are you ready to order?" A young woman who couldn't have been much older than Cassie smiled and held her pen in the ready position.

~*~

By the beginning of the third dance, her food came. Rusty certainly hadn't been mourning her loss. He'd been dancing the whole time.

The salad looked delicious, but the float looked even more so. She took a sip. It was almost as good as the ones from Dairy Delite. Before she could take another taste, her memories ambushed her, and her eyes filled. Not with tears of sadness, but with tears of gratitude for having known him, however brief the time. *Thank You, Father.*

Although she may never completely understand the purpose of their meeting again, their falling in love, and their going back to their separate lives, she would always be grateful it had happened. Knowing Sam had changed her, had pulled her out of the mire of routine and freed her to move on with life. Maybe one of these days she'd be able to thank him.

The verse about God working all things for good for those who love Him filled her heart. Good would come from this. It already had. And it was time for her, as she'd told Dad, to see what was on down the road.

In everything that had happened this summer, she had only one regret. She hadn't seen Sam since that night in the hospital in Oklahoma because they'd taken him to Dallas by ambulance the next day. She could have driven up to visit him over these past few weeks, but she hadn't. She'd needed some time to process her feelings. And now that she was in a place where she was ready to see him, he'd already left.

A tear tracked down her cheek and dropped onto the table. Even though she was content, she could still have regrets.

Dad might be right. Maybe she should plan a trip to London in the near future. More than anything, she wanted to see him one more time, to know he truly was OK, to confirm he had accepted the apology she'd made that night in Oklahoma—and above all that he had really forgiven her.

The fragrance of an ocean breeze overcame her before she realized anyone was there. As she looked upward into the Caribbean eyes she loved, she tried to speak his name, but no sound would come.

"Hi, Katherine." His voice was soft, his tone tenuous, unsure.

She quickly wiped her eyes and was barely able to muster enough breath to whisper. "Hi, Sam."

"Is this chair taken?"

As she shook her head, he sat down across from her.

"How did you know...?"

"Cassie."

She should have known. "So, I thought you were flying back to London tonight."

"How did you...?"

"Cassie." She'd missed his grin.

"I am, but I changed it to a later flight."

"I hope everything's OK."

"I just had some unfinished business to take care

of."

Her heart began to race. "You did?"

"Yeah. Seems you reneged on a bet I won at Balcones. I beat you downstairs that morning, remember? You owe me a root beer float."

She held her hand up and motioned for her server. "Please bring him a float."

"Yeah, and you can put it on her ticket." His eyes twinkled as he grinned. "She's buying."

"So what's new with you?" She was sitting across from the man she loved, the man who would always be Her One, and she couldn't think of anything better to say?

He didn't answer her question. "Did you ever get your job back?"

"Clark wasn't able to hire me as a permanent employee. I'm doing contract work for him, and I really like the flexibility. I can work from home most of the time, so that allows me to help my dad and be there for Cassie when he travels. I'll probably look for something else in a while. But then, maybe not. We'll see what's ahead."

The waitress set his float on the table. "Thank you, miss." He spooned some of it into his mouth.

"So what about you? Anything new?"

"Lots." He pushed the float aside and looked into the depths of her soul. "I can't play professional football anymore. My knee won't take it."

Before she could stop herself, she rested her hand on his. Her eyes searched his for some hint of devastation. Soccer had been the focus of his entire life. "Oh, Sam. I'm so sorry."

"It's OK. I've had a lot of time to think the last few weeks in Dallas, and I'm at peace with it. I got to live my dream for almost ten years, which is more than many people get. Besides, I'm not the same man I was even a few months ago, and I don't want the same things any more." He placed his free hand on top of hers. "Everything works together for a reason."

He was paraphrasing the Bible verse she'd called to mind earlier. "What will you do?"

"That's what's so great. They've asked me to stay on with the organization and do some scouting and recruiting. I'll be traveling all over, but the best thing is, I can live wherever I choose. They said I don't have to live in the UK unless I want."

So he could stay here in the States, but he was going back to London anyway. He took another spoon of his float, and just as that first night at Dairy Delite a small dot of foam remained on his upper lip. Then she'd wondered what kind of a kisser he was. Tonight, she knew. Passion burned through her whole body as she fought with her entire being the urge to lean over and kiss the sweetness away. Instead, she gently blotted it with a napkin.

Reaching up, he grasped her hand. "I do have one other bit of unfinished business."

The desire for him to ask her to go with him sprang from the deepest well of her heart. Her breathing quickened as she ached to hear the words.

"I want to thank you. You, your family, Brad and Josh, you've all helped me learn what life's really about. I was so wrong for so many years. Knowing you has changed me, and I will be forever grateful. I just had to tell you before I left."

The band began one of the songs they'd danced to in the Longhorn Suite that night with Juanita. He stood and offered his hand. "How about one more time before I go? Who knows when I'll have a chance to Two Step again?"

She placed her hand in his as he drew her closer, and they began moving around the floor. She was home—the place she was created to be. The entire restaurant faded away until only they remained. Juanita's teaching had not been in vain. She would have been proud had she been able to see them.

As the music ended, he dipped her. Their eyes locked, and time disappeared. Applause broke out. He drew her upright, and she began to applaud but then noticed she and Sam were the only ones left on the dance floor. The other couples had moved off to the sides and were clapping for them.

Rusty gave her a thumbs-up and tipped his hat.

The lights dimmed and the band began a slow ballad.

She stepped to head back to the table, but Sam stood firm. "Dance with me one last time?"

As he placed his arms around her waist and pulled her close, she snuggled up against him. He laid his cheek against her head, and she whispered, "I'm sorry, so sorry, Sam." She had to tell him, to know things were right between them before he left. "Please forgive me." The evening's earlier tears returned.

"Don't cry, Katy Beth. There's nothing to forgive."

If only she believed that.

He pulled her closer, and she tightened her embrace. No more words were exchanged, as memories were created in the silence. After he was gone, every cell of her body would be able to recall this moment and exactly how perfect his nearness felt. Contentment and desire were having a tug of war in her heart, and contentment was losing. "Don't go," she whispered.

His breath tickled her ear. "I have to."

The end of the song was approaching, and every inch of her prayed for the band to play one more chorus. But they didn't. She would not beg him. If he stayed, it needed to be out of desire and not pity.

"My ride's waiting. Gotta go."

By the entrance stood a man in black pants, a white shirt, and a black bowtie. A limo driver. Sam's car was probably already on a ship headed across the Atlantic.

As he led her back to her table, he squeezed her hand. "Promise me one thing."

Anything. Right now, she would promise him anything. She nodded.

He pulled a notebook about the size of a deck of cards from his pocket and placed it into her palm. "Save your dances for me?" He turned, and the back of his shirt retreated through the crowd on the dance floor until it disappeared out the door.

She sank down onto her chair. In one breath's time, he was gone. Really gone. She might never see him again. He was gone, and her heart was filled with a leaden emptiness.

She pushed the limp salad to the side. Her appetite had disappeared. The ice cream in the two floats had melted and the distinct brown and white layers had combined into one indistinct, room-temperature, tan mixture.

She lifted his gift, the tiny red notebook, up to her nose to breathe in the fragrance of him one last time. As she did, the pages spread open to reveal his handwriting. She closed the book, placed it on the table in front of her, and then slowly re-opened it. He'd numbered—no dated—every page and then printed something on each one.

The first page bore tomorrow's date and the simple phrase, Pray for Sam. Every following page for the next four weeks repeated the same phrase. Yes. She had been praying for him for weeks—months—and she wouldn't stop now.

She turned to the next page—the beginning of the fifth week. Pray for Sam. Go out on a date with Sam. Dance with Sam. How was she supposed to go on a date with him or dance with him when he was on the other side of the world?

She flipped over one more page. Another short list, but some of the words were different from those on the page before. She read them again, and as their meaning soaked into her heart, she fought to breathe. Springing up out of her chair, she threw some cash onto the table, grabbed her phone and the notebook. *Please, be there. The car needs to still be there.* She excused her way across the dance floor as quickly as she could and then burst through the door onto the sidewalk.

The street was empty. The limo was nowhere to be seen.

Opening the notebook, she reread the last page, just to make sure she hadn't misread the words. She hadn't. Pray for Sam. Help Sam move into his new apartment back home. Dance with Sam. She understood the words that composed the phrases but not their corporate meaning.

As her phone rang, his picture popped up.

"Sam!"

"You read my book yet?"

"Yes." An innumerable number of questions whirled around in her mind, all fighting to be asked first. But she couldn't voice them. Her heart feared what the answers might be.

"Sorry to leave you, Katy Beth, but I have to pack up everything in my flat in London so it can be shipped back to the States."

She could hardly breathe. "So, you're moving back?"

"Yes, after I get everything tied up in the UK."

"To where?" But what did it really matter? A few weeks ago, she'd been ready to pack up and follow him to London. Pretty much any place in the States would be closer.

"Well, let's see. I've thought about Chicago. Or maybe Atlanta—I hear it's a nice town. But then the weather in Seattle is a lot like the UK. I'd probably feel right at home there. Yep, Seattle's got to be at the top of the list."

Seattle. "Really?" Surely, he was joking. But then, Seattle was closer than London. She could move to Seattle.

"Yep. But there's only one problem with that."

"Problem?"

"Yeah. What do I do about the lease I have on an apartment in Crescent Bluff?"

"Lease?" Her heart pounded, and she struggled to keep her voice even. "Oh, yes. I can see how that would be quite a problem. Sleeping in Crescent Bluff and commuting to Seattle every day."

"Exactly. I'm glad you understand my dilemma."

She couldn't contain her laugh. "So tell me, Mr. Tucker. Why in the world would you lease an apartment in Crescent Bluff if you really wanted to live in Seattle?"

"Well, it seems I've got this bit of unfinished

business to attend to in Crescent Bluff. You see, there's this woman there who's absolutely crazy about me. I mean she really loves me. So much so that she proposed to me."

She tried to reply, but the happy tears stole her voice.

"Crazy thing is, I love her even more than she loves me. She's My One. The girl I've wanted all these years. So, Katherine Elizabeth Herrington, it's time for that answer I couldn't give you in Oklahoma. Yes. Yes, I will marry you. Yesterday, today, and forever, I'm yours."

"Oh, Sam." Her cheeks hurt from smiling.

"Sorry I made you wait so long, Katy Beth."

Every second, every minute, every hour she had waited was worth it. She loved him with an everlasting love. *Thank You, Father.*

"Love, I'll see you in five weeks."

"Oh, Sam. I'll be waiting."

Then you will know the truth, and the truth
will set you free. ~ John 8:32

When we begin to see the world through faith,
we work to achieve the desirable qualities that
God has appointed for Christians, and we expect
those qualities in others. When we fail to live up to
our higher standards, angst rides our hearts. Yes,
we work harder to be the person we think we're
meant to be—often to the point that we bury the
"old" us as if it never existed. It is true that once
God forgives our past sins, they no longer exist,
but sometimes, God wants us to revisit through
memory and sharing, without condemnation, the
old experiences that helped to mold us. Our
forgiven failings, lead to greater understanding for
others. Sometimes, what we see as negative is
exactly what God uses to minister to others. Just as
we must recognize this in ourselves, we must
recognize the same possibilities in others and
refrain from judging them based on their past.

In **The Waiting**, the unmarried protagonist
has a list of traits she requires in a husband. Any
man who doesn't meet the standard is dropped.
But then she meets someone, who, despite his less-

than-desirable qualities, tugs at her heart strings. The traits she initially sees as a drawback are speaking to others and bringing new Christians into the fold. Her perfect list is competing with God's perfect plans.

Have you ever judged another based on who they were and not who they are now? Have you ever tried to hide the person you once were, thinking that your past negates the Christian you are now? It's easy to forget that God uses flawed people every day. Remember that it is the truth which sets you free, not running from it. Your past experiences, coupled with your current understanding of God's grace might just be the thing He needs to bring another lost sheep home.

LORD, YOU REMAIN FAITHFUL EVEN WHEN WE FALTER, AND YOU WON'T JUST DROP US BECAUSE WE FAIL. ALLOW ME ALWAYS TO ACCEPT THAT TRUTH. ALLOW ME THE GRACE TO UNDERSTAND THAT MY OWN SHAMEFUL PAST CAN BE USED FOR YOUR GOOD IF I ALLOW YOU TO DO SO, AND ALLOW ME ALWAYS TO EXTEND GRACE TO OTHERS. IN JESUS' NAME I PRAY, AMEN.

You Can Help!

At Pelican Book Group it is our mission to entertain readers with fiction that uplifts the Gospel. It is our privilege to spend time with you awhile as you read our stories.

We believe you can help us to bring Christ into the lives of people across the globe. And you don't have to open your wallet or even leave your house!

Here are 3 simple things you can do to help us bring illuminating fiction™ to people everywhere.

1) If you enjoyed this book, write a positive review. Post it at online retailers and websites where readers gather. And share your review with us at reviews@pelicanbookgroup.com (this does give us permission to reprint your review in whole or in part.)

2) If you enjoyed this book, recommend it to a friend in person, at a book club or on social media.

3) If you have suggestions on how we can improve or expand our selection, let us know. We value your opinion. Use the contact form on our web site or e-mail us at customer@pelicanbookgroup.com

God Can Help!

Are you in need? The Almighty can do great things for you. Holy is His Name! He has mercy in every generation. He can lift up the lowly and accomplish all things. Reach out today.

Do not fear: I am with you; do not be anxious: I am your God. I will strengthen you, I will help you, I will uphold you with my victorious right hand.

~Isaiah 41:10 (NAB)

We pray daily, and we especially pray for everyone connected to Pelican Book Group—that includes you! If you have a specific need, we welcome the opportunity to pray for you. Share your needs or praise reports at http://pelink.us/pray4us

Free Book Offer

We're looking for booklovers like you to partner with us! Join our team of influencers today and periodically receive free eBooks and exclusive offers.

For more information
Visit http://pelicanbookgroup.com/booklovers